No Getting Over You

MacLarens of Fire Mountain

Contemporary Romance Series

SHIRLEEN DAVIES

Book Seven in the MacLarens of Fire Mountain

Contemporary Romance Series

For permission requests, contact the publisher.

Avalanche Ranch Press, LLC
PO Box 12618
Prescott, AZ 86304

Book design and conversions by Joseph Murray at 3rdplanetpublishing.com

Cover design by The Killion Group

ISBN: 978-1-941786-29-1

I care about quality, so if you find something in error, please contact me via email at shirleen@shirleendavies.com.

Description

No Getting Over You – Book Seven, MacLarens of Fire Mountain Contemporary Romance Series

Cassie MacLaren has come a long way since being dumped by her long-time boyfriend, a man she believed to be her future. Successful in her job at MacLaren Enterprises, dreaming of one day leading one of the divisions, she's moved on to start a new relationship, having little time to dwell on past mistakes.

Matt Garner loves his job as rodeo representative for Double Ace Bucking Stock. Busy days and constant travel leave no time for anything more than the occasional short-term relationship—which is just the way he likes it. He's come to accept the regret of leaving the woman he loved for the pro rodeo circuit.

The future is set for both, until a chance meeting ignites long buried emotions neither is willing to face.

Forced to work together, their attraction grows, even as multiple arson fires threaten Cassie's new home of Cold Creek, Colorado. Although Cassie believes the danger from the fires is remote, she knows the danger Matt poses to her heart is real.

While fighting his renewed feelings for Cassie, Matt focuses on a new and unexpected opportunity offered by MacLaren Enterprises—an opportunity that will put him on a direct collision course with Cassie.

Will pride and self-preservation control their future? Or will one be strong enough to make the first move, risking everything, including their heart?

No Getting Over You, book seven in the MacLarens of Fire Mountain Contemporary series, is a full-length novel with an HEA.

From the Author

Join Shirleen Davies' Newsletter to Receive Notice of:

- New Releases
- Contests
- Free Reads & Sneak Peeks

To sign up copy and paste this site address into your browser's address bar: http://bit.ly/1KqhKwm

Visit my website for a list of characters for each series.
http://www.shirleendavies.com/character-list.html

Acknowledgements

Thanks also to my editor, Kim Young, proofreader, Alicia Carmical, and all of my beta readers. Your insights and suggestions are greatly appreciated.

As always, many thanks to my wonderful resources, including Diane Lebow, who has been a whiz at guiding my social media endeavors, my cover designer, Kim Killion, and Joseph Murray who is a whiz at formatting my books for both print and electronic versions.

No Getting Over You

Prologue

Phoenix, Arizona

"Cassie, Matt left a note on the front door." Janie tossed the piece of paper on the bed. "Haven't you returned his calls?"

Cassie looked up from her computer. "Not yet, but he knows I'm swamped. I'll shoot him a quick text to say I'll see him Friday at dinner. I'm certain he's just as busy as I am."

"Yeah, but it's been days since you've seen him. The least you could do is call and speak with him." Janie shrugged. "Just saying..." Her voice faded as she closed the bedroom door.

Cassie's fingers stilled on the keyboard. Janie might be right. She'd ignored the messages Matt had left over the last three days saying he needed to talk to her. They'd known each other their entire lives, been together since high school. A year older than she, he had one more semester in college, and she'd finish a year later.

He'd talked of going into the professional rodeo circuit while she finished school, maybe staying in for a time after she graduated. They'd debated it over and over until she believed Matt had put that dream behind him, deciding to take the job her father, Heath MacLaren, offered at MacLaren Enterprises.

The job made more sense than chasing the fantasy he'd harbored since he was ten. In her mind, Matt had more going for him than wrecking his body and endangering his life competing in saddle and bareback stock competitions. Besides, Cassie had no desire to watch the rodeo bunnies fawn over him in city after city.

They'd spent a lot of time together in Fire Mountain at Christmas a couple weeks before. Their families were close, and although a few stayed silent, most seemed to have an opinion on his future. His reluctant admission over the Christmas holiday that the rodeo life might not be the sensible choice had sealed it for Cassie. Right now, she needed to concentrate on school, then they could take a short break between semesters.

Leaning to the side, she grabbed the note Janie had tossed on the bed. Opening it, she wasn't surprised to read he needed to see her right away. They already had plans to meet for dinner tomorrow night. Smiling to herself, she grabbed her phone, typed a quick text, and sent it. Surely he could wait twenty-four hours. Setting the phone on her desk, she got back to work, forgetting the urgency of his message.

******

Tapping her fingers on the table, Cassie glanced at her phone once more to make sure she hadn't missed a message. She checked the time—eight o'clock. Matt was now thirty minutes late. Growing impatient, she called him, waiting as it went to voicemail.

"Matt, it's Cassie. Where are you? Call me."

Sitting back, she sipped her beer and picked up a blue corn chip, nibbling on it, watching the activities around her. She recognized several people who had also made this a regular hangout, just as she and Matt had for the last couple years. It would be different when he graduated and took the job Heath offered. She'd still be at school, but at least the drive to Fire Mountain wasn't far. They'd see each other on weekends and holidays until she finished.

After another half-hour of checking her phone every five minutes, she sent him a curt message, telling him she'd decided not to wait any longer.

She continued to fume the following morning when he hadn't called or messaged her. Cassie could think of just one place that could hold his attention for so long, making him forget everything else—the rodeo grounds where he kept his horse. Anger turned into concern when she considered something may have happened to Thunder, the gelding he'd owned and trained since high school.

Showering and dressing, she picked up a latte at a neighborhood coffeehouse, then walked across campus. The rodeo grounds took up a good portion of what used to be vacant pastureland at one end of campus. Large and well-planned, it hosted collegiate and pro rodeo events. There were also a series of private stalls at one end. Ever since he had started school, Matt had rented one for Thunder.

Looking around, Cassie didn't see Matt's truck in the lot, nor did she spot Thunder in his stall. Checking again for messages, she continued to the office, hoping Matt's rodeo coach might be inside and know where to find him.

"Morning, Cassie. What brings you out on a Saturday morning?" The coach's deep voice greeted her the moment she stepped through the door.

"Morning, Coach. I'm looking for Matt. Has he been around today?"

He gave her a blank stare before clearing his throat. "He's gone, Cass."

"Gone? Do you mean he's running errands or drove into Phoenix?"

Standing, he walked around his desk, crossing his arms. "He packed up and left this morning. He's on his way to Texas. You are aware he graduated a semester early, right?" Seeing the stricken look on her face, he realized she knew nothing of Matt's plans. "Didn't he tell you anything?"

Lowering herself into an old wooden chair, she fought for air, trying to understand what she heard.

"Matt never said a word," she breathed out. "So…he's gone?"

Coach scratched his chin, his brows drawing together. "You mean he never told you? That doesn't sound like the Matt I know."

She tried to form a coherent thought as her chest squeezed. The idea he'd left her for the rodeo circuit without telling her, or saying goodbye, created an ache so intense, she thought her heart would stop.

"He left a couple messages saying he needed to talk to me, but I was so busy with finals, I…I…" Her throat closed as the news of Matt's departure became reality. Placing a hand over her churning stomach, she stood, heading for the door. "I need to go." Dashing outside, she broke into a run, heading for her car. She had to get to the apartment he rented a few miles from campus. Maybe she could still catch him.

Chapter One

MacLaren Enterprises, Fire Mountain, Arizona

Five years later...

"Cassie, they're ready for your presentation." Phyllis Jurgunsen, the senior executive assistant at MacLaren Enterprises, signaled for her to join the senior management team in the boardroom.

Picking up the folders she'd brought with her from the Cold Creek, Colorado, offices of MacLaren Rodeo, Cassie walked down the hall, once more reviewing her prepared speech. She'd been fighting the leadership's desire to partner with a rodeo stock company out of Houston, Texas, since learning who the company employed as their representative in the western states. But her personal objections would carry no weight for the business savvy MacLaren executives.

From her research, associating with Double Ace Bucking Stock gave them no significant advantages, and caused numerous disadvantages to their planned growth. At least that was her take on the findings. She knew her stepbrother, Cameron Sinclair, the president of the facility in Cold Creek, had a different conclusion. It would be quite a sales job to stop the momentum for partnering with Double Ace.

"Cassie, we're going to take a short break while you set up." Heath MacLaren, Cassie's father and chairman of MacLaren Enterprises, took a phone call as he headed into the hall.

"Do you need any help?" Cam asked as Cassie turned on her computer and opened her presentation.

"Do you mind passing these out?" She handed Cam the folders. When finished, he came up next to her, waiting until she looked at him.

"A heads-up. Heath, Jace, and Rafe are pretty set on working with Double Ace," Cam said, mentioning the senior MacLaren brothers. "It's going to take a good bit of persuasion to change their opinions."

"If they've already made up their minds, it sounds as if my presentation is a waste of time."

"Not necessarily, but it will take a lot to change their thinking."

"I know they all believe I'm pushing back because of Matt, but there are sound reasons for continuing with the path they set a few years ago." Cassie turned her attention to the presentation as everyone walked back into the boardroom.

Lowering his voice, Cam leaned closer. "Then stick to the business reasons and avoid any mention of Matt."

After a few successful rodeo seasons, Matt Garner sustained an injury serious enough to knock him out of the circuit. Taking a lucrative offer from

Double Ace to be their western states representative, he ran into Cassie for the first time in years at a meeting in Houston. They'd been able to avoid each other since then, and Cassie had every intention of keeping her distance. If this deal went through, however, she'd be his main point of contact, making avoiding him impossible.

"Cassie, are you ready?" Heath took his seat, motioning for her to get started.

Clearing her throat, she directed their attention to the folders, then launched into her presentation. Thirty minutes later, she closed her laptop and left. She'd find out their final decision soon enough.

******

Double Ace Bucking Stock Headquarters, Houston, Texas

"One more issue to discuss, then we're finished." Gage Templeton, vice president at Double Ace, sat forward, focusing his gaze on Matt. "We need to decide if we want to team-up with MacLaren Rodeo or move our efforts to another stock supplier."

"We do have other options that are as viable as MacLaren." Matt rested his arms on the table, looking at each person.

"Are you prepared to review them with us today?" Gage didn't believe any other companies had the resources and financial backing as strong as MacLaren. But knowing Matt's history with Cassie, he felt compelled to listen to alternatives.

"I am." Rifling through his notes, he stood, walking toward the whiteboard located at one end of the room. Taking a marker, he listed four companies, including MacLaren, then cited the pros and cons of each. An hour later, they'd debated until Gage felt he had what he needed for his boss to make a decision.

"Good job, Matt. I'll need to run all this past Ivan Santiago." Gage picked up his papers before he and Matt walked down the hall.

"What are your thoughts?" As much as he wanted to believe otherwise, Matt felt the debate had supported continuing talks with MacLaren Rodeo. From a business standpoint, they were the best choice. From a personal perspective, however, he couldn't think of a worse situation.

The icy welcome he'd gotten from Cassie's relatives a few months before, at Mitch MacLaren's wedding reception, told him they didn't know the whole story behind him leaving her for the rodeo circuit. Even his grandfather, Seth Garner, who'd raised Matt and his younger brother, Troy, had been disappointed in his actions. It had taken time, but his grandfather finally understood Matt's side, why he had to leave, and the frustration he felt near the end when Cassie wouldn't make time for him. He'd wanted to explain, but she'd shut him out.

"You presented good points for each company, and there's no reason we can't work with more than one. We aren't interested in an exclusive deal with MacLaren Rodeo—at least not yet. Santiago will want to kick the tires a bit before considering an exclusive with any outfit." Gage checked his watch before turning back to Matt. "Let's grab dinner after work. Stop by my office on your way out."

"Sounds good." Matt enjoyed Gage's company, always fascinated by the stories he told of his time competing in the rodeo circuit. Bareback and saddle bronc were his events, the same as Matt, although he'd gone a little further, winning a world championship in saddle bronc. He'd also been present the day Matt and Cassie saw each other for the first time since their breakup. It hadn't been pretty. The highlight being when she called him a sonofabitch and planted a right hook square into his face.

He'd probably deserved it for the way he'd left her. At the time, his decision felt justified. Looking back, he could've stayed a few more days, explained his reasons, and dealt with her arguments. Either way, the outcome would've been the same. She wanted one path for their life and he wanted another. Continuing to beat himself up over it wouldn't change the end result.

******

"How long did it take him to make a decision," Matt asked, nursing his second beer.

"About what you'd expect." Gage took a swallow from his glass, watching a redhead at the other end of the bar. He'd been through a nasty divorce a few years before and still dealt with the lingering fallout. He had no desire to get back into a committed relationship—now or ever. However, that didn't stop him from testing the waters for a woman interested in loose and casual, without strings.

"Five minutes?"

"A little less. I sent him a report of our meeting. By the time we spoke, he already favored negotiating the big rodeos with MacLaren for the coming season. After that, who knows?"

Matt pinched the bridge of his nose, feeling a headache coming on. "Yeah. I thought that would be his reaction. It was worth a try, even though I realize any other decision would've been doubtful."

"There's the option of swapping the account with someone else. One of the reps could take on MacLaren, passing off one of their big accounts to you. It's a little more traveling for both of you, but I'd be willing to give it a try if it will make the dealings easier."

"By easier, you mean for me?"

Gage chuckled. "Hell no. I mean for Double Ace. I can't afford to let your personal feelings for Cassie mess up what could be a lucrative deal for everyone."

"You don't think I can deal?" Matt swallowed the last of his beer, signaling for another as his jaw clenched.

"I didn't say that. I'm making certain you can handle being around her without screwing up a good contract. You tell me. I can make it work either way." Standing, Gage kept his gaze on the redhead, who'd been equally as intent on getting his attention. "Give me your answer first thing tomorrow morning." Without another word, he walked toward the far side of the bar, leaving Matt to his tangled thoughts.

"Hey, cowboy. You interested in buying me a drink?"

Matt looked up from his half-finished beer. Another night, he might be tempted to stick around, buy the lady a drink, and see where it went. Tonight, he wanted nothing more than to head home and clear his mind of everything, especially one stubborn, spoiled female who continued to plague him after all this time.

"Another time, darlin'." Standing, he tossed money onto the bar and stalked out.

******

"There's no reason Matt can't work with Skye up in Crooked Tree. We'll be partnering on all rodeo stock, not just bareback and saddle bronc." Cam sat at his desk, Cassie on the other side, listening to the reasons the MacLaren executives gave for continuing negotiations with Double Ace.

She'd prepared herself for the decision, knowing the outcome could be nothing else. Although she wished otherwise, a partnership between Double Ace and MacLaren Rodeo would be hard for rodeo committees to ignore. Two strong players in the stock business would knock the competition to the walls. They'd be hard to beat in quality of stock or price, especially for the large rodeos. No matter how she wished otherwise, Double Ace had entered the business strong and hard a few years before and was now considered a major player, same as MacLaren Rodeo.

"There's no need to bring Skye into this. I can work with Matt." Lowering her gaze to her lap, she resolved to keep telling herself that. Perhaps it would be true by the time she saw him again.

"Without punching him in the nose?"

Her head shot up. "You heard about that?"

"Cassie, everyone's heard about it." He shook his head, his mouth quirking up at the corners.

She could feel her face heat, knowing her cheeks would already be turning a deep pink. Jutting her chin out, she leveled her gaze at Cam. "He deserved it, although the timing could've been better."

"Yes, it could've been. It's a good thing Gage didn't judge you, and MacLaren Rodeo, by your action. This is a good opportunity for us and I don't want old feelings or your temper to mess it up." His voice had become stern, demanding an answer.

"You won't have to worry about me. I can handle myself around Matt. We've been over for a long time. I just needed closure and I've gotten it. I'm good."

Cam studied her, not quite believing Cassie had gotten closure. More like a small amount of revenge.

"All right. Let's start with Double Ace's latest proposal."

Chapter Two

Houston, Texas

"Garner." Matt picked up his phone on the fourth ring after checking caller ID. The last person he wanted to speak with tonight was the woman he'd been seeing the last couple months. He'd planned to call it off with her the last time they went out, but one thing led to another, then Gage had sent him out of town.

"Hi, Matt. It's Chelsea."

The slight waver in her voice tugged at his gut. Chels may not be the most exciting woman he'd been with over the years, but her sweet personality and willingness to please made their time together easy, undemanding. It made him wonder why he felt the need to call it off. She asked for nothing except a little of his time when he was in town. He'd never felt the need to string a woman along when he knew there'd be no future. She already had a hard time with self-esteem and he didn't want to add to it. He had to find a gentle way to let her go.

"Hi, Chels. What's going on?"

"Well...I just hadn't heard from you in a while and wondered if you were still out of town." She let out a nervous laugh. "Guess not."

"I drove back a couple days ago. Work's been hectic—like always." He swallowed his doubt, knowing he had to tell her. Glancing at the time, he made a decision. "If you haven't eaten, how about I bring over something?"

"Sure. Whatever you want."

It's the same response she always gave him. Chels never had an opinion and rarely made a decision, tending to go with what interested him. For some reason, it irked him more now that he'd seen Cassie again. Unlike Chelsea, he'd never had to wonder what was on Cass's mind.

"All right. I'll be there in a half-hour."

Ordering Chinese food, he slipped on his boots and grabbed his hat, going over what he'd say and at what point. She lived alone, worked in an office, and from what he could tell, had few close friends. They'd met through her aunt, a woman who worked at Double Ace. He and Chels hadn't been seeing each other long, but the break would still be a little tricky.

"Hi, Matt." Chelsea opened the door, motioning him inside, glancing at the bag. "Chinese."

"I remembered how much you like it."

She smiled over her shoulder while grabbing plates. "Chopsticks?"

"Of course," Matt grinned, again getting a sick feeling about what he needed to say.

Dinner passed with small talk of her work and his travels before she set down her chopsticks and picked up their plates.

"I'll get those, Chels." Matt started to stand, but sat back down when she returned to the table and took a seat.

"Matt, there's something I've been meaning to talk to you about."

"Sure, Chels." He pushed his chair back, stretched out his long legs, and crossed his arms.

"I, well...I suppose there's no right way to say this." Her voice shook and he knew whatever it was made her nervous.

"I've always found the best way is to just say it."

She took a breath, nodding. "Well, the truth is...I've met someone."

Nothing could've surprised him more. Sitting up, he pulled the chair back to the table, resting his arms on it. "Someone you want to date?"

"Well, yes."

He worked to keep his face impassive when all he felt was relief. "Tell me about him."

"We work together. He's, well...he's nothing like you."

That gave Matt pause. "How's that?"

"He's quiet, likes books and gardening." When she saw his brows arch, she rushed on, stammering. "Not that you don't like those, but you're always so, well...intimidating. You know exactly what you want and where you're going. You're so confident—nothing stops you." She hesitated long enough to take a breath. He'd never seen her so animated.

"We're so different. You're complicated with many layers. I'm a pretty simple person, not that interesting, and happy to stay at home. You need someone more like you—full of life, always charging forward." She glanced at him. "Does that make sense?" He could see her hands laced together in her lap, the knuckles almost white.

Reaching over, he laid a hand on hers and squeezed. "Yes, it does."

"I don't want to hurt you, Matt. You've been so good to me."

Pulling her up, he wrapped his arms around her. "Don't worry about me. I'll be fine. I'm just happy for you." Dropping his arms and stepping back, he gave her a stern look. "But you call me if he isn't good to you. I'll set him straight right away."

His comment got the response he hoped for. Chelsea laughed, giving him a quick kiss on the cheek. "I don't believe I'll need to worry about that, but it's always good to have you in my corner."

"Always, Chels." Picking up his hat, he walked to the door. "I'd better get going. You take care of yourself."

Sliding into the cab of his truck, Matt let out a relieved breath. Sometimes life *did* work in his favor.

******

"What are you doing tonight, Cassie?" Cam stopped inside her office door.

"I thought I'd pick up takeout and head home. Unless you have something you need me to do."

"Nothing like that. The local Search and Rescue team is meeting tonight. Lainey is meeting me there, and you've mentioned an interest in learning more about it." Cam and his wife, Lainey, met as SAR volunteers, marrying before he took over the Cold Creek operation. They'd continued to stay active volunteers, joining the local team.

"Can I bring my dinner?"

"As long as you get enough for Lainey and me," he smirked.

Not long afterwards, the three sat at the back of the room, sharing Cassie's food, and ignoring jealous looks from the other volunteers. Picking up the empty containers, she stuffed them in a bag as the SAR leader talked through the training exercises starting the following weekend. Stepping to the back, she tossed the bag in a trash can, leaning against a nearby wall, watching out of the corner of her eye as a man walked up next to her.

"I'm Kurt Dobson. I don't believe we've met." He held out his hand.

"Cassie MacLaren." Shaking his hand, she found herself staring at a scar on his neck, then looked back up to his eyes. "This is my first time at a meeting. My stepbrother, Cam Sinclair, and his wife are volunteers."

"That right? I've known Cam and Lainey since they came to town. Do you work at the rodeo stock company?"

"I do."

"Kurt, would you like to introduce us to our guest?" The SAR leader gave him a pointed look.

Ignoring the stare, Kurt smiled. "This is Cassie MacLaren. She's related to Cam and Lainey, but we'll try not to hold that against her."

Applause and laughter followed, several members offering greetings.

"Cam, anything you want to add?"

Cam stood, looking behind him at Kurt. "This is Cassie's first time at an SAR meeting. I'm hoping she'll decide to join us."

As the meeting broke up, Lainey joined Cassie and Kurt while Cam walked around, talking to several friends. "What do you think?" Lainey asked Cass.

"Kurt was just telling me about the fitness sessions. I didn't realize how much training it took to become a volunteer. Sounds like quite a challenge."

"Nothing you can't handle. I'm certain Cam would be supportive of whatever you needed to get started." Lainey watched her husband shaking hands with a few more people before making his way to them.

"Kurt's going to be doing an introductory session this weekend. You might consider attending." Cam slipped an arm around Lainey's waist, pulling her close.

"It'd be great to have you join us, Cassie," Kurt added.

Cassie sent him a quick glance. "Would it be all right to attend, then make up my mind?"

"Of course. It's not for everyone. The class will give you a good sense of what's expected." Tossing an empty cup in the trash, he turned back to Cassie. "Nice to meet you. Hope you decide to come on Saturday."

Watching him walk outside, she turned back to Lainey and Cam.

"He's single, you know," Lainey added. "A lieutenant with the fire department. According to Cam, he's on the fast track to becoming a captain. And...he's not bad on the eyes."

Laughing, Cassie followed them to the truck. "When would I ever have time to go out, especially if I decide to join Search and Rescue? My life is good the way it is."

Lainey sent Cam a look, telling him without words what she thought of Cassie's comment. "You may be right. It's just something to think about."

A couple hours later, Cassie lay in bed, unable to sleep, staring at the ceiling, and thinking about what Lainey had said. Kurt *was* easy on the eyes. The problem was when she closed hers, the only image in her head was Matt's.

******

Double Ace Offices, El Paso, Texas

"I'll not have this discussion over the phone. We'll meet where we can talk without fear of others listening." Ivan Santiago winced at the sharp reply to his request. One of his uncles had called with instructions on how to move the next group of cattle into the United States from Mexico, knowing his nephew wouldn't like the order from the senior members of the family.

"Fine. I'll meet you in Juarez for dinner tonight at nine o'clock."

Ivan ended the call as his office door opened, Gage and Matt entering for a meeting he'd requested. They'd flown in from Houston to the offices in El Paso. Double Ace had been started by American partners, as well as three Mexican families—the Santiagos, Castenadas, and Zamoras. The Santiagos held over fifty percent ownership, giving them the deciding vote for all operations. At this point, the other partners were happy to sit back and watch the money appear in their bank accounts.

Greeting Gage and Matt, Ivan sat back down. Their presence was a great diversion from the conversation he'd just completed, which he'd be required to continue in a few hours.

"Please, gentlemen, tell me what's happening with the MacLaren negotiations."

"We're already preparing proposals for the next season. Right now, we see a minimum of ten rodeos where we have an excellent chance of winning the bid. We'd prefer to bring MacLaren in on each of them for additional stock." Gage pulled out a list of rodeos, sliding it across the desk to Ivan. "The ones highlighted are those where we'd request their partnership."

Ivan studied the list showing the dates, location, number of stock needed for each category, and history of participation by either Double Ace or MacLaren.

"It appears one of the companies has worked with just two of these rodeos," Ivan commented, continuing to study the list.

"True. MacLaren was the contractor for one, and we were for the other. Each of us brought in two different stock subcontractors. We weren't pleased with the results on our contract. I don't know the MacLaren experience with their subcontractors." Gage pulled out another sheet of paper and passed it to Ivan. "These are the mid-sized rodeos MacLaren has won contracts with over the last few years using one subcontractor. If they retain the contracts for next season, we want them to use us."

"Why don't we go after these ourselves?" Ivan looked up, then leaned back in his chair. "Would that not be more lucrative for us?"

"Yes, but we'd be pitting ourselves against allies."

"Ah, yes. We will get to know how MacLaren operates, then exploit their weaknesses, correct?"

Matt shot Gage an uneasy glance, who nodded for him to go ahead and speak his mind.

"I've known the MacLarens all my life. If you form a solid partnership with them, my guess is you'll do well to keep it on good terms. You'll find no better long-term ally."

Leaning forward, Ivan rested his elbows on the desk, steepling his fingers. "I did hear about a slight altercation between you and one of the MacLarens at our Houston office. I trust the disagreement has been resolved."

Matt stifled a groan. He'd hoped the incident between him and Cassie had been forgotten. "I—"

Ivan held up his hand, stopping him. "I trust you, Matt. If you believe the MacLarens to be potentially strong partners, I will reserve judgment until later. Excellent work on this, Gage. You will be the one to negotiate the contracts?"

"I'll handle the initial agreements with the MacLarens. Matt or one of our other representatives will work directly with the rodeos and prepare the proposals. They will also be the main contacts at each of the MacLaren facilities."

Ivan looked at Matt, the corners of his mouth tilting upward. "So you will continue to have dealings with Ms. MacLaren. This will be a true test of your humility and patience."

"You're right about that, Mr. Santiago," Matt ground out, feeling the ghost from his past rearing up to haunt him.

Chapter Three

Cold Creek, Colorado

"Does anyone have questions?" Kurt Dobson stood at the front of the SAR training room, looking out at the fifteen attendees in his introductory class. "None? Well, if you come up with any, I'll pass around my card. Feel free to email or call."

Cassie hung back while the others filed out. She'd taken copious notes and had lots of questions, but didn't want to pepper Kurt with them all at once.

"Did the class help or overwhelm you?" Kurt asked, walking up to her.

"You do give out a lot of information in a short time." She brushed a strand of dark auburn hair from her face, tucking it behind her ear. "I do have a number of questions, which I could send you in an email."

"I have a better idea. Let's grab lunch and I'll answer each one."

He chose a quaint Italian restaurant in the middle of downtown Cold Creek, which she'd been to several times with Cam and Lainey. They ordered and ate at a slow pace as he answered each of her questions.

"Will most of the people today become volunteers?"

"From my experience, about a fourth of them will, at least for a period of time. Job changes, children, divorces, and other events all create a pretty high turnover of volunteers. If I get five from today's class, one or two will still be with us by this time next year. A year later, maybe one will continue." Kurt took a last bite of pasta and set down his fork. "Some are drawn to the challenge, some the excitement, and others because they just want to help the community. Most of the people today have good intentions, but once they experience the time commitment, they'll decide it's not for them."

"And you? What drew you to SAR?" Cassie leaned forward, more interested in his background than she wanted to be.

"I went to school to become a firefighter. It's all I've ever wanted to be. I tried for a few large city departments without success, finally getting on here in Cold Creek. Best job I've ever had. SAR came about a year later."

"Isn't it difficult juggling both?"

"Not as much as you'd think. My SAR team knows my job as a firefighter always takes precedence, so no one gives me grief about it. It would probably be more difficult for you to fit SAR into your travel schedule than for me to work around my job."

Cassie asked a couple more questions, then sat in silence for a few minutes before Kurt leaned toward her.

"I'm off this weekend. If you don't have plans, I'd like to take you to dinner."

She'd dated little since Matt took off. Nothing serious and she never found anyone special. This last year, she'd turned down each offer, citing work. Being alone had its advantages. However, complete freedom could also become a noose when nothing distinguished one night from the next.

When she'd seen Matt in Houston, her anger had gotten the upper hand. No matter how good it felt to take her pain out on him, she knew it had been wrong. She felt silly admitting it, but the worst part was she'd hoped he might reach out to her, even after she broke his nose, invite her for drinks or dinner or something. But it had been months without a word. Other than a few minutes together at Mitch and Dana's wedding reception, she'd neither seen nor heard from him since their meeting in Houston. All the dealings between Double Ace and MacLaren Rodeo went through Cam and Mitch MacLaren, who ran the two rodeo stock companies. She'd come to accept there'd be no getting over Matt, but the time had come to move on. Their time together ended a long time ago, and Cassie needed to find someone to help her sever all ties and reclaim her heart.

"I'd like to have dinner with you, Kurt. Be warned, though. I haven't been on a date in a long time." She could feel her nerves kick into action at the thought of putting herself out there with a man she found quite attractive.

"Not a problem, Cassie. I haven't dated much myself the last couple years." His mouth twisted into a wry grin. "I'll pick you up at seven tonight."

******

Houston, Texas

Matt's hand hovered over the phone on his desk. He'd been given the go-ahead by Gage to meet with Cassie, then travel to Montana to meet with her cousin, Skye MacLaren, who worked in the bucking bull stock part of the company.

Ever since the altercation that left him with a slight bend to his nose, he'd wanted to try and mend fences with Cassie. Instead of calling her then, he'd let the impulse pass. They were like oil and water in so many ways, yet so alike in others. No one would call either weak-minded, meek, or shy. Stubborn, driven, and determined were strong characteristics of both. The same traits Matt believed led to their split. There'd be no going back. The best he could hope for was a good working relationship that didn't escalate into a war of wills.

Taking a breath, he punched the speakerphone button and dialed her number.

"Cassie, it's Matt."

He could hear her breathing on the other end. For a moment, he thought she wouldn't respond, but then he heard her clear her throat.

"Hi, Matt. I understand an agreement for preparing joint proposals has been reached. I'm going to guess that's why you're calling." Her voice sounded calm, level, and devoid of emotion, which irritated him in a way he couldn't quite define.

"You'd be right. I'll be traveling up your way in a week, then going north to meet with Skye. I'd like to schedule time with you and anyone else who will be involved in preparing the proposals."

"Do you have any dates you can give me?"

He gave her the days he'd be in Cold Creek. "Let me know what works. I'll be in town three days, which will give me a chance to see your operation. Can you arrange for someone to show me around?"

"Um...sure. I'll arrange it. I'll check with Cam to see if he wants to get together with you, which I'm certain he will. Can I call you back by the end of the day?"

"Sure. If I'm not in, just leave the information on voicemail." Matt hung up, not wanting to prolong the discussion and risk setting her off in some way. Leaning back in his chair, his hands gripped the armrests, digging into the leather upholstery.

Instead of feeling content with the brief discussion, the pain of regret squeezed his chest. No matter how his mind knew they'd never be together, he still had trouble convincing his heart.

******

Cassie stared at the phone, hearing the dial tone at the other end. She wanted to scream, remembering the calm tone of his voice. He didn't seem to feel any of the inner turbulence she'd fought a losing battle with since seeing him for the first time after he'd left.

Well, maybe not the *first* time.

A few months after he graduated, she had learned of a rodeo he'd entered in Santa Fe. Sitting in the stands, never letting her gaze waver, Cassie had been so proud of him. He'd won the bareback event and scored well in the saddle bronc event. Enthusiasm replaced common sense as she dashed from the stands to the competitor area, searching for him in the crowd. Instead of one familiar face, she saw two. Becky, his old girlfriend from high school, the one he'd dumped for Cassie, had her arms wrapped around his neck, the kiss she gave him seeming to never end. After a moment, eyes glistening with tears, Cassie hurried to the parking lot and didn't look back.

"Hey, Cassie. How about grabbing lunch?" Janie, her college roommate, stood at the door, cocking her head to one side. She'd accepted a finance job from Cam right after Cassie moved to Cold Creek. "Are you okay? You don't look so good."

Taking a breath to clear her head, she wiped damp palms down her pants. "I just heard from Matt. He wants to meet with us now that the partnership is formalized."

"Ah. Well, you knew this would happen. When will he be here?" Janie had never disguised her irritation at Cassie for not returning Matt's messages before he left school. But, like sisters, she supported Cassie through the rough months that followed, knowing she'd never really gotten over him.

"Next week." Glancing up at Janie, she slung her purse over a shoulder. "I don't know if I can do this."

Stepping forward, Janie crossed her arms, taking one of her familiar, defiant poses. "Of course you can. You two loved each other, but it didn't work out. It's been years and no matter how much you'd like a do-over, I doubt either of you will let it happen. So you have no other choice except to move on."

Her brows crinkling together, Cassie stopped on her way to the door. "What do you mean you doubt either of us will let it happen?"

"Face it, girlfriend. You two are the most stubborn people I know. No matter how much you may still love him or he you, neither of you will be the first to let the pride go and reach out to the other. I'm not judging you, Cass. I'm just saying neither of you want to be the one to appear weak. It's just the way it is." Touching Cassie's arm, she squeezed. "Come on. I'm starving. You can beat me up after I've filled my stomach."

******

Taking a seat in the restaurant, Cassie pondered Janie's words. As much as her heart raced when she saw Matt or even heard his voice, there'd be no future—neither could ever go back. She hadn't understood it at the time, but Cassie now accepted each needed someone different. You couldn't put a spark to C4 and expect it not to explode.

She needed someone easy-going, who wouldn't challenge her at every step, who understood her drive to succeed. The thoughts conjured up an image of Kurt with his broad smile, unassuming ways, and steady character. They'd had a good time on their date, planning to go out again. Although committed to his work, she'd seen none of the overwhelming intensity she'd come to expect from Matt. None of the extreme self-confidence and power Matt projected. And none of the passion she felt when an image of Matt would pop into her head.

Reaching into her purse, she pulled out a small gold ring with a marquise cut ruby in the center. Matt had given it to her on her eighteenth birthday. She'd worn it until the day he'd walked away. Although she'd tried more than once, Cassie had never been able to put the ring where it belonged— buried in a box at the bottom of some random drawer.

"You still have that?" Janie's face lit up at the sight of the ruby, sparkling in the sun radiating through the window. "I thought you said you lost it."

Cassie's mouth twisted into a grim smile as she gazed down at the ring. "Yeah. Well, I lied about that."

"Good."

Cassie's head snapped up. "Why is that?"

"Because Matt was an important part of your life. Being with him made you what you are today. No matter what you keep telling yourself, sometimes the best person is one who pushes you, forces you to be better in all you do and not settle for average. Hate me if you want, but I think Matt was that person for you."

"And was I that person for him?"

Janie bit her bottom lip, deciding how best to answer. She'd wondered the same when she'd seen them together. A good question without a good answer. "Honestly, Cass, I don't know."

✳✳✳✳✳✳

León, Mexico

"It is good to see you, Tía Reyna. It has been too long." Ivan wrapped his arms around his father's younger sister. Still attractive with smooth skin and dark ebony hair devoid of the gray or silver streaks common in women her age, Reyna was one of his favorites, and he knew she felt the same about him.

"It *has* been too long. And whose fault is that?" She stepped back, looking up into his amused eyes.

Placing a hand over his heart, he let out a sigh. "Mine, of course. But your brother places many burdens on me, making trips home a rare event."

"Your father works too hard, as do his brothers. Don't they have enough land and money? They should pass the businesses onto you and the other cousins. It's time the younger generation took over." Placing hands on her hips, she turned toward the kitchen. As the youngest of five, one of two sisters, she'd learned to speak her mind at an early age, to the great embarrassment of her parents.

Shaking his head, Ivan followed her into the massive kitchen. Reyna lived with Ivan's father and mother in a beautiful home on the outskirts of León. Her only sister lived next door with her husband, in an equally beautiful estate. Each had massive yards,

35

gated entries, fountains, and guards roaming the properties twenty-four hours a day.

"Does father know you are doing the cooking tonight?" Ivan leaned over her shoulder, stealing a still warm handmade corn tortilla, tearing off a piece, and popping it into his mouth before she could shove him away. They'd been doing this ritual ever since she came from the United States to live with them many years before.

"No, mi sobrino, and you will not tell him. You know how much I enjoy cooking your favorite foods, but Javier will say it's not my place." Flashing him a smile, she turned back to her work. "You will slice the meat for me while we wait for your parents. They are returning from a meeting in town."

"Father told me he had to meet with his attorney. I'm surprised Mother went with him." Pulling a carving knife from a drawer, he speared the meat, placing it on a nearby cutting board.

Reyna laughed at the notion of Maria attending a business meeting. "She did not go to the meeting. Javier dropped her and a friend at the mall."

"Without a bodyguard?"

"No, no. He'd never let Maria go without one of his men to watch. I don't understand why a family dealing in exports and cattle needs bodyguards." Reyna's face scrunched in disgust. Even she had to have someone with her when she went out.

"It is not unusual for families with money to hire bodyguards, Tía Reyna." Ivan's muttered response held little conviction. His father did handle several businesses for the family, staying out of most of the rest of the ventures his two uncles had established over the last few years, including the bucking stock and cattle export business. Ivan wished he'd be more involved, hoping to speak with him about it during his visit.

"Yes, you are correct. His concerns for us make planning a trip difficult." Reyna thought of her desire to visit her son in the United States. Even though he wrote her often, she hadn't seen him in over two years. Much too long without seeing her only child.

"Where would you like to go? Perhaps we can arrange a time I may accompany you instead of father's men."

"You would do that for me?" Reyna glanced up, surprised.

"Of course. As long as there is time for me to make arrangements in El Paso—"

"Here you are!"

Ivan turned at the sound of his mother's voice, held out his arms, and wrapped her in a warm embrace. "You look well. Shopping agrees with you."

Slapping his arm, she laughed at his humor. "You know me too well. Your father has gone straight to his study. He asked that you join him there." The edge to her voice caused Ivan's brows to knit together as his eyes narrowed. "I will see you at supper."

Turning toward Maria, Reyna tossed a towel on the counter, resting her hands on her hips. "Is everything all right, Maria?" she whispered as Ivan disappeared down the hall.

Tearing her gaze from her son's retreating form, she straightened before casting a worried look at Reyna and shaking her head. "There is trouble coming our way. Of that I am certain."

Chapter Four

Cold Creek, Colorado

"Cassie, Matt Garner is here to see you. I'll show him to the conference room. Cam will join you in a few minutes."

"I'll be right there." She wiped damp hands down her slacks as her stomach tightened. Fighting her emotions ever since Matt called about a meeting, Cassie had used every trick in her arsenal to fortify herself. It wasn't right that he could still imprison her heart after all this time. Love, hate, anger, disbelief—they'd all come roaring back at the first sight of him. She'd do everything in her power not to let it show.

Taking her time, Cassie picked up the rodeo events folder, straightened her shoulders, and put on her best professional face possible as she walked down the hall. The way her stomach tumbled like a bingo basket, anyone would've thought she was meeting someone famous instead of the man who'd broken her heart. Peering into the room, she spotted Matt on one side of the oval table, pulling a pen from his pocket, then glancing at his watch. Letting her gaze wander over him, Cassie felt a sense of loss so strong, it threatened to buckle her knees. The mature creases in his face added to the masculine look he'd always worn with little effort. Her throat tightened, remembering the way he'd stare down at her when they made love, how he'd lift a finger to caress her cheek. If a door down the hall hadn't opened, she would've continued her concealed scrutiny of him a while longer. Cam's appearance signaled the time for reminiscing had ended.

"You certain you're ready for this?" he whispered as he joined her.

"Absolutely. He's just another one of our partners. No problem at all."

Cam nodded, although the skeptical look on his face told her what he believed.

"Good morning, Matt. Thanks for coming all this way." Cassie extended her hand, feeling an unanticipated jolt as skin touched skin. Resisting the urge to jump back, she allowed him to give her hand a slight squeeze before releasing her hold.

"Cassie, it's good to see you again." Turning toward Cam, Matt shook his hand, then sat down and waited. He'd learned a long time ago to let the host start the conversation, giving him time to gauge the tone of the meeting, and anticipate what to expect.

"Matt, we have a lot to cover. I figure we'll meet for an hour, break for lunch, then finish up, if that works for you." When Matt nodded, Cam took a seat next to Cassie, glancing at her. "Why don't you start?"

Matt took the folder she handed him, glancing over her notes, then listened as she recapped the rodeo committees who'd already agreed to meetings and those they still pursued. Leaning back in his chair, he forced himself to try and focus on the content of the meeting instead of letting her voice carry him back to the last time they were together in college. As her comments continued, however, he lost the battle, recalling how they'd spent their last evening together.

They'd been at his place. She'd cooked dinner, making her famous marinara sauce and ladling large spoonfuls onto angel hair pasta. He remembered preparing the garlic bread while she dished out salad. Afterwards, they'd watched a movie, one of the action-comedy ones they both liked. He'd intended to tell her about finishing his degree early and his decision to start the pro circuit while she completed her studies, but desire had intervened. One touch led to a heated kiss, and before he knew it, they'd woken in each other's arms hours later.

"Matt, what do you think?"

Silently cursing himself for letting the past intrude, he straightened, thankful he'd already read her information.

"First, I'd like to ask you and Cam to review these lists."

"What are they?" Cassie asked, picking up the paper he passed to her.

"A list of rodeos we've been the prime contractor for in the most recent years. We'd propose that Double Ace enter the proposal process as the lead with you as the subcontractor. The second list is where *you've* held the lead position. We'd like to be included as the subcontractor if you plan to provide a proposal."

"Sounds reasonable," Cam offered as he scanned the list. "Cassie, do you have any issues with this?"

Pursing her lips, she read the list of rodeos she'd already targeted for a proposal. Most were on the list Double Ace had already prepared. "Well, I'd like to suggest we review the lists in detail. Make certain it's good for both parties."

"All right." Cam checked the time, then glanced at Matt. "I apologize, but I have an appointment. Cassie, how about you take Matt to lunch, review the lists and anything else needed to keep this moving. We'll meet back here afterwards."

"Sure, Cam," she replied, trying to hide the fact she wasn't happy about him not joining them. "Are you certain you can't come with us?"

"Not this time." Without another word, he stepped out, closing the door behind him, leaving them to stare at each other.

"Don't feel you have to join me for lunch, Cassie. I can grab something and meet you back here in time to review the lists." Matt tried to make the request sound casual, hoping she wouldn't detect how much he wanted to put distance between them. They were fire and ice. No matter how much he still wanted her, he couldn't let her know it, and wouldn't act on his desire.

Standing, she crossed her arms, shooting him a mocking smile. "Can't handle being near me, Garner?"

"I can handle being around you fine, MacLaren." Walking toward the door, he pulled it open. "After you."

Following her outside, he chastised himself for taking the bait. She'd always been able to goad him into doing what she wanted. The fact she'd done it again didn't sit well with him.

"We'll take my car."

"No. We'll go in my truck," Matt countered. "It's closer."

"They're almost next to each other," Cassie protested, walking ahead of him.

"Yeah. We're still taking mine." He walked to the passenger side, opening her door.

Cassie came to a stop, refusing to be pulled into such a juvenile argument. Nodding, she climbed onto the seat, grabbing the seat belt and clicking it into place with more force than needed.

"Where to?" Matt glanced at her as he got in and started the engine, feeling a bit guilty and childish at the slight jolt of victory pulsing through him.

"There's a grill down the street with burgers, salads, sandwiches—the usual lunch fare. Unless you want something fancier," she smirked, knowing he'd prefer pizza and beer if she mentioned it.

"Lead on."

It took no more than five minutes to navigate the short distance and be seated at one of the few remaining tables in the center of the crowded restaurant. Glancing around, Matt noted the odd combination of horse and auto racing memorabilia decorating the walls. Picking up the menu, his gaze landed on the name of the place—Horse Power. Okay, so the eclectic motif now made sense.

"Ready?" a waitress asked, staring down at Matt while ignoring Cassie.

"A club sandwich, fries, and diet soda," Cassie bit out, irritated at the slight. She'd been used to it during their time together. Young women drooling over Matt, doing all they could, short of crawling up his body, to get his attention. Now it just ticked her off.

"The same," Matt added. "Except I'll take a real soda." He flashed the average-looking, but well-endowed brunette one of his devastating smiles, getting a throaty giggle in response. He all but fell out of his chair as he let his gaze follow her back to the kitchen.

"Get over yourself, Matt," Cassie ground out, flashing him a severe look of disapproval.

"What?" His eyes widened in feigned innocence. Cassie's snort told him she didn't buy his act for a moment.

"Never mind." Reaching into her purse, she pulled out the lists Matt had prepared. "Let's review these while we wait for our food."

"You start. It sounds like you have issues with some of my suggestions."

"All right." Scanning the list again, she checked off certain names and dates with her pen. "We already have proposals ready to go to the committees for these rodeos. I don't think we should exclude ourselves from submitting." Shoving it toward him, she held her breath as he looked it over.

"We also have proposals ready to send. The difference is Double Ace has won the awards at least the last two years on all of these." He held up his hand when she started to object. "And each of those years we've gone against MacLaren Rodeo."

"That doesn't mean you'll be as competitive as we are this year. Perhaps we've sharpened our pencils…"

"You could say the same about us. I'll be blunt. There's no way in hell we're backing away from any of these, Cassie. You want to submit, go ahead. Just understand you may tick off those in charge at Double Ace to the point they don't include MacLaren when we win the award."

Glaring at each other across the table, both were glad when the waitress set their food down.

"Anything else?" the waitress asked, bending a little too low as she set down his glass and flashed Matt another suggestive smile, not bothering to hide the intention behind it.

"No. Thank you," Cassie snapped, sending the woman a withering look.

Stifling a laugh, Matt picked up his sandwich. "Why don't we call a truce long enough to eat?"

"Sure. Whatever." Gritting her teeth, she grabbed her glass of soda, taking a long swallow in an attempt to curb her irritation at both Matt, with his hard line on the rodeo proposals, and the loathsome waitress, who was too thick to take a hint and back off. It wouldn't be so bad if her body could control its response to him. She hadn't been able to calm the storm raging in her stomach or take in a solid breath since she'd seen him in the conference room that morning. Cassie needed a distraction, something to take her mind off the man across the table.

Picking up his glass and stretching out his legs until they rested against Cassie's, he seemed oblivious to the instant heat that shot through her at the contact. Contact which seemed all too familiar. She wanted to rub her leg against his, prolong the desire ripping through her. Instead, she tossed her napkin down and stood.

"I'll be back in a minute." Dashing to the back, she disappeared into the ladies' room, slipping into one of the stalls. She didn't need the facilities, just space and time to bring her feelings under control. Taking deep breaths, she leaned against the stall door and closed her eyes.

******

Matt watched her disappear, certain he'd been the cause of her quick departure. He shouldn't have pushed it, but he couldn't resist brushing his leg against hers, feeling the heat build until he either wanted to draw his leg back or reach across the table to take her hand in his. The need for contact, to touch Cassie, be near her overwhelmed him, creating a fire in his gut he couldn't control. It didn't matter how much he told himself they were no good together. His body took no notice, forcing him to face how much he still desired her, wanted her in his bed.

Glancing around him, he noticed a group of men being seated a few tables away. All wore shirts showing they were with the same organization, although he couldn't make out the name. Ignoring them and the laughter from their table, he poked at the last few fries, then picked up his glass, glancing up at the sound of chair legs scraping against the tile floor.

"We can head back to the office whenever you're ready," Cassie announced as she sat down, unmindful of her almost full plate of food.

"Sure. I'll just get the check."

"Hey, Cassie. I thought that was you."

Looking at the man standing next to her, she smiled, then stood to give him a brief hug. "Kurt. I didn't know you were here."

"We just arrived." He nodded toward his table as Matt stood.

"Kurt, this is Matt Garner. Our companies are working together on some proposals. Matt, this is Kurt Dobson. He's with the fire department, and he's..." Her voice trailed off as she tried to decide how best to describe her relationship with him.

"I'm the man she's dating," Kurt supplied, spearing Matt with a cautionary look as they shook hands. "Which reminds me, Cassie. How is Saturday night for going to the new restaurant we talked about?"

"Sounds good."

"Great. I'll pick you up at seven. Guess I'd better get back to the table. Good to meet you, Matt." He leaned down, placing a quick kiss on Cassie's cheek before turning away.

Matt's face had turned to stone when he learned about the relationship between Kurt and Cassie. Before he could gain control, his mind conjured up images of them in bed, their bodies hot and sweaty.

The jealousy he felt couldn't be more out of place, or more real. It should be him in her bed, not some firefighter who knew nothing about her and didn't love her the way Matt did. *Love*, he thought, cursing himself for letting the fact she had someone else in her life get to him.

"Matt, you ready?" Cassie watched his expression turn from what appeared to be surprise to indifference within a matter of seconds. Blinking, she stared at him, wondering if the news of her dating bothered him at all. If it did, he hid it pretty well.

"Yeah. Let's get out of here."

Driving back to the office, Matt couldn't get his mind off Kurt. All those years they were apart, he never allowed himself to dwell on what Cassie might or might not be doing. Now, faced with the reality of another man in her life, he felt an unexpected anger build within him. Gripping the steering wheel almost painfully, he took slow breaths, hoping Cassie didn't notice.

"How long have you been seeing him?" *Damn.* He didn't mean to ask that out loud.

"A few weeks. I met him through Cam and Lainey at a Search and Rescue meeting. He's one of their trainers." She tried to sound casual, inserting a tone of fondness for Kurt she didn't quite feel. They'd gone out three times. Two of them had been interrupted by emergency calls for arson fires. In total, she figured they'd spent maybe five hours together. Not much time to get to know each other, yet she knew he wasn't for her. She'd planned to tell him before he'd surprised her at the restaurant, asking her on another date.

"Seems like an okay guy." Matt didn't want to like the guy, and he sure as hell didn't want Cassie to be with him.

"What about you?" Cassie had been waiting for the right time to ask, her curiosity fueling her courage.

"What about me?"

"Are you dating? Engaged?" *Married?*

"Not me," he snorted, feeling his body relax a little. "No encumbrances of any kind."

"Oh." Somehow the news deflated her more than providing relief. He sounded pleased about having no attachments, no one to tie him down, like she would have if they'd stayed together.

Pulling into the parking lot and killing the engine, Matt jumped out, his mind whirling with thoughts of Cassie and Kurt. The guy was new in her life, while he had no woman in his to worry about. Matt refused to analyze why those realizations brought him a measure of comfort, but they did.

Chapter Five

"Jerrod, why don't you provide us with an update on the fire investigations."

"Be glad to, Captain." Jerrod James, their fire and arson investigator, and a close friend of Kurt's, stepped to the front of the room where a portable bulletin board held photos of the last two fires. "This is the fire from a week ago. The owners weren't on the property at the time. I believe the cause to be unattended candles accompanied by a gas leak." Picking up his cup, he took a sip of coffee, letting his gaze roam over the people in the room. "In other words, an accidental fire with an identified cause." Seeing Kurt at the back, he nodded before continuing.

"The fire from three days ago is still under investigation. As you know, it occurred in an abandoned barn five miles from the station. We believe it may have been started by teenagers. The point of origin is dead center in the barn's first story. Accelerants were combined, poured over a pile of old hay, then road flares were tossed inside. Simple, efficient." He glanced up and nodded, seeing Kurt raise his hand.

"What accelerants were used?"

"I still need confirmed results from the lab, but in my opinion, it was a combination of gasoline and diesel."

"Do you believe the two fires are related?" Captain Vassar stood to the side, a bad feeling building in his gut.

"At this time, there's no indication they are. As I said, one appears to be a simple case of unattended candles, while the barn fire looks to be arson set for excitement, maybe a prank that got out of hand. Any other questions?"

"Thank you, Jerrod." Captain Vassar finished with a few station updates before adjourning the meeting.

"How's it going, buddy? I heard you have a new lady." Jerrod clasped Kurt on the shoulder, following him to the day room.

Stopping in the hall, Kurt turned, letting a few others pass by. "No big deal. I don't know her really well. We're taking it slow." They'd been out a few times, yet Kurt felt a detachment he didn't expect. Smart and funny, Cassie was also so guarded, their conversations were stilted and forced. The chemistry he expected never materialized, leaving him with a sense he was out to dinner with his sister rather than a date. He figured they'd go on one more date, see if he could get her to relax and open up. If not, he'd let her know he didn't see them as a fit.

"Anyone I know?"

"Doubtful. She's new in town. Works for MacLaren Rodeo." Kurt didn't want to discuss Cassie at the station. It didn't take much for his fellow firefighters to blow anything involving a woman out of proportion. "Let's meet for drinks later. For now, join us for lunch. I'm cooking."

"Sorry, buddy. I can't today. I've got to drive north to help with another suspected arson fire. Their investigator is out of commission...broken leg and concussion from falling down a flight of stairs." Jerrod scrubbed a hand down his face. "Couldn't come at a worse time with our recent fires. I'll be back in time for beer, though."

"Hey, Dobson. You going to feed us or what?"

"Guess I'd better finish lunch before the beasts revolt. They get grumpy when they aren't fed on time. I'll see you tonight." Kurt turned toward the kitchen as Jerrod left the station.

He finished assembling a large salad, setting it on the bar, along with two huge dishes of lasagna and baskets of bread. All the while, he pondered Jerrod's report on the latest fire. They expected a fire call every couple months, more in the dry summer season. Two in such a short span of time was unusual, even if one had been caused by recklessness. Brushing aside his concerns, Kurt grabbed a plate, deciding to feed his own beast before returning to work.

******

"We worked it all out, Gage. Cam stepped in and made the final decision since Cassie refused to budge from her position." Matt set his phone on speaker and placed it on the dresser in his hotel room as he poured a glass of water.

"Are you going to be able to work with someone who's so determined to have her way? Seems she's pretty intractable."

Matt chuckled. "You don't have to tell me. She's changed little from when the two of us were together." He chugged the water, then poured another glass. "To answer your question, yes. It takes more time to wear her down than most people, but Cam wants this to work and so do we. She's a cog in the wheel, Gage. Nothing more."

"I hope you're right. Keep in mind, though, that cogs have been known to break. When that happens, the entire journey can come to a halt."

Matt cringed at Gage's observation. "I've got this handled. Don't worry."

"It's in your hands, man. Don't let us down."

Matt shoved his fingers through his hair as the call ended. Letting out a breath, he sat on the bed, falling back to stare at the ceiling. If today's experience signaled the way their working relationship would go, he was in for a long, crazy rodeo season. She'd argue and push him to his limits, all the while setting him on fire more than any woman he'd ever known. A combination of exasperation and exhilaration all in one gorgeous, sexy package. The comprehension frustrated and excited him, even as his brain sent out warning signals.

He couldn't afford to show either anger or desire, no matter how she triggered both feelings. Closing his eyes, he thought of how difficult today had been. He'd struggled keeping his hands to himself during the drive to the restaurant and back to the office. Seeing her sitting an arm's length away flooded him with memories—he accepted most were good, a smile curving his mouth.

He couldn't count the number of times they'd parked in his truck, catching glimpses of a sunrise or sunset while steaming up the windows. Their sessions had risen to a new level when he'd saved enough to spring for a motel room, then again when she'd joined him at college. By then, he had a studio apartment where she stayed most Friday and Saturday nights. Regret ripped through him as he remembered how he'd held her close all night, legs and arms tangled together, then wake her with heated kisses and gentle caresses.

Groaning, Matt pushed himself up, scrubbing a hand down his face. Looking at the clock, he decided it wasn't too late for a visit to the local bar. A cold beer had his name on it...a *very* cold beer.

******

Tossing down her pen, Cassie struggled to focus on the work before her. She'd read the agreement they'd received from one of their longtime rodeo committees three times. Each time, her mind wandered to thoughts of Matt. It made no difference how much she schooled herself to concentrate on the work before her. Her mind, well...had a mind of its own.

She'd been pushy, obnoxious, and outright rude several times, garnering warning glances from Cam, grimaces from Matt. The awareness was there, but the ability to control the combative responses vanished each time he questioned her ideas.

Over the years, she'd worked hard to become more of a team player, rein in her competitive nature, and tone down the way she approached opposition to her concepts. None of that effort came through today. Matt seemed to bring out every negative characteristic still buried deep inside. She'd been surprised Cam hadn't called her into his office for an official dressing down.

"What's going on?" Janie peered over her shoulder, spotting the numerous scribblings Cassie had created on a pad of paper. None of them meant a thing. "Maybe a glass of wine will calm your nerves."

"I'm not nervous," Cassie huffed, pushing back from the table and standing.

"No? Then what are you? I haven't seen you this worked up since Matt took off for the rodeo circuit." Janie crossed her arms, resting a hip against the table.

"I don't know. It's just..." Her voice trailed off as she tried to form a coherent thought. "I guess I thought it would be easier to be around him after all this time."

"And it's not?"

"No. If anything, it's worse. Having him back in my life emphasizes all I lost when he walked away. What's wrong with me that I can't get him out of my system after all the pain he's caused? You'd think I'd hate him."

"But you don't."

"Believe me, I'm trying." Cassie paced to the refrigerator, grabbing a bottle of water and taking a long swallow. "He's just so...I don't know...more than I remembered."

"Well, he has filled out some, has muscles he didn't have before, along with a maturity in the way he carries himself. He may even be more handsome than when you two were together."

Cassie buried her face in her hands and groaned.

Janie tapped her chin with a finger. "And his smile. He sure has learned to use it to his advantage."

Cassie stared at her roommate, head tilted to the side. "You've talked to him?"

"Not me, but I had to get a look at him after all this time. I peeked around the corner while he carried on a long conversation with the receptionist. She couldn't stop talking about him after she showed him to the conference room. I think she's in lust."

"You're not helping, Janie." She plopped into an armchair in the living room, knowing she felt too agitated to stay seated for long.

"Sorry, hon. But I know how you are about me telling you how I really feel. The guy's a hunk *and* single. What's a girl to do?"

Standing, Cassie walked to the table, looking down at the papers spread out next to her computer. Except for a continual stab of longing she couldn't control, she had nothing to show for the last hour.

"Maybe you need to take Skye up on her offer to visit her in Montana. Cam and Mitch have both said they want the two of you to make more joint calls. It may be time to go with it." Janie pulled out a chair, sitting down, resting her arms on the table. "After today, Cam may even *require* you to take off."

"What do you mean? Did he say something to you?" Turning her chair toward Janie, she sat down, leaning forward.

"Of course not. But the walls of the conference room aren't that thick and your voice does carry..."

Cassie let out a sigh, chastising herself again for letting her temper get the best of her.

"Look, it's not that bad. If it were, Cam would've called you into his office before he left today. But if you don't think you can handle being around Matt, it may be best to confront it with Cam now rather than let the whole partnership fall apart."

Shutting her eyes tight, Cassie rubbed her temples in an attempt to stop the throbbing headache she'd had all day. The effort didn't help.

Standing, she grabbed her purse. "I need some fresh air."

"You aren't taking off at this hour, are you?"

"It's not that late and I won't be gone long. I just need to clear my head, get away for a bit." Pulling the door open, she stepped outside before turning. "Thanks, Janie. It's good to have a friend who's honest with me." Shutting the door, she headed to her truck, wishing she could start the day over.

******

Twenty minutes seemed like an hour as Cassie drove aimlessly around town, her windows down, radio playing the country music she loved. Tonight, she didn't even change channels when songs Matt and she had both liked came on. Instead, she forced herself to listen, remembering the good times...and the bad. Truthfully, she couldn't remember much of the bad.

Giving up, she turned into the parking lot of a neighborhood bar a few blocks from her apartment. She and Janie came here a couple times a week after work to grab a quick meal and watch whatever sports were on the numerous televisions mounted to the walls. Her spirits brightened, noticing the lot was half empty. She might even get a seat at a secluded table where she could sip a beer and not have to converse with any of the locals.

"Hey, Cassie."

She glanced up to see the owner wave a quick greeting. Smiling, she walked over, leaning against the bar.

"Hi, Marcus. How's it going tonight?"

"Slow," he answered, grabbing a glass and filling it with her favorite craft beer. Sliding it across the bar, he took a good look at her. "You look beat. Long day at work?"

"Long, frustrating, embarrassing...you name it and I probably felt it today." Lifting her glass, she tilted it to him, then took a sip. "I had to get out for a bit. Clear my head."

"Good decision." Leaning over the bar, Marcus dropped his voice to a whisper. "There's a new guy down at the end of the bar. Never seen him before, but it might be worth striking up a conversation." He paused when he saw Cassie's eyes widen. "You know, to get your mind off today."

Her mouth twitched at the corners. "Are you trying to set me up, Marcus?"

Touching his fist to his chest, his face sobered. "Not me, darlin'. My only aim is to get you back to your normal, smiling self. Anyway, he's down that way if you change your mind." He nodded to his left toward the darkest corner of the bar.

Ignoring the suggestion, she settled onto a stool, deciding against a table. She'd have one beer, then head home, crawl under the covers, and pray for sleep. Staring at the big screen in front of her, she had the strangest feeling of being watched. Telling herself it wouldn't be unusual in a bar, she focused on the television again.

It didn't take long for the feeling to return—stronger this time. Glancing around, trying not to look obvious, she spotted a couple at one table and three men sitting together at the bar. Then her gaze wandered to where Marcus had indicated the new guy sat. Blinking, she let her eyes adjust to the dark section of the bar, then gasped when a pair of eyes she knew well stared back.

Turning her head, hoping he hadn't recognized her, she pulled several bills from her purse and set them on the bar. "Here you are, Marcus. I need to run."

"It's already taken care of, sugar."

"What? By whom?"

Marcus nodded behind her, then turned toward another customer.

"Good evening, Cassie."

Turning slowly in her seat, she swallowed the lump in her throat. "Matt. What a surprise."

"Mind if I take a seat?" He lowered himself onto the stool next to her. "Do you live around here?"

She didn't want to talk with him. Didn't even want to see him. The sole purpose of getting out was to rid her mind of Matt, clear her thoughts, and get back to normal. Now she had to contend with her heart beating so hard, she thought it would burst from her chest.

"A few blocks. Are you staying nearby?" Her voice sounded much steadier than she felt.

"Across the street. I just needed to get out for a bit." He let his gaze wander over her, not caring if she noticed or what she thought of his open appraisal.

"Well, I should be going. Thanks for the beer." Slipping a hand under the strap of her purse, she paused when Matt's hand gripped her arm.

"Don't leave yet. Stay and talk to me for a while."

Glancing down at his hand, feeling the same jolt she'd always felt when he touched her, she bit her bottom lip, then pulled her arm free. "I really should head out."

"Please, Cass."

She'd seen that look before, knew he needed the comfort only a familiar soul could provide. For a brief moment, she wished he wanted her to stay because he still had feelings for her, not just because he needed the company of someone familiar. Pushing the foolish thought from her mind, she settled back on her chair.

"All right, for a little bit." Pulling her unfinished beer toward her, she took a sip, looking up at the television.

"We got a lot accomplished today."

She could feel his gaze boring into her, causing her skin to prickle with heat.

"Yes...yes, we did." She could hear the slight rise in her voice.

"I think we can wrap up tomorrow."

Clearing her throat, she glanced over at him. "Then where will you go?"

"Crooked Tree to meet with Skye. Possibly Mitch and Sean," he answered, mentioning her cousins. "Do you ever go up that way?"

"I've been there twice. I'm due to go again. Skye wants us to meet with some of the rodeo committees together. She believes it will make a stronger impact on them if we both show up." Cassie gripped her glass tighter, quelling the almost overpowering urge to reach out, run her fingers up his neck, and play with the long hair at his nape.

"You're welcome to ride up with me."

"What?" Her eyes widened as panic rippled through her. "No. I couldn't do that. It would be crazy to..." Her voice trailed off as she gulped down the last of her beer, reaching for her purse again. "Look, I really have to leave." She headed for the door, not looking back.

"Cass, wait up." Matt dashed ahead of her, holding the door open. "I'll walk you to your truck."

"It's not necessary—"

"Yes, it is." He placed his hand on the small of her back, ignoring the heat which flamed at the contact as they walked the short distance to her truck.

Rummaging in her purse, she pulled out the keys, groaning when they slipped from her hand.

"I'll get it." Matt grabbed the keys and unlocked her door, then held it open, but blocked her entry. "I'm sorry if I said something wrong."

Wanting only to get inside and get away, she shook her head. "You didn't say anything wrong. I just need to leave." She lifted her face, chin jutting toward him.

"Always in a hurry. Always somewhere to go." He lifted his hand, letting a finger trail down her cheek, along the line of her jaw, then down her neck.

Excitement mingled with fear at his touch, causing what felt like a swarm of butterflies to pool in her belly. She had to get away from him. Now.

"Matt, I really should go." Her voice held little conviction, even as she knew staying longer would be foolish.

His hand wandered to the back of her neck, drawing her closer. "Do you ever take time to enjoy yourself, relax and have a little fun?"

She could feel the heat flame in her cheeks as he pulled her closer, but she couldn't seem to find the strength to push him away. It had been so long, and she missed him terribly.

He bent his head, moving toward her until their mouths were a mere inch apart. Seeing her eyes close and feeling no resistance, he covered her mouth with his. The kiss was tentative at first, his lips brushing across hers, becoming more possessive as she dug her fingers into his arms. Wrapping his arms around her, pulling her tight, he let his hands roam over her back, settling on her waist. Groaning in pleasure, he deepened the kiss, taking whatever she'd give him.

Heat streaked through her at the feel of his hands, warm and familiar as they stroked her back, moving to her hips to align her against him. She could feel her knees tremble. His taste, scent, the feel of him after so long sent her nerves humming. Seeking closer contact, she wrapped her hands around his neck, sliding her fingers through his hair as she pulled him closer.

"Ah, Cassie, baby. I've missed you," he murmured against her ear.

Her heart tripped over the words as doubt crept into her mind. She knew he no longer wanted her, had walked away without a backward glance. The realization of what they were doing hit her like a slap in the face. Breaking the kiss and lowering her hands, she pushed against his chest.

"Matt, stop. We can't do this." Pushing again, she finally broke his hold on her and took an unsteady step backward, drawing in a breath.

Dragging a hand through his hair, he locked his gaze on hers, feeling as if his heart had seized. Breaking eye contact, he moved away, giving them both space.

"You're right. We can't."

Her stomach plummeted at his quick agreement, blinking to fight back tears. Nodding, she climbed into the truck, not allowing herself to look at him. Starting the engine, she pulled away, leaving him to stare after her.

Watching her disappear down the road, he cursed at himself and his foolishness. Passion, desire, lust. None had any impact on why they weren't together. No matter how much his body craved hers, how much his heart ached at not having her, they were poison together and that wouldn't change.

From now on, he had to keep a tight rein on his feelings, ignore the insistent pull she had on him, and forget how much he wanted her.

Chapter Six

"This is lovely, Kurt. I've been wanting to try it since first moving to Cold Creek." Cassie glanced around the elegant restaurant. It had been a long time since she'd been taken to such a nice place. A wave of guilt hit her, knowing she planned to tell him they had no future together.

"I'm glad you like it. Let's hope the food is as great as I've heard."

Opening the menu, she took her time reading each selection, never seeing such an interesting number of choices. Ordering the eleven-spiced venison and grilled quail with tamale tart, apple-braised cabbage, grilled eggplant, and juniper sauce, she handed the menu to their waiter, picking up her glass of Argentine Malbec.

"How's your wine?" Kurt watched her over the flowers and candles in the center of the table, wondering what troubled her. The usual smile was in place, bright as always, yet it didn't quite reach her eyes. It should have made him feel better about his decision to not ask her out after tonight. Instead, it made him curious about what weighed on her.

"Excellent." She took another sip, then set down her glass. "Tell me what you've been doing."

"We had another fire. You probably read about it in the paper." He recounted what had been found at the scene and their efforts to determine if the blaze was arson.

As he spoke, Cassie found herself thinking of a few nights before and her encounter with Matt. Each had gone through their meeting the following day as if nothing had happened. They'd been professional, polite, and distant. Matt had excused himself when they broke for lunch, declining an invitation to join her at a restaurant a few blocks away, saying he had other plans. His rejection stung. When the afternoon session ended, he'd left for Montana without any hesitation and with no more than a cursory goodbye.

Most of the last few nights, she'd lain in bed, unable to sleep, and unwilling to erase the feel of his lips on hers, his arms wrapped around her. He'd felt so right, as if their time apart had been scant seconds instead of years. But a part of her knew it was wrong, which was why she'd pushed him away. Matt didn't want her for more than a night to fill his time while on the road. She felt certain he'd leave without a backward glance if she gave into her desire, giving him what they both wanted.

"Cassie. You with me?" Kurt watched her, his brows meeting in a frown.

Face heating, she fought to recall what he'd been talking about. "Yes, of course. You're continuing to investigate and believe you have one case of arson."

"Close enough. Excuse me a minute." Reaching in his pocket, he pulled out his phone. "Dobson." He listened before responding. "Yes, sir. I'm on my way." He pulled out his credit card, signaling their waiter. "Sorry, Cassie. There's another fire. Stay as long as you like. I'll leave the amount open if you want another drink or dessert." Standing, he walked around the table, placing a kiss on her cheek. "I'll call you."

Watching as he dashed outside, she felt no remorse at his departure. No matter how much she liked him, she'd yet to meet anyone who could compare with Matt. She wondered if she'd ever meet a man who could trigger the intense passion she felt with him. The reality hurt, knowing he was now part of her life whether she wanted him to be or not.

******

Kurt helped put the apparatus back together as the men finished the overhaul, tearing down ceilings and exposing walls to check for any type of fire extension. It had been another abandoned building. This time on the edge of town in a defunct industrial park. He couldn't remember the last time he saw activity in this area, guessing the fire had been set for thrills, not for monetary gain. Perhaps they did have a gang of teenagers setting fires for the adrenaline rush of watching a building destroyed by flames.

"Three fires in less than two weeks. That must be some kind of record around here." Captain Vassar stood next to Kurt, surveying the damage. "Jerrod is on his way to start the investigation, although I doubt he'll be able to detect much until morning."

"He likes to get a fast start, taking pictures as soon after containment as possible." Kurt continued to watch the scene, letting out a breath when a member of their crew gave an all-clear signal.

"At least no one was in the building," Vassar commented, walking away.

Kurt stepped a few paces closer to the building before turning at a shout from behind him.

"Hey, Kurt. Wait up."

Jerrod grabbed a camera and backpack, along with the rest of his equipment, and jogged toward him. "What do you know so far?"

"Not much. Abandoned building. No one inside. No equipment, furnishings, or trash. Partition walls and general debris kept the fire going once the fuel flamed out. Point of origin appears to be in the far corner office. I'll go in with you."

Jerrod stepped inside and glanced around. "It's large by Cold Creek standards."

"Close to eight thousand square feet is what the captain said. About a third of the space had been offices, while the rest might have been warehouse or manufacturing space. Doesn't make sense to set fire to a building unless..."

"Unless someone wanted to get their kicks by watching stuff burn," Jerrod finished, already suspecting the barn fire and this one were related. Following Kurt to what had been a corner office, he took pictures and made notes, taking samples for testing. Finishing, he turned back toward the entrance. "Not much else I can do tonight. Feel free to join me at six tomorrow morning for a more detailed investigation."

Kurt smiled at the prospect. He'd taken the courses necessary to become a fire investigator. All he waited for was the funding needed to become Jerrod's assistant. Given the current economic environment, he wasn't holding his breath.

"I thought you had plans with your lady tonight," Jerrod uttered, looking around.

"We were at dinner when I got the call. Doesn't matter. I doubt we'll be seeing each other again, at least not on a date." Kurt sighed, wishing he had a chance to discuss it with her. Now that he'd met her ex-boyfriend, he felt certain some of the friction between them had been due to unresolved feelings for Matt. Even though she'd said they were long over, the reality felt different once Kurt met him.

"Tell you what. Once you get cleaned up, meet me for a beer. You can whine about your dating problems, and I'll whine about my *lack* of dating possibilities. It's gotta be better than nursing a beer alone."

"Done. I'll see you in about an hour."

******

Houston, Texas

"Of course, Ivan. I can bring on as many men as you need to handle the additional stock. Keep me posted on the delivery schedule. I'll take care of everything from this end." Gage hung up the phone, jotting down a few notes.

The owners in Mexico had an annoying habit of sending their rodeo stock in the same trucks as cattle meant for specific buyers. The increase in cattle imports from Mexico would require several new hires to cull the herd before sending the contracted number to buyers in the United States. Grateful for the expanded business and success of a company relatively new in the stock business, Gage still felt a twinge of uncertainty about what he considered haphazard practices. Interestingly, he'd gotten the same vibe from Ivan Santiago, as if he also had qualms about some of the orders coming from the two active majority owners—his uncles. It couldn't be easy taking orders from family.

"Gage, you have a call from Cassie MacLaren. Should I take a message?" The receptionist stood outside his office, leaning against the doorframe, flashing him a warm smile.

"No, I'll take the call. Thanks." He watched her walk away, believing she communicated more than just a fashion statement with the short skirts and provocative tops she wore each day. Single and attractive, he allowed himself to look. Anything more held little appeal. He'd learned through hard experience you don't date someone you work with every day. "Hello, Cassie."

"Good morning, Gage. Hope I didn't interrupt anything."

He could hear a slight quiver in her voice and hoped this had nothing to do with Matt.

"Nope. How can I help you?"

"Cam asked that I give you a heads-up. He'll be in Houston tomorrow and wondered if you'd have time to meet with him."

"No problem. Give me his number and I'll set it up."

"That's why he asked me to call. He's in meetings at the corporate offices in Fire Mountain today. Heath had them all hand over their phones." Cassie laughed, imagining the looks on all their faces when her father made the request. "If you'll give me some times, I'll make sure he gets the information, then confirm back with you."

Gage chuckled. Like many companies, he knew the three elder MacLaren brothers ruled a pretty tight operation, but confiscating phones before a meeting was new to him.

"If he has no plans, let's meet for dinner tomorrow night."

"Great. Oh, here's his number in case you need to reach him tomorrow." Cassie rattled it off, fidgeting with her pen, glad Gage couldn't see her. Knowing he and Matt were close friends, she kept the call short, not wanting to move into any topic that might include him.

"I assume all went well with Matt."

She groaned inwardly at Gage's offhanded comment. "Fine. No problems at all. Everything went just great. From what I heard, he's in Montana meeting with Skye." She took a breath, feeling her face color at the way she rambled. "I'll let you go and will pass your request about dinner along to Cam. Thanks."

Hearing her click off, Gage hung up, guessing he'd hit a sensitive spot. He'd known Matt a long time, yet over all those years, he'd mentioned Cassie only in passing—until the day she belted him outside Gage's office. Afterwards, he'd learned much more, hoping he wasn't making a mistake assigning Matt as the contact point for MacLaren Rodeo. Shaking off the thought, he grabbed the phone again.

"It's Gage Templeton. I need to speak with Montgomery."

******

Crooked Tree, Montana

MacLaren Rodeo, Bucking Bull Group

"Have a seat, Matt. Sean is out in the yard. I'll go get him." Skye gestured to a chair as she left to get her brother.

On the drive from Colorado, he'd made a few stops, meeting with the chairs of two rodeo committees and another supplier providing bull stock for rodeos. Double Ace had worked with them before and he hoped to continue, even with the association between MacLaren and his company.

Glancing around, he noticed the walls were covered with pictures of Rafe's children—Mitch, Skye, Sean, and Rhett, the youngest one still in college. Like Cassie's family in Fire Mountain, they'd competed in various rodeo events while growing up. Matt grinned, a crooked, regretful twist of his lips. Seems he might never break his ties with the MacLaren family. At this point, he didn't believe he wanted to.

"Matt, it's good to see you." Sean entered the office first, extending his hand.

"Same here." Matt gripped his hand. "Will Mitch be joining us?"

"Not today. He was unexpectedly summoned to a meeting in Fire Mountain yesterday."

"Seems Heath called the presidents of the different groups together. They're meeting with the brothers and top people at MacLaren Enterprises." Skye referred to her father, Rafe, and his brothers, Heath and Jace.

"Sounds mysterious." Matt drew his brows together, wondering what new deal they might be discussing, then pushed it from his mind. He had other business to discuss.

"It is. Those men are always working on some deal." Skye set a bottle of water in front of each of them. "Seems you're doing a lot of driving lately."

"I left Houston a couple weeks ago. Visited some customers along the way, met with Cam and Cassie over two days, then came here. The plan is to take another three weeks on the way back to Houston." Although he enjoyed the job and working with Gage, it didn't quite fill the void left after his rodeo days.

"How's Cassie doing?" Skye did her best to make it a casual question. She'd been there the day Cassie and Matt had seen each other for the first time after the split, witnessed the punch Cassie landed to his face, and sympathized with her cousin over drinks that night. It had been plain she'd never gotten over Matt, but duty called. No matter her personal feelings, Skye had to put her own aside and work with him.

"Good." Matt squirmed in his seat, lifting the bottle of water to his mouth to deflect more questions. He'd spent the entire last day in Cold Creek and the ride to Montana thinking of their kiss, wishing he hadn't started it, then wishing he'd pushed it further. He figured it was God's punishment for whatever misdeeds he'd committed. The one woman he couldn't get enough of and couldn't forget was also the one woman who could drive him crazy with her strong, competitive personality.

"Well, I guess we should get started." Skye watched his expression twist and wondered if her question about Cassie triggered unease or regret. Either way, it was a private issue between Matt and Cassie.

******

"Guess that does it. Unless you have more to talk about," Skye said.

"I think that's it," Matt answered, ready to get out of the office.

"Good. How about dinner?" Sean asked, standing and grabbing his hat.

"I'm in, as long as it includes a beer." Matt picked up his own well-worn hat.

"Don't they pay you enough at Double Ace to get yourself a decent cover?" Sean asked, a grin splitting his face.

Matt took another look at his old Stetson. "Hey, this hat has seen me through a lot of tough times and worse rides. Besides, breaking in a new hat is almost as hard as breaking in a new pair of boots."

"Fair enough. What kind of food—" Sean broke off as his phone rang. Glancing at the caller ID, he answered immediately. "Good evening, Heath... Yes, he's here." He handed Matt the phone, then turned away. "We'll be in the lobby when you're ready." Sean and Skye stepped into the hall, leaving Matt to wonder what was going on.

"Heath, it's Matt." Listening, his body tensed, going on alert as Heath explained the reason for the call. "Tonight? But I have my truck here in Crooked Tree and meetings planned—" His mouth drew into a thin line when Heath interrupted. "Yes, sir. I understand. I'll be at the airport in an hour."

Walking down the stairs to the lobby, he handed the phone to Sean, knowing his face conveyed the confusion he felt.

"What's going on?" Skye walked up next to them.

"I wish I knew. Heath has sent the company jet to pick me up in an hour at the airport. I'm to go to Fire Mountain and meet with him, Jace, and Rafe."

"Tonight?" Sean's bewildered expression mirrored Matt's.

"He said it's important we meet tonight."

"Nothing about your grandfather or brother, I hope." Sean had met Seth Garner and Matt's younger brother, Troy, at Mitch's wedding reception and knew Seth had raised his grandsons after their parents died in an accident.

"No. Heath said the family is fine, but he wouldn't give me any other details."

"Well, when any of the brothers request a meeting, it's best to get it over with. At least that's the way it is with our dad. I suspect it's the same with the other two," Sean said. "Come on. We've got an hour. We'll grab dinner, then take you to the airport."

Chapter Seven

"Can I get you anything to drink?" the co-pilot asked after the plane had leveled off. "We have a full bar, sodas, water."

"Water would be fine. Thanks." Matt sat back in his seat, unable to come up with a good reason for Heath's summons. He'd known him his entire life. His parents and Cassie's had been best friends until the accident. Over the years, Heath had become a father figure, a man Matt looked up to, wanted to please. The break with Cassie had been difficult on many levels, not the least of which was losing Heath's respect. Now he wanted to meet with Matt, and there was no way he'd refuse.

According to the pilot, the flight would take a little more than two hours, giving him time for some much needed sleep. Folding his arms across his chest, he stretched out his long legs and closed his eyes. It was the best way he knew to rid his mind of unwanted thoughts of Cassie and his curiosity about the upcoming meeting.

"Mr. Garner, we're about to start our descent into Fire Mountain." The co-pilot touched his shoulder, making certain Matt was awake, then disappeared into the cockpit. He stared out the window at the nighttime view of Fire Mountain. It had been several years since he'd flown into the small airport. Not much had changed.

As they came to a halt after a smooth landing, he grabbed his overnight bag, then walked down the steps, spotting his grandfather standing next to his extended cab, long bed pickup. A relieved breath escaped his lungs.

"Pops." He wrapped Seth in a hug. "I didn't expect to see you here."

"I called Heath about the new construction project we're doing for them and he mentioned you flying in. He said a car would be sent for you," he scoffed. "I told him to forget it. I'd deliver you to him after we had a few minutes to catch up."

Tossing his bag in the back seat, Matt climbed in, spotting the expected folders on the seat between them. "MacLaren keeping you busy?"

"Those boys know how to create more work than any three men I've ever known. I've had to hire two new crews to keep up with the load." Seth's grumbled response hid his pleasure at keeping the construction business going. Before the accident which killed Matt's parents, he'd planned to pass it along to his son, who'd worked for years to help keep it successful. Matt had no interest in following his grandfather into the business, although he didn't rule out ending up there someday. His younger brother, Troy, wanted nothing more than to get his degree and work for the company.

"Is Troy in town?" Matt leaned his head against the seat, letting his body relax.

"Left last weekend. You know he finishes grad school at the end of the year." A year younger than Matt, Troy had always planned to get his MBA. It had taken a few years longer than he'd planned, but Matt couldn't be more proud of him.

"I'll be at the graduation if that's what you're asking." Matt glanced at Seth, a grin turning up the corners of his mouth.

"You'd better be. Without you sending a good chunk of your rodeo winnings a few years ago, who knows if he would've ever made it this far." The economic crash had impacted Seth's construction business, bringing some projects to a grinding halt. Between Seth's savings, Troy's part-time work and college loans, and Matt's help, they'd all made it through.

"And now Heath has you working harder than ever."

"True. It's good for this old heart." Seth thumped his chest a couple times, chuckling. Turning into Matt's favorite drive-thru, they ordered, then parked the truck down the block by one of the MacLaren projects. "Pass me my burger, boy. I haven't eaten since lunch."

They ate in silence for several minutes, Matt studying the construction work. "What is it?"

"The MacLarens are building senior housing." He indicated the building in front of them. "Next to it is low-income apartments for people who are struggling but don't yet qualify under the senior category. I don't know how they do it, but even with reduced rent, they still make money."

"How about the high-end stuff?" Matt knew MacLaren Enterprises was also heavily invested in pricy condominiums and retail space in several towns in the western U.S. He figured the profits from one entity helped pay for the lower rents in others.

"We only work on the Arizona projects. We've got two large ones going in the valley. The rest are built by out-of-state contractors." Seth tossed his empty wrapper aside, clutched the steering wheel with both hands, and pulled out into traffic.

Driving in silence to the MacLaren offices, Matt could feel the tension begin to build in the cab of the truck. He knew to wait it out when his grandfather had something on his mind.

"You know, Matt, I'm not getting any younger." Seth stared at the road, wishing they had more time. "Troy is going to do a real fine job running this business someday."

Matt waited for him to continue. When Seth stayed silent, he turned in the seat to stare at him. "What are you trying to say, Pops?"

Seth's mouth formed a thin line, his expression not changing, although Matt knew he struggled with something. "I've got some health issues going on."

Matt's eyes widened, then narrowed at the news. Seth never talked about his health. Never. "Tell me."

Clearing his throat, Seth shifted in his seat, still not looking at Matt. "Something about my prostate."

Matt muttered a curse. "Pull over. We need to talk about this."

"Heath wanted you at the office by nine. We'll barely make it as it is. We can—"

"Pops, right now, I don't give a damn what Heath has to say. This is more important." He turned to look out the windshield. "Take that turnoff. We can talk there."

Pulling over and cutting the engine, Seth got out of the truck, pacing to the front, and leaning against the hood. Reaching in his pocket, he pulled out a package of cinnamon gum, handing a piece to Matt.

"Look there." Seth pointed to the sky. "A shooting star. Some people would take that as a sign."

"A sign? You want to talk about a sign, Pops? We need to talk about what the doctor said." Matt tried to control the worry building inside, knowing he was taking his fear out on his grandfather. "Please. Tell me."

"A year ago, the tests and exams came back positive. The doc and I spoke, and when a second opinion came back with the same findings, we made the decision to have it treated with radiation." Seth glanced at Matt standing a few feet away, his arms crossed, legs shoulder width apart.

"Go on."

"Seemed to work, but it's come back. Looks like I need surgery."

Matt couldn't stop the stream of curses as he dropped his arms and paced several feet away. Settling his hands on his hips, he looked up at the sky, wishing he could have any other conversation. Walking back, he leaned against the truck.

"I want to speak with the doctor."

"What?" Seth growled. "You think I can't handle my own health problems? I didn't decide to talk about this because I wanted your opinion."

"Then why did you tell me?" Matt shot back.

"Damned if I know. Guess I thought it was time—in case something goes wrong in surgery, or they can't get all the cancer. Hell, Matt, I don't know. Just seemed like the right thing to do." Pushing from the truck, Seth turned toward the door. "Come on. You need to get to your meeting."

"Wait, Pops." Matt jogged up beside him, putting his hand on the doorframe to stop Seth from pulling it open. "You are having the surgery, right?"

"It's scheduled for the end of the week, but I may call it off and go for more radiation."

"Like hell. You're going ahead with it and I'm staying here until we have the results." Lifting his hands from the door, he opened it for Seth, then walked around to his own side. "Drop me off for the meeting. I'll be staying at your house until I know what's going on."

Still shaken from the conversation, Matt finished a call with Gage, requesting at least a week off to take care of his grandfather, then walked through the double glass doors of MacLaren Enterprises, surprised to see Jace at the front.

"Hello, Matt. Glad you could make it." Jace stood, extending his hand as he walked around the desk. "Did you have time to visit with Seth?"

"I did." Matt started to say more, then clamped his mouth shut. He didn't know whom his grandfather had confided in, so until they spoke again, he decided to keep it quiet.

"Heath and Rafe are waiting upstairs."

He followed Jace, his thoughts on his grandfather, the surgery, and what he'd do if Seth didn't make it. His chest tightened. More than anything, he wished he could still confide in Heath, ask for his advice. But he'd thrown that opportunity away when he'd broken up with Cassie.

Jace stopped at a closed door, pushing it open. "Go ahead."

Stepping inside, he got his first look in a long time at Heath's office. What he noticed first was the size. It was bigger, having large windows and more furniture, including a small conference table. It suited Heath.

"Matt, it's good to see you. Hope you had some time to visit with Seth. Will you be staying with him tonight? I can offer you a bedroom at my place."

"I'll be staying with Pops, but thanks for the offer." Matt's brows furrowed at the invitation. The last time he saw Heath, they'd spoken only a few sentences. The tone of the welcome tonight didn't compare.

"Have a seat. I know you must be tired, so we'll get started. You've probably been wondering what had us sending the plane for you on such short notice."

"Well, yes." Matt didn't try to hide his curiosity.

"It's all right here." Jace slid a folder across the table. "I'll give you the short version. MacLaren is growing and we see no reason to rein it in. We're studying ten acquisitions right now, expecting at least three to go through. To integrate the new acquisitions, we need experienced people." He stopped, nodding at Rafe to continue.

"We've been developing a system for cross-training our key people. This will become even more important as we bring on new companies. If our expansion plans materialize, the pace will be quick, the learning curve steep. We foresee rotating assignments, up to six months in each group. Keep in mind, this has not been announced outside of senior management." Rafe looked at Heath.

"Jace and I have always known we wanted you working at MacLaren. As you know, life got in the way, but we can now go ahead with an offer we hope you'll find intriguing. Go ahead. Open the folder. We'll step out and give you some time to absorb the information."

The three filed out, leaving Matt dazed, staring after them, then at the folder on the table. His hands shook as he opened it and started reading. Finishing, he read it again, too stunned to sort through his thoughts. If their acquisition plans were successful, he'd be one of the key people in the rodeo stock division, managing other representatives. He assumed he'd be working closely with Cam, Mitch, and Kade, Rafe's oldest son who'd been unknown to the family most of his life. Now Kade was thoroughly ensconced in their horse and cattle breeding business, also heading up their security group.

Matt sucked in a startled breath as he looked at the bottom line. The salary came to twice as much as he made now.

"Hope you've had enough time to read through it and come up with questions."

Matt looked up as the three took their seats again, not sure how to start. Instead, he leaned forward, resting his arms on the table.

"This comes as quite a shock. I didn't even have this on my list of possible reasons you wanted to see me." He pursed his lips, focusing his attention on

Heath. "There must be several people you could approach about this opportunity. Why me?"

"Simple. Jace and I have known you all your life. We know your background, education, interests, and ethics. You're a straight shooter, Matt, a quality we value. We know you won't be afraid to give us unwelcome news, but you're flexible enough to support whatever decision is made. You already know we are a loyal bunch. You'll be paid well, but you'll be expected to hit your goals like everyone else. And they will be high."

"I would expect nothing less." Leaning back, he crossed his arms, taking another look at the offer. "Gage and Double Ace have been good to me. I don't know that I can leave at this point without waiting to train a replacement. And I'd like to see the partnership continue between MacLaren and Double Ace, as I believe it could be lucrative for everyone."

"We can all agree on that," Heath answered. "As far as the timing, we'd need you as soon as possible. Three weeks, if you can make that work. We'll do whatever we can to smooth your departure with Gage. He's a businessman. I believe he'll understand."

"Where would I be living?"

"Here, in Fire Mountain. We have one of the cabins available, but you're welcome to live wherever you want." Jace slid a photo of one of the cabins in front of Matt. They'd built several for company and family use, each with two bedrooms, one bath, full kitchen, small laundry, and views of the MacLaren ranch. "There would be travel."

Matt chuckled. "I doubt it would be more than I'm doing now." The lightness fled his voice when he thought about the most glaring issue. One that might well kill the entire deal. "We still have the biggest obstacle to discuss."

"My daughter." Heath stood, walking to the bar and taking down four glasses. Filling each with whiskey, he passed them around. "Right now, the people in this room, plus Cam, Mitch, Eric, and Kade, are the only ones who know of this offer."

"And our executive assistant, Phyllis," Rafe added.

Jace nodded, his mouth curving into a smile. "You'll find she's the one to go to if none of us are around. The woman keeps tabs on all of our lives and business dealings."

"So Cassie knows nothing about this?" Matt picked up his glass and stood, walking to the window. "You know, she won't like it. I'm not her favorite person."

"My question to you is can you work with her? If not, we'll understand and shred this offer right now. No hard feelings." Heath joined him at the window, setting a hand on Matt's shoulder. "We know none of this will be easy for either of you."

Matt downed his drink, setting the empty glass on the bar a few feet away.

"Do I have time to think about it?"

"How much time?" Heath asked.

"I've decided to stay through the end of the week. Will Friday afternoon be all right?"

"Done. We'll set a time to meet Friday." Heath opened his computer to the calendar. "Say three o'clock?"

"I'll be here."

"Great. Here, take these." Rafe held out a set of keys. "It's a truck you can use while you're in town. It's parked in a visitor spot."

Matt took the keys, shaking hands with each of them, then grabbed his hat and started for the door before turning back around. "No matter how this turns out, I want to thank you. It's a generous offer."

******

"I can't imagine why Dad wanted to fly Matt in for a meeting. It must have something to do with the association with Double Ace." Cassie hit the speaker button on her phone, setting it down next to her on the sofa as she picked up her glass of wine. Skye had called, asking if she knew any reason the executives would want to speak with Matt.

"That's what Sean is guessing, but it makes no sense to me. I thought it was a done deal and all we had to do was work out the specifics."

"Which is what we've been doing," Cassie interjected.

"Exactly. Regardless, whatever is going on..." Skye's voice trailed off for a few seconds. "Let me call you back. Sean's calling me."

Cassie walked into the kitchen, refilling her wine glass, and checking the dinner she had warming in the oven. Her mind worked over the various possibilities of why Matt had been called to Fire Mountain. It seemed too soon for senior management to rethink the relationship with Double Ace. The companies had agreed to give it a year, then review its success, deciding to either make adjustments or scuttle the deal. She didn't think it had to do with Seth or Troy. If either had been in an accident or had a serious illness, someone would've called her. No matter what had transpired with Matt, the Garners were like an extended family and were treated as such.

From what Skye had said, the call came as a complete surprise to Matt, eliminating the possibility he'd called Heath for a meeting. Dishing enchiladas onto a plate, she picked up her glass and settled herself back on the sofa as the phone started to ring.

"Hey, it's me," Skye said. "Sean got a call from Dad saying Matt wouldn't be flying back here until this weekend or early next week."

"Did Rafe say why?" Cassie asked, setting her plate aside, her brows knitting into a frown.

"Sean asked what was going on. All Dad told him was it had to do with company business, which is strange because he doesn't hold much back from us."

"I don't like it, but there's not much I can do short of calling Cam and asking."

"Dad told Sean neither Mitch nor Cam were involved in the meeting, so not to bother either one of them. The whole thing gets weirder by the minute. Well, I'm headed to bed. It's been a long day."

"What, no date tonight?" Cassie asked, knowing how much Skye hated dating.

"Cass, it's almost ten o'clock and you know my feelings on dating," Skye laughed. "Call me if you hear anything."

"You do the same." Cassie smiled as she hung up, then sobered, remembering the night she'd seen Matt in the bar.

Touching a finger to her lips, a shiver ran through her as she relived their kiss. It seemed natural, easy, and right, even though she knew it was all wrong. From now on, she wouldn't let herself be alone with Matt. They'd complete their work using phone calls and email, spending as little time as possible together. There would be no reason for meals, drinks, or anything else. All she had to do was keep her guard up, stay professional, and remember their past.

No problem, she thought, then bit her lower lip, hoping she wasn't deluding herself.

Chapter Eight

In a daze, Matt drove to his grandfather's house, one hand on the steering wheel, the other resting on the folder holding the offer. He didn't know what he'd expected, but it sure wasn't an offer like the one they dangled in front of him.

He wanted to accept, making the most of the opportunity. The work he'd done at Double Ace had prepared him for the next step in his career, the money was beyond good, and he knew he'd get top level support from the MacLarens. Plus, it would keep him close to Fire Mountain, allow him to keep an eye on Seth, making certain he followed doctor's orders and had someone around who would take care of him. He chuckled at the thought of his grandfather allowing anyone to fuss over him.

Matt felt certain Gage would understand. At some point, maybe he could even talk to Heath about making him an offer. He knew Gage would fit right in without a single misstep.

His hesitation came from what he guessed would be Cassie's response. She'd see it as a betrayal—her father siding with him. She'd be wrong, but her stubborn streak and pride wouldn't let her see the truth. In the meantime, he'd have to deal with her distrust and still do his job. Heath would expect nothing less.

Pulling to a stop in front of the house, he killed the engine. A sense of peace and rightness drifted over him at the thought of coming home after so many years. College had taken him away, then the rodeo circuit, followed by his job at Double Ace. It had been close to ten years since he'd lived here. He missed home and his grandfather more than he'd realized.

Grabbing the folder, he stepped out of the truck, walking the short distance to the front door, then turning in a slow circle. A cool breeze washed across his face as he gazed at the star-filled sky. Houston was a fine city with many great points, but it would never be Fire Mountain. This was home and he felt ready to return. Cassie would just need to figure out a way to live with it.

******

"The surgery went well. He's in recovery now, but they'll be taking him to a room within the hour. I'll make certain someone notifies you." The doctor wrote on the chart, then looked up. "He'll need to take it easy for a few days, and I'll want to see him in a week. Call my office and they'll schedule it for you." He shook Matt's hand before exiting through the double doors leading to the surgery area.

"Good news, I gather?"

Matt turned to see Heath and his wife, Annie, walk up beside him. "He told you?"

"Let's say I persuaded him to tell me while discussing one of the projects."

"Heath does have ways of getting information," Annie joked, engulfing Matt in a warm hug.

"I'll buy us all coffee while we wait for him to get out of recovery." Heath put a hand on the small of Annie's back, guiding them to the cafeteria.

Choosing a table that looked out onto an enclosed patio, Matt stared outside, knowing he had to call his brother to let him know about the surgery. He'd honored their grandfather's wishes to keep it quiet, but Matt saw no reason to keep Troy out of the loop any longer.

"Is there anything we can help you with, Matt?" Annie laid a hand on his arm, giving it a gentle squeeze. "He's welcome to stay at our house while he recovers." Even though the split with Cassie had occurred several years before, she still saw him as another son, an extension of their family.

"Thanks, Annie, but I have it covered. If all goes well, he'll be released Monday or Tuesday, then he'll have to take it easy for two to three weeks. Keeping him from going back to work too early will be the hard part. Plus, he isn't supposed to lift anything heavy for several weeks."

"Do his supervisors know about the surgery?" Heath sipped his coffee, trying to formulate a plan to keep Seth inside the next few weeks rather than letting him follow his tendency to visit each job site daily.

"One does." Matt squeezed the bridge of his nose. "Guess I should tell the others."

"He'll fight anyone trying to baby him," Heath chuckled.

"It's a lot better than him going around trying to do what he shouldn't." Matt's phone vibrated in his pocket. "Looks like they've moved him to his room. I'd better go up."

"We'd like to come with you if you're okay with us being there." Annie slid her hand into Heath's as they stood to follow Matt.

"Fine with me. I can use the reinforcements."

******

Cold Creek, Colorado

"Cassie, your firefighter is out in the lobby, talking to Cam."

"He's not *my* firefighter, Janie. We've been out a couple times. We're friends and that's it."

"I thought you were interested in him." Janie stepped into Cassie's office, closing the door.

Twisting her mouth into a wry grin, she shrugged. "He's a nice guy. But..."

"He just doesn't do it for you?" Janie lowered herself into a chair, crossing her arms.

Cassie shook her head. "Not really."

"You sure this doesn't have to do with a certain rodeo rep from Houston?"

"No. Absolutely not. Matt is someone I work with and that's all." Cassie surged to her feet, adjusting the blinds, then paced toward a cabinet, fiddling with some files.

"You know, Cass, you're like a sister to me. As such, I hope you will accept I'm saying this with love. Honey, you're delusional. Any woman with any sense would see Kurt Dobson as a real catch. And I mean a screamer. The fact you're willing to pass him off says a lot."

"I'm delusional because one specific man doesn't get me all hot and bothered?" Cassie snorted, crossing her arms and spearing Janie with an incredulous look. "Matt and I are over and there's no going back. Besides, he has no interest in me. He's carefree with no encumbrances, and loving it."

"How do you know that?" Janie challenged, her brows creasing.

"He told me." *No encumbrances of any kind,* he'd said without a trace of regret. "And Matt has no part in my decision to tell Kurt I'm not interested. I don't want to lead him on or have him waste another dollar on dates." Sitting down, she picked up her pen before tossing it back down. "I know," she gasped, her brows rising. "Why don't I set him up with you? Gosh, why didn't I think of this before? You two would be great togeth—"

Jumping from her seat, Janie slammed both hands on Cassie's desk. "Don't even think about it."

"And why not?"

"One, you're dating him, and two, he has no interest in me."

"How do you know if you've never actually met him?" Cassie countered, liking the idea more with each passing second.

"Well...I just know. I'm nothing like you, Cassie. If he's attracted to you, he sure wouldn't be attracted to me. You're slender and petite, with dark auburn hair. I'm none of those." Janie tugged on her braided light brown hair, then placed her hands on her ample hips, emphasizing another difference. "Forget it. What you do about Kurt is your business, but don't push him toward me."

Cassie watched her leave, a smile tugging at her mouth at Janie's warning. Well, it would do no good. She'd already made up her mind about Kurt, deciding on what she thought was an excellent way to let him down easy.

******

"Thanks again for being at the hospital today, Heath." Matt took a seat at the table, waiting for Jace and Rafe to arrive.

"I don't know that it helped, but it was worth it to see the cantankerous look on his face when Annie and I walked in. You know, Annie's offer still stands to have him recuperate at our place."

"Thanks." Depending on how this meeting went, Matt might change his mind and have his grandfather stay at the MacLaren's a few days next week.

"Hope we didn't miss anything," Jace joked as he and Rafe walked in, taking seats.

"Not a thing." Heath glanced from them to Matt and nodded. "This meeting is about you. Why don't you tell us what you've decided?"

Clearing his throat, Matt leaned forward, resting his arms on the table. "It's a big step for me, walking away from Double Ace." He paused a moment, collecting his thoughts.

He'd called Gage late the night before, explained the offer, and waited for his friend to tell him all the reasons he shouldn't leave. Instead, Gage surprised him by encouraging him to go for it, saying the money alone was worth the risk, not to mention having Matt with MacLaren would almost assure a long-term partnership with the rodeos. He assured him if it didn't work out, Double Ace would find a place for him again.

"It would be a big move for anyone," Rafe said, remembering the angst he'd gone through after his brothers had found him after years of estrangement, making an offer to buy the bull stock business his partners and he had started. He'd been adamantly opposed to the sale, but he'd been outvoted. He'd lost the battle, but won the chance to reunite with the rest of the MacLarens.

Matt nodded before continuing. "It's a great offer. Nothing I'd counter. There is one part that has me hesitating."

"What's that?" Jace asked, his gaze narrowing.

"Cassie. Understand, I don't want to be the cause of any more trouble with the MacLarens. She's excited about her new position, works harder than anybody I've ever known, and is a real asset. If me accepting the offer changes that, I'd have to say it's not worth it."

Heath leveled his gaze at Matt, already knowing his daughter would be the reason for any hesitancy on accepting the offer. Jace, Rafe, and he had already discussed it at length, deciding Cassie might be upset, but she'd get over it. Her family and the company meant everything to her. She'd gotten through college with the goal of working for MacLaren Enterprises, and not even Matt's decision to come on board would derail her.

"I don't believe you're giving Cassie a fair shake, Matt. She's a strong, independent woman, used to dealing with difficult situations. You may see her as pampered and coddled in some ways, but she has a core of steel. My suggestion is you decide without worrying about her reaction. Do what's best for you and your family."

And there it was. The reference to his grandfather. Seth had dropped everything, changing his life to raise two young boys. A widower, he'd never dated the entire time they were growing up, focusing his days on Troy, him, and the business. Now Seth needed him, and Matt was going to be there.

"In that case, I accept."

"Excellent." Heath's smile came a second before he reached across the table to shake Matt's hand, which was followed by congratulations from Jace and Rafe. "We're pleased to have you with us. Now, let's get down to details so you can get back to the hospital."

An hour later, they'd discussed the specifics of his new role, answering his questions and asking a few of their own. Knowing about Seth's surgery, Gage had already given him the go-ahead to start at any time.

"If the offer is still open, I'd like to see if Pops would agree to stay at your place next week. That will give me time to get my truck down from

Montana and arrange to have my gear shipped from Houston.”

“No problem at all having Seth stay with Annie and me.”

“We’ll take care of getting your furniture and belongings here,” Jace offered.

“There isn’t much. I rented a furnished place. It even came with all the kitchen stuff.” Matt shrugged at how little he owned. “Guess the rodeo life never really left me. If we’re done, I’ll head back to the hospital.” Standing, he grabbed his hat, starting for the door.

“Oh, one more thing, Matt.”

Turning, he took a few steps back toward the table, taking a piece of paper Heath held out to him.

“We’re moving up the timeframe of when some other changes will take place. Because of that, you’re going to be managing some people sooner than planned.”

“No problem. Do you know who’ll be reporting to me?”

Heath cast a quick glance at Rafe and Jace. “Skye...and Cassie.”

******

"I'm glad you had time for a drink."

Cassie had been surprised when Kurt called her that afternoon, asking if she'd meet him after work. No mention of dinner or a movie. She'd taken his request as an opportunity to make one other call to set up the rest of the evening.

"Thanks for asking. I'm actually meeting my roommate, Janie, here in a little bit, so the timing is great. You'll finally get a chance to meet her."

Kurt shifted on the stool, trying to remember Cassie mentioning her friend. "Is she the one you roomed with in college?"

"She is. Janie is also part of the finance team at work." She sipped at the margarita Kurt had already ordered, trying to come up with the right words to convey her decision.

"Cassie, we need to talk about something." Kurt turned toward her, his gaze sincere, open.

"Sure. What is it?"

"First, I want you to know you're a wonderful person and I've enjoyed our time together. You're beautiful, smart..." His voice trailed off when he heard her snicker. Focusing on her, he noticed her mouth curl up in amusement. "Is something funny?"

"Oh, Kurt. This sounds so much like a brush-off."

Squirming in his seat, he cleared his throat. "I guess I don't know what to say to that."

"Am I right? Are you wanting to call off dating, maybe just be friends?"

"Well...yes. I guess that is what I was trying not so eloquently to say."

This time, Cassie did start laughing, shaking her head when she saw the confused, hurt expression on his face.

"It's just that I planned to say the same to you tonight."

His eyes widened in a combination of surprise and relief. "That a fact?" He grinned, taking a swallow of his beer.

"I didn't want to hurt your feelings, but..."

"Say no more, Cassie. It seems we've come to the same conclusion. I'm glad we recognized it sooner rather than later."

"Hey, Cassie. Sorry I'm late, but the traffic light stopped working a few blocks back and parking is horrible on a Friday." Cassie turned in her seat, letting Janie get a good look at the man next to her. "Oh, it appears I'm interrupting something. I'll just—"

"You're not interrupting anything." Kurt stood, walking around Cassie and holding out his hand. "Kurt Dobson."

Taking his hand, Janie almost jumped back at the immediate and intense sensation coursing up her arm. By the shocked look on Kurt's face, he'd felt it, too.

"Hey, why don't you two take a few minutes to get to know each other while I go to the ladies' room." Cassie slid from her stool and disappeared toward the back before Janie could object.

Pursing her lips, Janie let out a sigh, taking a seat in the empty stool next to Kurt. "I probably should leave you two to your date."

"Nonsense. Besides, Cassie and I are no longer dating."

"What? Since when?"

"Just before you arrived. Seems neither one of us felt a real connection to the other. What can I get you to drink?"

Chapter Nine

Houston, Texas

"There wasn't much I could do about it, Ivan. He'd already asked for a week off to take care of his grandfather when the MacLarens sprang the offer on him. He told me he'd be glad to give us two weeks, but I told him to forget it. I can handle his load until a new person starts." Gage had already spoken to someone, a friend from his rodeo days who could step into Matt's place with little training. "Of course I'll set up a meeting with you as soon as I confirm his interest." He turned up the volume on the phone's speaker and sat back.

"The increased deliveries of cattle will start next week. Do you have men ready?" Ivan's voice, rich and cultured, a reflection of his Ivy League education, came through clearly.

"All set. One full additional crew has been hired. I can bring on more, if needed."

"You may have to do that, my friend." Ivan still hadn't discovered what his uncles were up to, but he did know these additional shipments weren't supported by any sales figures he'd seen. His father had been quiet about what his brothers were doing, either from lack of information or something more. Either way, Ivan's sense of unease rose as the dates of the increased shipments drew near.

"I still don't have any information on where the cattle go after arriving in Houston. How long before you can get that to me?" Gage asked.

"I'll check on it myself today. You will have the information by the time the cattle arrive." Ivan clenched his fists, knowing he'd already asked for the list of buyers more than once. His uncles had put him off each time.

"Good. On another matter, I've made arrangements to travel to the MacLaren bull stock operation in Crooked Tree, Montana. Matt began meetings before his grandfather's surgery. I'd like to keep those moving and believe the best way is to meet with them in person."

"Excellent idea, Gage. Just because Matt is going to work for them, we cannot assume the relationship will stay intact. They may have other plans of which he is unaware."

"Maybe, but from what Matt said, they're pleased so far. I'd rather err on the side of caution."

"When do you leave?" Ivan asked, wanting him back in Houston for the cattle deliveries.

"Early next week. Don't worry. I'll be back in time for the shipments."

Ivan breathed a sigh of relief. "I may even join you in Houston. It's been too long since I've checked on the facility there."

"Anytime. Give me a day or two notice so I'm in town and not visiting one of Matt's clients."

"I must take another call, Gage. I will get you the information you need."

Gage ended the call. Something in Ivan's voice didn't sound right, and he wondered if his boss had any of the same reservations about the increased shipments. Usually, Gage's people would've been the ones identifying additional cattle buyers in the United States, not Ivan's uncles. None of his people had heard anything about buyers wanting anywhere near the number of head Ivan projected.

Knowing he could do nothing about it, he grabbed the phone, punched in some numbers, and waited. He hoped his contact, Thad Montgomery, had some information for him.

******

Cold Creek

"I'm so glad you called me, Annie. It's good to know Seth is doing so well, even though he must be a bear under the circumstances." Cassie loved Seth, considering him her surrogate grandfather. "I suppose Matt is there with him."

"Matt left for Montana this morning. That's why Seth is staying with us. Heath said Matt had been in a meeting with Sean and Skye when he found out about Seth. I understand he plans to drive his truck back to Fire Mountain and stay with him for a while." Annie couldn't say any more. Heath had confided in her about Matt's decision to leave Double Ace, swearing her to secrecy.

"Seth and Matt are lucky to have you there. With Troy in school, and Matt, well...wherever he is during any given week, there wouldn't have been anyone to keep watch on Seth. My guess is he'd be up and around, back to work way before he should."

"Troy's driving up this week, and Matt should be back by Wednesday."

"Yeah, but no telling how long he'll stick around. He's a wanderer, Annie. Everyone knows that." The edge of bitterness to Cassie's voice didn't surprise Annie. Her stepdaughter had a hard time hiding her emotions, especially when they concerned Matt. "I'd better go. I've got a meeting in a few minutes."

She'd just hung up the phone when it rang again, her father on the other end.

"Hello, Dad. I just hung up with Annie. She told me about Seth."

"I sure hope he doesn't give her too much trouble. He's a cantankerous old bird when he's laid up."

Cassie laughed. "You and I know he won't get away with anything as long as Annie's watching him."

"So true," he chuckled before his voice turned serious. "We're going to need you in Fire Mountain on Thursday for a general meeting. You can fly down with Cam. Mitch, Sean, and Skye will also be here, as well as the key people in our other groups."

"Whoa. Must be big news." Cassie's mind reeled at what could be happening to require everyone to fly to Arizona and how much business would be put on hold during their time away.

"You'll get nothing more from me," Heath warned. "Plan to spend the weekend. I think Annie's ready for another one of your shopping trips."

"She's always ready for that, Dad. I look forward to seeing you. Love you."

"Love you, too, Cassie."

She had little time to ponder the reason behind the summons. Knowing her father and uncles, it could be another large acquisition, some kind of merger, or the announcement of a new bonus plan. Thinking of the last made her smile.

"Hey, Cassie. You planning to join us?" Janie stood in the doorway, a large folder in her hand. "It's finance day, you know." She grinned, knowing how much everyone loved to spend their time reviewing numbers.

"Wait and I'll walk with you. We haven't had time to talk since you decided to spend so much time with Kurt. I guess the introduction worked out well." Cassie watched as Janie's face reddened, something she'd almost never seen.

Janie's steps slowed as she glanced around. "This isn't a conversation for the hallway. All I'll say is yes, we hit it off very well. In fact, I'm seeing him again tonight."

Cassie stopped outside the conference room, turning to face Janie. "That's wonderful news and I hope wonderful things come from it."

Janie wished the same as she followed Cassie into the room.

******

Crooked Tree, Montana

"Good to see you." Matt held out his hand to Gage, who'd flown in from Houston for a transition meeting with Mitch, Sean, and Skye. Per Heath's request, they wouldn't be telling them why Gage would be taking over the account, just that changes had been made. From what Matt understood, the formal announcement would occur on Thursday in Fire Mountain when all the executives and managers would be present. "How was the flight?"

"No problems. Thanks for picking me up." He slid into Matt's truck. "Tell me more about the people I'll be meeting."

Matt chuckled as he thought about the team in Montana. "Like all MacLarens, they're independent and smart. It will be a give and take situation as they won't let anyone railroad them. Mitch is the second oldest and a real hardnose when it comes to business. After what happened with their bull stock a few months ago, he's being extra cautious. Sean is more laid back, but equally concerned about growing the company. Before Skye took over the position, he was the one meeting with the rodeo committees. Rhett is still in college, so I don't know much about him other than he'll come to work for the company when he graduates."

"Tell me more about Skye. I understand she'll be my main contact." Gage leaned back, trying to remember more about her from their brief meeting in Houston months before.

"She seems to be a combination of Mitch and Sean. Bright, doesn't seem to miss anything, and has no problem standing up to anyone she encounters. Very professional. More social than Mitch, and a little more competitive than Sean."

"Sounds like an interesting and tough lady," Gage commented, conjuring up his own memory of her. He looked forward to the prospect of getting to know her better.

"She can be. I guess it's built into their genes." Parking the truck, Matt waited for Gage to join him. "Let's get this transition going."

******

"Thanks to all of you for changing your plans on such short notice. The executive team has been tackling some tough issues lately, making some changes based on what we believe is best for the company. First, however, let's go over last quarter's reports." Heath indicated the spreadsheets before each of them.

Trying to keep his gaze from wandering to Cassie, who sat directly across from him at the large conference table, Matt flipped through the stack of documents as Heath continued. He'd arrived in town the night before after a long, tiring drive. The trip had been needed. They'd had a good meeting, transitioning Gage to take his place. Mitch, Sean, and Skye now sat around the same table, eyeing him with curiosity. He'd said nothing about being invited to this meeting. Although he held firm in his acceptance of the offer, he couldn't help but be concerned at the possible fallout when Heath made the announcement.

"Any other questions?" Heath asked once he finished going over the latest financials. "No? Then we'll move to the main reason for this meeting. Rafe, why don't you start?"

Matt shifted in his seat, focusing on Rafe as he stood and sauntered forward. At the table sat a slew of younger MacLarens, including spouses who worked for the company. The news would impact them the most. He prepared himself for what he knew would be dismay, confusion, and definitely anger. Glancing around, he noted Heath hadn't taken a seat, and Jace had positioned himself at the back of the room.

"For those of you who may not remember, the executive team consists of Heath, Jace, our chief financial officer, me, plus the corporate attorney and two outside directors. The approved changes will impact every person in this room. By the end of the meeting, we hope you'll understand why we've made these decisions and support the changes." Rafe nodded at Phyllis, their executive assistant, who brought up the old and new organization charts on the screen, then passed around copies. He pointed to each.

"This is the current structure. We'll be moving to this one. As you can see, we're realigning and combining entities to streamline reporting and speed our decision-making." Rafe paused a moment, letting them study the changes before signaling Phyllis to bring up the next screen.

"As you can see, the top tier is shown first. Phyllis will add to this as we move through the changes. First, Heath will continue as the chairman with all administrative services groups reporting to him. Jace will take over all aspects of cattle and horse operations, including livestock, ranch services, horse breeding, and bucking stock.

"All operations involving real estate will now fall under me, including our new Resort and Community Group. Eric will report to me, but all day-to-day operations involving all real estate and development operations will go directly to him. Sean, you'll also report to me, but be in charge of all day-to-day operations of this new group."

"No offense, Pop, but what the hell is that?" Sean asked, as confused as everyone else.

"We're moving several small, one-off businesses having to do with foster children and dude ranch services into an operational unit. I'll go over details with you and Eric after this meeting."

Eric Sinclair, one of Heath's stepsons, leaned forward, his brows drawing together. He'd expected to head up that division at some point. He thought he'd report to Heath when it happened and couldn't quite hide the disappointment. Rafe noted his reaction, but moved on.

"Cam will be moving back to Fire Mountain. He'll continue to report directly to Heath, but will be in charge of business development, marketing, and technology services for all of our groups."

"Moving..." Cam muttered, then reigned in his reaction. Although honored to take over three groups, it was a change from being president of his own division.

"We'll go into more detail on all this, Cam. It will work out," Heath interjected, knowing Cam might not be happy with the change.

"Kade will be taking Mitch's place in Crooked Tree—"

"To hell with that. He knows nothing of the bucking stock business." Mitch's hands fisted on his thighs, his eyes sparking at the news.

"Mitch, you're moving to Fire Mountain. You'll report to Jace in the cattle operations group, as will Kade, who will also retain his position as head of security. In that role, he'll report to Heath."

Jace moved from his spot near the wall, clasping Mitch on the shoulder. "We'll talk after this meeting."

The one thing keeping Mitch from commenting was the realization he and his wife, Dana, would be able to spend more time together as most of her work involved frequent trips to Fire Mountain.

"Time for questions. Whatever you're thinking, toss it out now." Heath and Jace joined Rafe at the front, forming what appeared to be an impenetrable wall.

Cassie glanced at Skye. They'd been silently communicating during the announcement. With both Cam and Mitch moving, neither had a clue what would come next for them, nor had they any clue as to why Matt had been included in the meeting. The longer it went without mention of his name, the more Cassie's stomach knotted. Clearing her throat, she looked at Heath.

"Is now the time to ask why Matt is in this meeting?"

Matt's gaze flew to Cassie. She had done her best to ignore him, forcing her attention anywhere but at him. He could only guess her reaction when Heath broke the latest news.

"Now is the perfect time. You all know Matt Garner and his extensive experience on the pro rodeo circuit and the bucking stock business. He's been offered a position in the Bucking Stock/Horse Breeding Group, which he accepted. He'll report directly to Kade, but will be in charge of the day-to-day operations of the bucking stock segment. Skye and Cassie, you will report directly to Matt."

Cassie froze as her mind tried to wrap itself around the bomb her father had dropped. Clamping her mouth shut, she gripped the edges of the table, her unwavering gaze never leaving Heath's face, a feeling of betrayal coursing through her.

Heath shifted, knowing he'd have a lot to explain, hoping Cassie wouldn't bolt and turn in her resignation. The move had been a gamble and he prayed his daughter would give it a chance.

"Welcome aboard, Matt." Eric held out his hand. "Talk about getting thrown to the lions."

"You don't have to tell me," Matt grumbled, sending Skye a bleak smile. "If nothing else, it will make for an interesting Christmas party."

"Cassie, you and Skye will meet with Matt after we adjourn." Heath glanced around the table, making eye contact with each person. "In fact, let's take a break, then everyone will meet in the office of the head of their new group. Phyllis has a completed chart with your names. Grab one before you leave."

Her legs feeling a bit shaky as she stood, Cassie took the handout from Phyllis, unable to form a coherent thought. She walked from the room, barely cognizant of Rafe leaving ahead of her, Sean next to him, with an arm around his father's shoulders.

"Seriously, Pop. You're putting me in charge of a *dude ranch*?"

Chapter Ten

Unable to think, Cassie disappeared into the employee lounge, grabbed a cup and filled it with hot coffee. Standing at the counter, she dumped in sugar and creamer, stirring absently, not noticing someone entering.

"Hey, Cassie. How's it going?" Dana MacLaren, Mitch's wife, filled her own cup with coffee.

"Have you seen Mitch since our meeting?"

Dana's eyes narrowed. "No, why?"

Letting out a sigh, Cassie took a seat at a nearby table, waiting until Dana joined her.

"The brothers announced some big changes. Very big. I'll let him tell you what's going on."

Dana leaned toward her. Normally cheerful with boundless energy, Cassie sounded down, almost adrift. "Are you all right?"

She shifted her gaze to Dana, blinking. "No, but I will be. I just need some time to let the changes settle in. I'll make a decision then."

"A decision?"

"Sorry, Dana. I don't mean to be vague, but I can't talk about it now. Besides, I'm supposed to meet with Kade, the new head of the bucking stock group, and the others who've moved under him."

"What?" Dana gasped, pushing her chair back and standing. "I'd better go find Mitch."

"He may already be meeting with Jace, his new boss."

"Jace? Jeez, this just keeps getting more and more interesting. I'd better run."

Cassie nodded as she watched Dana leave, wishing she could just get in her truck and drive away with no destination in mind. Maybe take an actual vacation and think through all the changes, deciding if staying was best or if applying at another company might be wise. The thought of leaving her family behind felt wrong, but working under Matt didn't work for her. Not at all.

Before he'd left for the rodeo, they'd talked of taking a month off after she graduated. Maybe drive to the east coast, see the sights, and enjoy the beaches. Each figured they'd earned the chance for some time together before taking regular jobs after graduating. The idea had disintegrated when he'd moved on without her. Burying herself in school, then her new job had been her way to forget him. The changes would make it impossible to keep her distance now. Perhaps the time had come for Cassie to branch out and find her own way.

"I thought I'd find you in here." Skye walked in, taking a soda from the refrigerator. "Wow, can you believe the changes?" Glancing at the clock on the wall, she laid a hand on Cassie's shoulder, her voice softening. "It's time to leave for our meeting."

Cassie let out a deep breath. "You go ahead. Tell Kade I'll catch up with him later." Cassie stood, dumping her untouched coffee in the sink, tossing the cup in the trash.

"Hold on a minute. Do you think that's wise? Kade's being thrown into a new position, as is Matt. And Mitch...I don't even want to think about what he'll say during our meeting. Besides, I'm not going to let you throw me into the fray alone. I could use a little female support."

Cassie's mouth turned up at the corners. "You're the last person who needs another woman's support. But you're right. I don't want Matt to see me as a coward."

"Come on then. We'll take this opportunity and shove it up Matt's..." Skye trailed off, smiling, letting Cassie's imagination finish the thought.

"You're on."

******

A somber Matt sat at a neighborhood bar, nursing a double whiskey, wishing he could take back the last two weeks and start over. The meeting had gone as expected, with everyone spearing Jace with pointed questions. He'd been firm in his responses and the reasons behind the changes. Even the hard lines on Cassie's face softened when she understood the long-term plans behind the restructure. She'd even spared him a few glances devoid of the animosity targeted at him when she first entered the room.

The problem was Matt felt like a complete outsider. After the meetings concluded, everyone had been invited to Heath and Annie's for supper. Everyone except him. He knew it was a way for the family to reconnect after a tough day, but being excluded grated on him in a way he couldn't quite describe.

He'd swung by Seth's house, made sure his grandfather had taken his medication and not pushed himself too hard, then taken off. The Tavern had been a regular hangout when he and Cassie came back to town during school breaks. They'd meet friends from high school, catch up, then drive to a buddy's house who had a spare bedroom. Most times, they wouldn't leave until just before dawn. The memory didn't improve his already deteriorated mood one bit.

"Where the hell did you go?"

Mitch's rough voice pulled Matt to the present. Glancing over his shoulder, he spotted Mitch, Kade, Eric, Sean, and Cam. All pulled up chairs, gesturing for the waitress.

"You think you're the only one who's had a crap day?" Eric asked, grabbing a handful of peanuts from the bowl on the table.

"I don't know what you're complaining about. You get to take over almost all activities of the real estate group. It's what you wanted. I have to help Lainey sell her preschool business and move back here." Cam accepted his drink from the waitress, taking a long sip.

"Hell. You're all wusses." Kade tossed back his shot of whiskey. After time serving in Special Forces, then with the DEA, he'd seen things these guys could only imagine. "Suck it up, boys, and roll with it."

"Are you telling me you're ready to move back to Crooked Tree?" Mitch stared at his older stepbrother. They'd come a long way since Kade, the offspring of their father's first love who'd disappeared before Rafe knew she was pregnant, had surfaced. He'd married another, having four children. The reality of Kade's existence had changed the family dynamics, requiring everyone to make adjustments.

Kade shook his head. "You heard Jace. I won't be required to move unless I want to, which Brooke will never agree to." His wife, Annie's daughter and Heath's stepdaughter, held a position at the company not impacted by the changes. "This works out great for you, Mitch. Dana won't have to travel as much, and Jace will give you plenty of autonomy. I've worked for him for a while now, and he's great. More laid back than either Heath or Rafe. Go with it, man." Kade shot him an evil grin and laughed.

"You may be right, but it doesn't sit well with me that they made all these changes without talking to any of us. It's as if they wanted us to mutiny." Mitch tossed back his drink, letting the amber liquid burn down his throat.

"And I'd wager you would've been the one to start it," Sean added, understanding Mitch's frustration.

"I was tempted." Mitch slammed his empty glass on the table.

"Come on, boys. Time to fill our stomachs and enjoy the family." Eric stood, stretching his arms above his head to relieve the ache from a full day of meetings. When Matt remained seated, he shoved his shoulder. "You, too. You're not leaving us to face Skye and Cassie by ourselves."

Matt hesitated a moment, then shrugged. "Why the hell not?" he joked, following them to their cars, then the ranch, bracing himself for whatever Cassie might throw his way.

******

The men heard women's laughter as they entered the ranch house. Matt paused inside the foyer, glancing around, looking for Cassie. He hoped to pull her aside for a private talk, try to air out their differences and make the most of the changes. She stood with Skye, Brooke, and Dana at the end of the long breakfast bar, holding a glass of wine, laughing. Spotting him, her expression soured before she turned her back in an attempt to block him out.

"Grab plates and fill them up. Everything is ready." Annie and Jace's wife, Caroline, placed the last of the serving bowls on the counter, motioning them to get started.

Matt piled on the food. He'd forgotten what a great spread Annie always prepared. Heath's oldest, Trey, and his wife, Jesse, along with their son, Trevor, were the only ones missing. Both naval aviators, their tours would end soon. He knew Heath hoped they'd return to the ranch and work in the company.

"I'm going to need all the help I can get with the bucking stock business." Kade set his plate next to Matt's and took a seat between him and his wife, Brooke. "Your background is going to be a huge benefit."

"You wouldn't think so the way Skye and Cassie took the news." Matt shoved a forkful of enchiladas into his mouth, chewing slowly, his gaze riveted on Cassie at the other end of the table.

"They'll get over it. Both are professional and understand the reasons behind the moves." Kade had noticed the shocked expressions on both women's faces when Rafe made the announcement. He hoped each would step up and accept the changes, but something about what Cassie had left unsaid during their meeting bothered him. She'd asked questions but he never once felt she'd bought into the new structure. Listening to his gut had saved him more than once while in Special Forces and his gut knotted each time he glanced at Cassie.

"They might understand them, but Cassie is a long way from embracing them." Setting his fork down, Matt picked up his bottle of beer, tipping it back and taking several swallows. "Can't say as I blame her."

"You're going to need to have a hard talk with her about what you expect. She's headstrong, but from what I've seen, she takes direction well." Picking up his empty plate, Kade stood. "I'm going for seconds before Mitch beats me to it."

Matt followed him, but instead of going for more food, he stopped next to Cassie. "When you've finished, I'd like to talk."

Even before hearing his voice, she knew who had stopped beside her. As always, it sent a ripple of excitement through her, a response she couldn't stop, no matter how hard she tried.

"I'll meet you in Dad's study in five minutes."

He nodded, grabbing a bottle of water, bracing himself for the expected fireworks.

******

Staring at the MacLaren family pictures on the wall, Matt waited for Cassie to join him. It had been over thirty minutes, and given her usual insistence on being punctual, he had to attribute the lag to a desire to let him stew. It didn't faze him one bit. He'd wait her out, no matter how late it got. At some point, she'd have to face him.

"Okay, I'm here now. What do you want to discuss?" Cassie breezed into the room, not making eye contact as she lowered herself into a chair.

Matt held her gaze, uncaring of how stern his next words would sound. "Your thoughts on the changes. Specifically, if you'll be able to accept I'm your boss and you'll be reporting to me."

"And if I don't?" She lifted her chin, daring him to threaten her.

"You'll be gone, the same as anyone else."

Cassie blinked, knowing if she didn't produce results, her father would agree to a termination. He'd give her no special privileges. Treating family different than regular employees wasn't tolerated at MacLaren Enterprises. You were professional, showed respect, and did your job. No excuses. If not, you were gone.

"Fine." She stood, turning toward the door.

"Hold on a minute, Cass."

"What? There's more?"

"I want to know what you mean by *fine*. Are you saying you've bought into the program and are on board? I don't want any misunderstandings between us." He took a step forward, then stopped when he saw her eyes narrow in frustration...or resentment...or possibly desire. He couldn't tell which.

All she wanted was to leave. Get out the door and away from Matt. She'd made him wait for her to join him, not because of the changes, but because her traitorous heart wouldn't stop pounding like a bass drum. Being this close to him did dangerous things to her body. Breathing became difficult, labored, the walls closing in around her. Ever since she'd spotted him coming through the front door, she'd fought the attraction so hazardous to her health. She could deal with him, but only if he kept his distance and didn't require face time. Taking a couple steps closer, she tilted her face up, fisting her hands at her sides.

"What I'm saying is I'll report to you and do my best to meet your expectations. But I'm warning you, Matt. If you start feeding bullcrap reports about my work to Dad and the others, there will be hell to pay!" Cassie's face reddened as her eyes sparked.

Holding up his hands, palms out, he took a step back. "Calm down, Cassie. No one is trying to sabotage you."

"Oh, right. That's easy for you to say. You waltz in here after disappearing for years, and all of a sudden, you're the golden boy, handed a promotion which vaults you above Sean, Skye, or even me. We've all been paying our dues. What the hell have you done?" Crossing her arms and planting her feet, she glared at him, daring him to explain.

"I didn't ask Heath for a job. He came to me. What would you have done?"

Without missing a beat, she took a step toward him, stopping within inches of his face. "I would've realized I'd be jumping headfirst into a firestorm. Do you have any idea what it's like to be in my position with the change? Of course you don't. You're still a selfish sonofabitch without a clue of how your actions affect others. It's always all about Matt and what he wants. No one else matters, and no one gets in your way. Well, I have news for you, hotshot. Your job won't be some easy ride where you can float to the top on Skye's and my achievements. You damn well better show everyone how good you are or you'll be out on your butt just like anyone else." Her voice had hardened with each sentence until she'd gotten out the ball of frustration knotted inside her.

The clear combination of anger, betrayal, and pain on her face hit Matt like a punch in the gut. He'd had his share of disappointments, knowing how it felt to be shoved aside.

"Cassie...I—"

"Save it, Matt. I'll do the best I can, but it won't be for you. My best will never be for your benefit *ever* again." Turning, she froze at the sight of Heath,

Jace, and Rafe standing in the doorway. Pushing past them, she didn't explain further. She was certain they hadn't missed a word.

The brothers watched her retreat, then turned back to Matt.

"Well, that went well," Heath muttered, stepping into the room, his chest tightening. He knew Cassie wouldn't be thrilled about the changes, but he never imagined the deep resentment, anger, and pure hostility she'd buried inside until hearing it for himself. Perhaps their brilliant plan to realign divisions, move family around, and bring Matt on weren't as dazzling as they'd let themselves believe. He wasn't prepared to lose Cassie over the changes.

"What did we miss?" Jace asked, walking past Matt, who still stood frozen in place.

"Uh...that was pretty much the heart of it. I'm an S.O.B., I'm out to get her fired, and I don't give a damn about anyone except myself." He glanced at Jace. "I think that covers it." Scrubbing a hand down his face, Matt slumped into a nearby chair, resting his arms on his legs, and hanging his head.

"Going into this, we knew some wouldn't be happy with the changes. It's a business decision and not meant to slight anyone, especially Cassie. She's done a remarkable job with no training. Her gut instincts are extraordinary, her work ethic is as good as they come, and her ambition, well...we all know how competitive she can be." Heath crossed his arms, resting a hip against the edge of his desk. "Except..."

"No one considered she might walk out over this," Matt supplied, his throat tightening at the raw emotions she'd directed at him. "I suppose I should go after her. Try to smooth things over."

"Forget it. What she needs now is space and time to adjust." Heath pursed his lips, wondering if she would bend.

"She believes we stabbed her in the back. Maybe we did." Jace closed his eyes, conjuring up an image of Cassie as a little girl, running around, laughing, never letting anything get her down. Tonight, all he saw was a defeated woman who believed she'd been betrayed.

Standing, Matt walked to the door. "You hired me to do a job and that's what I'll do. I don't want to lose Cassie any more than the rest of you, and I'll do all I can to make things up to her. That's the best I can offer." Closing the door behind him, he didn't see the looks passing between the men at his parting words. All he could focus on was the hatred on her face and what he had to do to fix the damage he'd caused.

Chapter Eleven

Cold Creek, Colorado

"I heard the meeting didn't go so well." Janie closed the door behind her, taking a seat in Cassie's office.

"I won't ask how you found out, but no, it didn't go well. At least not for me." Cassie stared at her computer screen, trying to focus on the data in front of her. She'd honored her commitment to stay in Fire Mountain over the weekend, begging off most activities Heath suggested, including supper with him and Annie, knowing she wasn't up to a quiet meal with just the three of them.

Somewhere in the distant parts of her brain, she knew her actions were immature and had hurt her father. If her brother, Trey, were at the ranch, he would've lit into her big time. Instead, she did the best she could, accepting her father had been the one to betray her trust and set her up to fail. He knew being in touch with Matt daily and traveling with him would push her to resign. She had to assume that's what he wanted. Now she had to make a decision to shove it back in his face or leave, as Heath planned.

Getting on the plane the night before had allowed her the first amount of relief she'd felt since the bomb had been dropped.

Cassie looked up at her friend. "I tapped on your bedroom door when I got home last night. Seems you were out."

A grin tipped up the corners of Janie's mouth, recalling what she and Kurt were probably doing when Cassie got home. "I spent the night at Kurt's."

"I figured as much." A smile lit Cassie's face, the first one she'd had since her explosive tirade aimed at Matt. It felt good to relax and enjoy Janie's obvious happiness. "I'm so glad it's working out between you two. Kurt's a great guy."

"It's so odd, but I feel as if I've known him all my life. I can say anything to him, be myself, and not worry about what he'll think. We're enough alike not to grate on each other, yet different enough to keep things interesting. Does that sound crazy?"

"Not at all." Cassie's face clouded. She once had all those ideas about Matt. It often felt as if they knew each other's thoughts, could anticipate each other's needs and desires. The reality still stung. "Maybe he's the one for you."

"Wouldn't that be something? A firefighter in an out-of-the-way town in Colorado. My parents would have a fit."

"What do you mean?" In all the years she'd known Janie, Cassie heard little about her family, and had never met her parents. Most times, she would stay at school during breaks or go home with Cassie. When asked, Janie closed up, not offering much information. All Cassie knew was she was from Ohio and her parents had money. Lots of it.

Janie bit her lower lip, wishing she'd kept quiet. "Nothing, except they believe I shouldn't marry anyone who gets their hands dirty for a living."

"That leaves Sean out," Cassie joked.

"Sean?"

"Mitch and Skye's brother. You weren't at Mitch's wedding reception, but trust me. Sean is *hot*."

Janie burst out laughing. "You know you're talking about your cousin, right?"

"So? He can still be hot, can't he?"

"Absolutely." Checking the time, Janie stood. "Guess I'd better get to work." Her face sobered. "What are we going to do without Cam?"

"Trust me. It's all going to work out. Kade is taking over both bucking stock groups. He may not have much experience with bucking bulls, but neither did Cam when Heath sent him here to handle the bucking horse group."

Thinking more about it as Janie closed the door, Cassie admitted Kade had considerably more experience with horse stock than Cam. Also, if she were being honest, she conceded Matt had more experience and more rodeo contacts than she or Skye.

Spurning most of the family's invitations over the weekend had allowed her time to think through the changes, accept the reasons behind the moves were sound, and attempt to work through her issues. She'd thought of going to Kade, asking about reporting directly to him, then discarded the idea, knowing her cousin would see it as a wimp move. *Suck it up, kid*, he'd say, then dismiss her, which would be embarrassing on so many levels. In truth, he'd have been right. She needed to pull her big girl pants up tight and move on.

The anger she felt toward her father hurt the most. She'd worked hard, done all he'd asked, yet he wanted her out. The intense pain at his decision would take a long time to heal. She needed to make a decision about her future, and soon.

Cradling her head in her hands, she let out a deep groan, knowing she was better than some whiny, weak female who couldn't get over a lost love. MacLarens didn't moan about setbacks or obstacles. They confronted them head-on, found a way around them, and kept going. And that's just what she'd do. No one needed to know if she began to send out résumés, confidentially inquiring about other jobs. Perhaps something away from Arizona and outside the ranch and rodeo industries. A clean break where her father and ex-boyfriend could no longer hurt her. The last gave her the first smidgeon of hope about her future since the announcements.

Feeling better, she opened an old résumé and began to read through it. Jotting down notes, she picked up her phone on the first ring, not taking the time to check the caller ID.

"Hey, Cassie, it's Matt. Kade and I are flying to Cold Creek tomorrow."

Staring at the phone, she let out a low groan.

******

Houston, Texas

"Good morning. I assume you had an uneventful trip." Gage extended his hand, grasping Ivan's in a firm grip.

"Ah, yes. Pleasant and short." He'd left El Paso, touching down in Houston less than two hours later.

"As you can see, the newest delivery is being unloaded. Care to inspect the cattle with me?"

Ivan walked alongside Gage as they made their way to the stockyards, hearing the unmistakable sounds of bawling cattle.

"Gonzo, you remember Ivan Santiago." Gage stopped next to his stock manager, Eddie Gonzalez, waiting as the two exchanged greetings. "How's it going?"

"Good, except I can't match the time the truck left the border with their arrival here." Gonzo glanced at a clipboard, his face twisting into a frown.

"What do you mean?" Ivan asked, moving closer to him to get a look at the schedule.

"Based on the distance and speed, there is almost an hour of lost time." He glanced up at Gage. "It doesn't add up, boss."

"Have you asked the driver about it?"

"Not yet."

"Where is he?" Gage walked toward the truck as the men herded the last of the cattle into holding pens.

"I'll get him." Gonzo walked toward a trailer used for breaks, returning a few minutes later with a rail thin man with leathered skin, wearing a well-used ball cap announcing his support of an American football team. "This is the driver, Hector Garcia. He only speaks a little English, so I'll translate."

"Ask him about the discrepancy." Gage watched Hector's reaction, seeing his gaze drop to the ground as he shook his head, mumbling a reply to Gonzo. Digging in his pocket, he pulled out a crumbled piece of paper and handed it to Gonzo.

"He says his boss asked him to make a stop about an hour out of El Paso. This shows a freeway exit, but nothing else."

"What boss?" Ivan asked in Spanish, stepping forward.

Although Gage's Spanish was passable, he couldn't understand the driver's rapid reply, but he did comprehend Ivan's mumbled curse.

"What is it?"

"He said his boss was ordered to stop by another man. This man is a worker. He does what he's told."

"I'll do some checking, Ivan," Gage offered. "It may mean nothing."

Ivan nodded, although his gut told him the additional stop *did* mean something. "I will also ask questions. I am certain we will find a satisfactory explanation."

******

Cold Creek, Colorado

"Cassie, wake up. We have to get out of here."

Opening her eyes, Cassie tried to focus. "Janie?" she croaked out. "What time is it?"

"It doesn't matter. There's a fire in the abandoned building next door. Kurt is out front with his crew. He says we have to evacuate. Now!"

"Evacuate?" Her muddled brain finally kicked to life, her eyes flying open. Throwing off her covers, she fumbled for the jeans and shirt she'd tossed on a nearby chair.

"He says not to take anything with us," Janie called from the living room.

Right, Cassie thought as she packed up her computer and slung it over her shoulder. Grabbing her jewelry case, phone, and purse, she dashed toward the front door, then stopped, turning back to her bedroom.

"Cassie, we need to leave."

"Just a minute." Rifling through a drawer, she found the small album hidden at the bottom, stuffing it into the computer bag before dashing out the front door. "Okay. Let's go."

Smoke blanketed the air, making her eyes burn as they maneuvered the steps to the parking lot. Like Cassie, Janie had grabbed several of her own personal belongings, which shifted as she took the final few steps.

"Come on." Kurt gripped Janie's arm, guiding her and Cassie to a cordoned off area where other residents waited, watching the flames from the nearby building. "You should be fine here unless the flames jump to your building, which is doubtful. Do *not* try to go back upstairs until I come back and get you." He leveled a stern stare at Janie, then Cassie before leaving them to join the rest of the crew.

Even from this distance, Cassie could feel the heat from the burning building, sense the fear of those standing around her. She'd never seen a fire of this magnitude or one that threatened human life. The flames seemed to have a life of their own as they danced in and out of an open window. She reached out and gripped Janie's arm.

"Was there anyone in the building?"

"I don't know." Looking around, Janie spotted the flickering strobes of squad cars and an ambulance. "But there's an ambulance over there."

"I suppose we should make ourselves comfortable. This could be a long wait." Cassie reached into her purse, pulling out the keys to her truck. "Come on. Let's wait in the truck."

"I don't know..."

"It's right there." She nodded to a parking spot not twenty feet away. "We'll still be able to see what's going on and keep an eye on Kurt." Cassie knew he would be foremost in Janie's mind. She'd never seen her so taken with a man. And from Kurt's behavior, it appeared he felt the same. "Let's get out of this smoke and drink some water. I always keep several bottles in the truck."

"I suppose it could be a long time before they let us back in our apartment." Janie followed Cassie, slipping inside the truck. "It is good to get out of the smoke. The wind really carries it."

Handing Janie a bottle of water, Cassie leaned her head against the seat back and closed her eyes, stretching her legs out as far as possible. She'd just dozed off when the sound of her phone jerked her awake.

"Hello?"

"Sorry to be calling so late, but there's been a change in the schedule for tomorrow."

"Matt?"

"Yeah, it's me." Listening to her sleep-filled voice, Matt felt a sharp pain in his chest, recalling all the times he'd woken her from a deep sleep to make love. She never refused, always welcoming his caresses. They'd fit together perfectly. "Did I wake you?"

Sitting up, she shook her head to clear her mind. "Not really. The fire did that." She knew her response was curt, but she didn't care.

"What fire?" Matt asked, jolting to attention.

"The one at a building near our complex. Janie and I are in my truck."

Matt paced back and forth in his grandfather's living room. "Are you all right?"

"Fine. We're both fine. Just waiting to get back into our apartment." She watched as Kurt walked toward them. "Kurt is here to give us an update. Can I call you back?"

Matt stopped in his tracks. He'd completely forgotten about her firefighter boyfriend.

"Sure. Talk to your boyfriend, then call me back."

"He's not—" She started to tell him Kurt wasn't her boyfriend, but the sound of the dial tone stopped her. Brushing a strand of hair away from her face, she fumed for an instant before realizing who she dated was none of Matt's business. Nothing about her life was his business. What did she care if he thought she and Kurt were together? It made no difference to her. Shoving the phone back into her purse, she joined Janie and Kurt outside, having no intention of calling Matt back.

"You should be fine to go back inside. We've got it under control." Kurt settled a hand on the small of Janie's back, letting her lean into him. "I'll try to come up and check on you before we pull out." He brushed a quick kiss across her lips, then turned and jogged away.

Janie's gaze followed him all the way back to the charred building.

"Come on," Cassie said, gripping Janie's arm and tugging her toward the stairs. "I'll make you a cup of hot chocolate."

"Ugh...nothing hot," Janie grumbled as they trudged up the steps.

******

Cassie had finally drifted off to sleep when her phone rang, startling her awake. Reaching out, she knocked the phone to the floor, mumbling a curse as she slid to the floor. Seeing Matt's number, she groaned, almost deciding not to answer before reconsidering.

"Yeah?"

"You were supposed to call me back."

"There's been a lot going on. They finally got the fire under control and let us back into our apartment. And no, neither Janie nor I were hurt, thanks for asking." She paused, taking a breath and reining in her frustration. "I hope there's a good reason you have to talk to me tonight," she snapped.

Matt's jaw clenched at her snarky response. "Why? Am I interrupting something?" As soon as the question was out, he wanted to pull it back. It wasn't any of his business who she spent time with or welcomed into her bed. Cursing to himself, he waited for a harsh response.

"Only my sleep." Cassie closed her eyes, not feeling up to arguing with him tonight.

"Sorry. That was uncalled for. And I'm glad you're safe and back in your own place."

"Whatever, Matt. Is there a reason you have to speak with me tonight?"

"There is. Kade has an early meeting with Cam and the company's local banker, so we'll be flying in earlier than we first thought. I'll pick you up at your place and take you to breakfast."

"I don't think—"

"Nothing to think about. We've both got to eat. Besides, it will give us some time to talk before we meet with Kade and Cam. See you in a few hours."

Cassie stared at the phone. She couldn't believe Matt had cut her off twice in one night. Being her boss did not mean he could be a complete jerk. She didn't want to have breakfast...or lunch...or any meal with him.

Rubbing both temples with her fingers, she stretched out on the bed, her heart pounding as fast as her head throbbed. She hated the way his voice could trigger such immediate and painful emotions. Ever since he'd reentered her life, Cassie felt as if she was on an unending roller coaster ride. She'd rocketed out of the starting gate, but couldn't seem to find the finish line. Now she lived in a constant state of turmoil, as if the ground shifted beneath her, causing her to remain off balance.

Grabbing her computer case from the floor, she reached inside, finding the album she'd stuffed inside and opening it. Two smiling faces stared back at her, arms around each other. They were in their early twenties when they'd driven to Tucson for the weekend, hiked the nearby mountains, and spent their nights making love until neither could move. It had been one of the best times of her life. As soon as she had the chance, she'd toss it in a dumpster.

Shoving it back in the bag, she glanced at the clock. Six hours until Matt picked her up. Six hours to find a way to defend her emotions and traitorous body from the sight of him. She shut her eyes, knowing it wasn't enough time.

Chapter Twelve

"Good morning, Janie. I'm here to pick up Cassie."

She stared at Matt, not moving from her position blocking him from entering. Glancing down the hall toward Cassie's door, she looked back at him, tilting her head.

"Are you certain she knew you were coming? I've been up a while and haven't heard her stir."

"We talked after you got back into your place last night. Is it okay if I come in?"

"Um...sure. Help yourself to coffee while I check on Cassie." Tapping on the door, she cracked it open, leaning inside. "Hey, Cassie. Are you awake?"

"No." Turning onto her stomach, Cassie grabbed the pillow and covered her head.

Janie walked to the side of the bed, prying the pillow from her fingers. "Do you remember agreeing to have breakfast with Matt this morning?"

Still lying on her stomach, Cassie opened one eye a crack, peering up at Janie before pushing herself up. "I guess the alarm didn't go off."

Picking up the clock, Janie turned it over. "Maybe because you didn't set it?" She cocked a brow at Cassie. "Do you want me to tell him you aren't well?"

Brushing hair from her face, she stood, grabbing clothes. "No. He'll know you're lying and that I'm trying to avoid him."

"Both would be true."

Cassie narrowed her gaze, sending Janie a withering glance. "Just keep him occupied so I can get across the hall to the bathroom."

A few minutes later, she stood under the warm spray, letting the water sluice over her body, rinsing away the last smells of smoke from the night before. She had no desire to spend an hour in casual conversation with Matt over breakfast.

No matter how hard she tried, their encounters always ended with one or both of them angry, continuing to avoid the elephant always present between them. She'd lain awake too many nights, trying to force what they'd once had into a compartment hidden deep in the recesses of her mind. It had been a waste of time and sleep.

Although the one conclusion didn't thrill her, nothing else would ever bring her peace. Until she confronted him about how they'd split, about the pain and anger his leaving had caused, she'd never be free to move on.

Clearing up the past would change nothing. He'd still feel nothing for her, and she'd never again be able to trust him with her heart. It might, however, allow her to put some logic to his leaving, allowing her to finally move on. And she so desperately needed to move on.

******

Matt paced around the small living room, glancing at the framed photos on bookshelves, studying posters on the walls, even flipping through a coffee table book featuring images of Colorado before his gaze landed on an object tucked behind a vase. Picking it up, his palm almost burned at the memories flooding through him. Staring at the geode they'd found on a weekend trip to a mountain town two hours east of Fire Mountain, Matt turned it in his hand. He'd known when he picked it off the rocky trail, tapping it against the ground and hearing the hollow sound, that there'd be treasure inside the nondescript rock.

The size of an ostrich egg, Cassie scoffed at his enthusiasm, more intent on completing their hike than the journey before them. They'd always been different in that way. She tended to focus on the end goal, while he enjoyed the journey. Her eyes had widened when he took a chisel from the truck, striking the rock with several taps until it split in two, displaying a beautiful combination of white and amethyst crystals. He still remembered her gasp, then how she'd reached out, taking the larger half from him. Memories of the smile she'd shot him still caused his heart to trip over itself, his chest tightening.

"Sorry to keep you waiting."

Matt set the geode back in its hiding place as Cassie walked toward him, grabbing a jacket off a chair, oblivious to the stroll he'd taken into their past. Checking his phone, he glanced at her.

"We still have an hour before meeting with Kade and Cam. Anywhere in particular you'd like to go for breakfast?" His appreciative gaze wandered over her from the cowboy boots, to the tight, deep blue jeans, then the peach-colored blouse with a deep V-neck that hugged her curves, to the white jacket in her hand, which seemed to be more for show than warmth.

"There's a mom and pop pancake place a few blocks from the office." Cassie stopped a couple feet away, fidgeting with the purse slung over her shoulder, catching her bottom lip between her teeth. He always looked so blasted hot and tempting in his Wrangler's and chambray shirt with the top buttons open, revealing a sprinkling of hair. She couldn't count the number of mornings she'd been settled on his chest, letting her fingers run through it, enjoying the silky crispness before letting her hand wander lower.

"Cassie?" Matt snapped his fingers before her face. "You with me?"

"Um...yeah," she breathed out. "Let's go."

Matt's lips curled up into a wry grin, as if he'd been able to read her thoughts and knew how his closeness affected her. Turning toward the door, she glared at him over her shoulder. "Well, are you coming?"

******

Seven-thirty and the diner already bustled with activity. From the vehicles in the parking lot, Matt figured it attracted a good mix of locals, truckers, and those passing through on their way to somewhere else. Not known as a tourist town, Cold Creek still enjoyed its fair share of travelers looking for remote places to scour for antiques, or hoping to find solace in a trek through the thick forests.

"Any table that's open." The waitress stood to the side, menus in her hand, waiting for Cassie and him to pick a spot.

Cassie spared him a quick look before selecting a table near the back.

"What do you suggest?" Matt glanced at the menu, already knowing he'd go for any item, including eggs and bacon.

"I always order eggs and hash browns, but Janie goes for the pancakes or waffles. She never leaves a scrap on the plate." She flashed him a quick smile, then covered it by picking up her coffee and taking a sip. Grimacing, she added sugar and a little cream, then tried again.

"Better?"

Looking over the rim of her cup, her brows furrowed before she understood his question had to do with her coffee, not her personally. "Um...yes. Much."

Cassie had no idea why he insisted on meeting for breakfast. She figured he must have a list of items he wanted to discuss before including Kade or Cam. Well, she had one of her own, and her goal was to at least put it before him, let the request roll around in his head, then invite him for cocktails at her place tonight. By the time he left, she hoped to have answers and perhaps a little peace.

"Tell me about what happened last night," he asked a moment before the waitress brought their food.

"There's not much to tell. Janie and I were in our apartment when a fire broke out at an abandoned building close by."

"I saw it. There doesn't seem to be much that's salvageable."

"Probably not. I was asleep when Kurt and his crew arrived, ordering us to evacuate. We waited in my truck until they contained the fire. That's about it." She mashed her eggs with her potatoes, mixed them together, then took a bite.

"I'm surprised you didn't stay with your boyfriend last night." Matt didn't glance up from his plate. He'd told himself not to bring Kurt into the conversation, but for some perverse reason, he couldn't manage it.

Tilting her head, Cassie set down her fork, giving him an impassive stare. "First of all, both Janie and I were beat. Secondly, he's not *my* boyfriend. He's Janie's."

Matt choked on a piece of bacon, then grabbed his coffee, taking a swallow. "Didn't he introduce himself to me a few weeks ago as the guy you were dating?"

Shrugging, Cassie took her time swallowing her last bite before answering. "It didn't work out for either of us, so I introduced him to Janie. They hit it off right away."

"Sorry. It must have been hard."

"Not really. We'd only gone out a few times, and never, well...you know." She bit her lower lip, stopping herself from revealing anything more. It was none of Matt's business. "I'm glad for Janie. I've never seen her this happy." Pushing her plate away, she leaned forward. "So what did you want to talk about?"

Matt sat back, allowing himself to feel relief at her announcement. He'd hated the knowledge Cassie may have found someone else. As ridiculous as it seemed, the worst part about being back in her life had been the realization of how much he still loved her. It made no sense.

He'd left because of her staunch determination to see their lives melding together in a plan of her own making. Her rare acknowledgment of what he wanted or needed played little part in how she saw their lives playing out. He knew she believed his leaving had been all about him, and perhaps in some ways it had. The truth was, he'd been willing to give her anything she wanted, but he needed her to give him the chance to prove himself in the pro rodeo circuit. Not only had she balked at him taking the time between his graduation and hers to give it a shot, she refused to spend time discussing it. He wondered if she ever looked back and regretted cutting out his dreams to concentrate on her own. Now that they were older, had experienced more of life, he contemplated whether they could have a second chance to right the mistakes of the past.

"Kade wants us to travel around the Midwest and West, meet with the main contacts on the various rodeo committees, and try to cement relationships. We could be gone for a week at a time over a period of a couple months."

"Just the two of us?" Cassie choked out. "I don't think—"

He shook his head. "Skye would travel with us much of the time, figuring we have a better chance of at least one of us hitting it off with the contacts."

"I don't know. The logistics seem pretty difficult with you in Arizona, Skye in Montana, and me in

Colorado." Besides, she didn't like any idea that included Matt and her spending significant amounts of time together, even if Skye could act as a buffer.

"First, only the big rodeos would require us to partner. We'd approach the smaller ones as we always have, hoping to keep as many as possible and add others. It's the big ones we want to grab. Mitch and Cam worked through the details with Kade so we'd have a starting point. The three of us would begin in the northwest and move on from there. What do you say?"

He made it sound so simple, as if the two of them could be in the same space for significant amounts of time without the past encroaching. And from where he sat, Cassie understood. She had to remind herself he didn't share the same regret she did about their parting. He'd wanted it, and she hadn't. She still loved him, whereas his feelings for her had burned out long ago.

She needed to focus on her new goal of obtaining a significant role within another company. After focusing for so long on building a career within the MacLaren companies, the thought gave her no comfort. Traveling with Skye and Matt wouldn't hinder her plans of searching for a new job, and might actually help her achieve it.

"Whatever you and the others want. If this is the plan, I'm in."

"Great. We'll work out the details during the meeting today." Matt hadn't expected her to agree to it so easily, being prepared to counter each of her arguments. "If you're ready, we should head to the office."

"Wait, Matt. There is one more item I want to talk about."

"Sure. Lay it on me."

The lump she'd felt building in her chest had grown until it threatened to choke her. Still, she needed to get this said. "I want to have some time alone with you. Not in a restaurant or other public place. Maybe my place tonight for cocktails...if you don't have other plans." She waited, her hands tightly clasped under the table.

The request couldn't have come as more of a surprise. It took all his concentration to control the hope he felt, knowing he had to keep his wits about him and his desire reined in until he knew what she wanted.

"Tonight is fine. What is it you'd like to discuss?"

"I need to understand why you left me."

******

"That wraps it up. Matt will schedule the meetings, set up the logistics, and get back with you and Skye. Is there anything else?" Kade sat back, glad to have the meeting end without fireworks

157

between Cassie and Matt. This would be Cam's last involvement in the division before moving back to Fire Mountain and his new responsibilities. Kade didn't want him to carry any doubts about them to his new assignment.

Matt and Cassie shook their heads.

"Everyone up for dinner tonight?" Cam stood, stretching his arms over his head. "Lainey's invited you all over to our place."

"Works for me," Kade answered, watching a look pass between Matt and Cassie.

"What time?" Matt hoped it wouldn't interfere with cocktails at her place. The subject of their talk didn't appeal to him, but time alone with Cassie did.

"Lainey asked if it could be a little later. Is eight o'clock all right?"

"Perfect," Cassie blurted out. "At least for me."

"Done." Kade pushed from the table. "I have some calls to make, so I'll see you at the house."

Cam and Kade filed out, leaving Matt and Cassie alone in the room. Neither spoke as they put away their laptops and walked out to Matt's rental car.

"Are you still okay with coming over to my place?" Cassie looked at him, wanting him to know she hadn't changed her mind.

"Sure am. How much time will we have before Janie gets home?" He unlocked the car, opening Cassie's door for her.

"She has plans with Kurt. I doubt she'll even *come* home."

Shutting the door, Matt glanced at his watch. They had over three hours before dinner at Cam's. Sliding behind the wheel, he glanced at Cassie sitting erect, her hands clasped in her lap, her body radiating with tension. He would reach over and place a hand on hers, but now wasn't the time to show his concern. They had a difficult conversation awaiting them, and he had no idea how she'd respond to what he intended to be an honest discussion about why he'd left. If that was what she wanted, he'd give it to her full force and expected the same in return. They were adults, more mature, and able to deal with tough talk.

Matt didn't know why his stomach knotted at the last thought.

Chapter Thirteen

"I have wine, beer, whiskey, water, or soda. What would you like?" Cassie stood at the refrigerator door, her hand trembling as she rested it on the door handle.

"Water would be great."

Pouring herself a glass of wine and grabbing a bottle of water, she joined him in the living room, waiting for him to take a seat.

"Not much of a cocktail." She held the bottle toward him, a smile that didn't reach her eyes curving the corners of her mouth.

"I'll follow it with a whiskey, assuming we have time before leaving for Cam's." Uncapping the bottle, he gulped down half, then lowered himself onto the sofa. "Why don't you sit here?" He smiled, patting the cushion next to him, unperturbed when she shook her head and sat in one of the overstuffed chairs.

"Look, Matt, I know you would probably rather be anywhere but here with me, so thanks for giving me some time."

"This is exactly where I want to be, Cassie." His face grew serious as his penetrating gaze caught hers. "Our talk is long overdue." Finishing his water, he stood and walked into the kitchen. "Guess I need that whiskey sooner than I thought."

"It's in the pantry. Glasses are next to the sink." Cassie stared down at her wine, noticing the glass shake. Even the alcohol hadn't helped control the nervous tremor in her hands. She'd been fighting the butterflies ever since breakfast. The need for answers drove Cassie to seek closure. She thought his agreeing to talk would be the first step. Now she wasn't so sure.

Tipping his glass toward her, Matt took a sip of whiskey, but didn't sit down. Instead, he walked to the shelf holding the geode he'd seen that morning and set down his glass. Crossing his arms, he rested a shoulder against the cabinet, his face impassive.

"So you want answers."

Glancing up, she searched his face, swallowing the lump in her throat. "I thought I did, but now I'm not so sure. Maybe it would be best to leave it all in the past."

He'd never seen Cassie so cautious, so unsure, and although she did her best to hide it, the reality she still hurt from their breakup pained him. It had been years. Matt had moved on, sort of, by dating other women, having a couple brief relationships. No other woman had affected him like Cassie. No one had filled the empty spot in his heart reserved only for her.

Picking up his glass, he walked toward her, indicating a nearby chair. "May I?"

Cassie nodded, scooting back in her chair, creating a defensive distance.

"You deserve to know the reasons I left, but there are things I need to know, too. This has to be a two-way conversation, Cass. I need this talk as much as you."

"All right, if you're certain."

"I am. Go ahead. Ask whatever you want."

Lifting her chin, she began. "What did I do to make you stop loving me and go back to Becky?"

What the hell? His jaw tightened at the mention of Becky. "I don't have any idea what you're talking about. I never went back to Becky. My leaving had nothing to do with another woman."

Leaning forward, she rested her arms on her legs, her eyes sparking. "That's not true and you know it. I saw you with her not even two months after you took off."

"Exactly where did you think you saw me with Becky?" he ground out, fists clenching at the outrageous allegation.

"I heard you entered a rodeo in Ft. Worth, so I hopped a plane, hoping we could talk. I thought perhaps we'd still be able to work things out."

"I don't remember seeing you." His rough voice lowered to almost a whisper. He had no idea Cassie had tried to seek him out. He'd checked his phone, email, and texts daily for weeks, hoping for some indication she cared enough to reach out.

"That's because when your events were over, I found you wrapped around Becky. And well...let's just say the kiss I saw was more than friendly." Brushing hair from her face, she took several breaths, desperate to hold on to any amount of dignity she could. She pushed out of the chair, moving away from him, wrapping her arms around her waist.

"Cassie, I don't remember..." Matt's voice trailed off as he thought back, realizing it had to be the first rodeo he'd entered. He'd won one event and made the top three in the other. Becky had been waiting when he'd left the arena. They hadn't seen each other in years. His emotions had been so high, he grabbed her around the waist, lifting her up and swinging her around, sharing a celebratory kiss. That had to be what Cassie saw. Mumbling a curse, he took a couple tentative steps toward her.

"It's true, isn't it? You left me to go back to her." Although she hoped it wasn't, Cassie knew what she saw.

"No, it isn't true. I left the arena and there was Becky running up to me, her arms wide. Yes, I kissed her, but it didn't mean what you thought. After high school, she left for college on the east coast. I hadn't seen her in years."

"So you didn't know that right after you left, she transferred to State and tracked me down on campus?"

His eyes widened. "I had no idea she'd moved back to Arizona. She never said a word about it in Ft. Worth. I'm telling you, Becky had nothing to do with my decision to leave."

"That's interesting because she knew you'd left me. After I returned from Ft. Worth, she made a point of telling me the two of you had reconnected and to stay away."

His face hardened at the blatant lie Becky had fed Cassie. He couldn't imagine what had gone through her mind when she faced Becky after seeing them together at the rodeo.

"She lied, Cass. I don't know what else to say, except Becky and I never got back together."

"And I'm supposed to believe that after what I saw? You're saying you shook her hand, thanked her for coming, and let her head home?"

No, he hadn't sent her on her way, but he hadn't slept with her, either, even though he knew she wanted and expected him to take her back to his motel.

"We had a couple beers at a nearby bar where I made it clear she and I wouldn't be hooking up. She wasn't happy, but didn't push and left with her friends. I haven't seen her since."

She'd always been able to tell when he was trying to con her. His eyes would give him away each time. Listening to his explanation and watching his face, she saw no sign of deceit.

Cassie slipped onto the sofa, trying to wrap her mind around the fact Matt might be telling the truth. "If not because of Becky, why did you leave?"

"I had dreams, Cass, and you refused to accept them. Every time I brought up what I wanted, you pushed back, reminding me our plan was to graduate and work for your dad. You always called it *our* plan, even though I'd never agreed to it. What *I* wanted was to enter the pro circuit, give it a chance until you graduated, then decide my next step. I never intended to break it off with you, but I needed my time, just like you wanted yours. I didn't leave because I didn't love you. I left to pursue a dream you were determined to extinguish." Threading fingers through his hair, he stood, pacing away. "Not once did you take me seriously when I told you my plans, which *did* include you. You were too damned focused on your end goal, what you thought was best for us, never once considering my dreams." Scrubbing a hand down his face, he took a breath, trying to control his anger. "Do you know how many times I tried to get you to talk to me the last week before I left?"

Her heart clenched, knowing he'd reached out to her for several days. She'd been too busy to see him.

"No," she muttered.

"Eighteen times. Voice messages, emails, texts. Hell, Cassie," he thundered, "I even left you a written note and told Janie it was critical I talked with you."

All the frustration he felt at the time came rushing back. "Still, you ignored me."

Cassie shut her eyes tight. She remembered all the times Matt mentioned his desire to compete in the circuit for a year, maybe two. Long enough to get it out of his system before settling down. She had blown him off, including all his attempts to reach out to her during his last week on campus. Preparing for finals consumed her time, giving her what seemed a convenient excuse for not discussing the subject which always triggered an argument.

Her biggest fear was the likelihood of him getting hurt or killed. The thought of losing Matt to an accident had kept her awake each time he'd talked about his rodeo dreams. Fear, almost paralyzing in its intensity, caused Cassie to ignore his desires and focus on what she felt was best and safest for both of them.

In hindsight, the second reason she pushed his desires aside seemed more of an excuse, but it impacted her thinking at the time. She'd trusted Matt, but the thought of him being on the road alone, tempted by all those rodeo bunnies bothered her. Even married men had a hard time refusing what was offered. The odds were high they'd hook up with the bunnies who made it their mission to bed as many cowboys as possible. Knowing Matt, those worries seemed to be just one more of her excuses for not wanting him to leave. Her immaturity and selfish actions had pushed him away, making him feel he had no choice but to leave.

"I'm so sorry. If I could get the past back, there's so much I'd do differently."

Seeing the misery on her face, the fight in him vanished, but not the need to protect his heart. Matt remembered the desolation he'd felt after leaving her, the battles he'd fought with himself about whether to go back or stay his course. He'd held firm, continued with his plan. After a while, the sharp pain when she entered his mind became a consistent throbbing, then an occasional ache. He filled his days with work and his nights with women who demanded nothing of him. The life he'd built felt right, solid...and lonely.

Taking a seat beside her, he reached out, grasping her hand in his. "We both made mistakes. I wasn't perfect—"

"You tried harder than I did."

A sad chuckle escaped his lips. "I'm not sure about that, but I always knew you were the best thing to ever happen to me. Leaving you...nothing has ever been so hard."

Tightening her hand around his, she sought courage, knowing she had no right to ask the question hanging between them. "How do you feel about us now?"

The pained expression on his face, the hesitancy to answer, told Cassie all she needed to know.

Pulling her hand from his, she plastered on a forced smile and stood.

"It's all right, Matt. I had no right to ask." Turning, she picked up her coat, swiping at the tears pooling in her eyes, hoping he didn't notice. "We should probably leave for dinner," she called over her shoulder, hearing Matt walk up behind her, not daring to look at him. Tensing at the feel of his hands on her shoulders, she tried to pull away, feeling his grip tighten.

"It's not what you think, Cassie." He leaned down, brushing hair from her neck, grazing kisses along the soft skin, feeling her shiver. Moving up, he nibbled at her ear, breathing in the scent so uniquely hers. "There's risk in trying to reclaim the past," he whispered.

She melted against him, dropping her coat on the floor as she sighed in pleasure. "Are you afraid of risk?" she breathed out, then inhaled a sharp breath when his teeth grazed a path across her shoulder. Unable to concentrate, she gave into the sensations.

He turned her toward him, brushing his knuckles down her cheek, watching her eyes close. "I'm afraid of anything involving you, as you should be of me."

Opening her eyes, she studied his face, seeing the same doubt and confusion she felt. "I am afraid, but you're worth the risk."

"Am I?" He lowered his mouth, taking hers in a soft caress.

Moving her hands tentatively up his arms, she wrapped them around his neck, drawing him to her. Holding Matt felt so right. She trembled at the intensity of her need, the desire he created with each touch. Parting her lips, she heard his deep growl as he plunged in, deepening the kiss, creating heat that flashed through her.

Tightening his hold, he let his hands move down her back, feeling her tremble against him. *How had I ever thought I could live without this?* he wondered, letting his hands settle on her hips, pulling her close, letting her feel his desire.

"Cassie, you home? Oh my. I guess you are." Janie stopped inside the door, amusement crossing her face as they slowly pulled apart, faces flushed. "Sorry. If I'd known, I would have stayed away longer." Her smirk told them both how much she enjoyed catching them. "I certainly hope this is the start of something which should never have ended."

Cassie's jaw dropped. "We, uh..."

Matt saved her, tilting her face to his and placing another quick kiss on her lips. "We were just on our way out."

"Uh, yeah. Like that was obvious," Janie laughed, tossing her purse aside. "Where are you headed?"

"Cam's. Lainey invited Kade and us to dinner. I'm sure you're welcome to come, too." Cassie felt a sense of triumph at the sound of her level voice, then sobered at the look on Janie's face. "What is it?"

"Kurt and I were having dinner at his place when he got an emergency call. Another fire in an abandoned building. He asked me to stay at his place, but I didn't feel right being there without him. He might not get home for hours. It seems this one jumped to another building with people inside." She slumped into a chair. "I just hope they get everyone out."

Cassie knelt beside her, resting a hand on Janie's knee. "I'll stay. Matt can explain to everyone what happened."

"No. You go ahead. There's nothing you can do here, and it may be hours until I hear from Kurt. Besides, I'd make terrible company tonight."

"All right, but call me as soon as you hear anything." Standing, Cassie's gaze locked on Matt's, wondering if she'd made a monumental mistake with him. He hadn't mentioned anything about still being in love with her. In fact, his signals had been the opposite. At least until he'd kissed her.

"We'd better leave before Lainey wonders what happened to us." Matt took her arm, guiding her to his car.

"Should I take my truck?" she asked, her chest tightening at the set look on his face. All the warmth of minutes before had vanished.

"No. We'll go together." Opening her door, he waited until she slid onto the seat, then slammed it shut with more force than he intended. Cursing himself, Matt stormed around to his side, not believing how close he'd come to lifting her into his arms and taking her to bed. And he knew she wouldn't have stopped him.

Shoving the key into the ignition, he backed out and entered the street without once glancing her way. He could feel her gaze on him, knowing she must be wondering at his abrupt change in mood.

"Look, Cassie. What happened back there, well...shouldn't have."

Biting her lower lip hard enough to almost break the skin, she nodded. "Okay."

"It's just..." He hesitated, tightening his grip on the steering wheel, not sure what he wanted to say.

"You don't need to explain. We were both caught up in the moment. I know it meant nothing." She swallowed the lump lodged in her throat, hoping her voice concealed the distress she felt.

He started to speak, then clamped his mouth shut. Until he understood his own feelings, figured out if he could try again, it would be better to keep his distance. Having the same chemistry and passion didn't guarantee they could work through their differences or overcome the problems that doomed them in the past. Love didn't solve everything.

They rode the rest of the way in an uneasy silence, each lost in their own thoughts. Their history hung between them as thick as a dense fog. On occasion, the visibility seemed clear, indicating a sure path. Other times, no matter how much each wanted to try again, the past clawed at them, slicing through their desire, halting their progress.

Parking at the curb, Matt turned off the engine, shifting toward her. Cassie refused to look at him, her gaze fixed on some real or imagined object outside. Even in the dark and two feet away, he could see the sheen of moisture on her cheek.

"Cassie, look at me."

Shaking her head, she grasped the door handle. Pushing the door open, she turned to look at him. "You don't need to explain. I get it. We were over years ago. We had our talk, and all is good. Each of us can move on." Shutting the door, she focused on escaping into the refuge of Cam's house. At least she knew where she stood, and it wasn't beside Matt. The heat and passion of their kisses meant nothing to him. He'd done it to comfort her, nothing more.

"Cassie, wait."

The sharp stab of pain served to speed her actions, not slow them. She knocked once on the door, then turned the knob to let herself in.

"Oh no you don't." Matt grasped her arm, turning her around. "You aren't shutting me out this time."

"I wasn't..." Cassie started before Matt placed a finger on her lips to silence her.

"We *will* finish our talk, just not now."

Her eyes wide, she nodded, feeling a little of the tension seep away.

"Good." He brushed a kiss across her cheek, although the spell of earlier had been broken. Her heart sank at the sadness in his eyes.

Straightening her spine, she plastered a smile on her face, knowing whatever else he had to say wouldn't bring her any joy. The outcome might not be what she hoped for, but at least she'd have answers—and that would be more than what she'd had all these years.

Chapter Fourteen

Houston, Texas

Ivan hung up, deciding to call his father. He needed to persuade him to confide about what his brothers were doing. Depending on what he learned, Ivan might have to make arrangements to isolate himself from any dealings that hinted at what he expected might be happening. It might mean being disowned by the family and forsaking his legacy, but he knew he'd take that chance if his uncles were doing what Ivan suspected. Until he received confirmation, though, he wouldn't pass judgment.

"Are you ready to finish reviewing the sales figures?" Gage joined Ivan in the office his boss kept in Houston. It was one of three Gage knew about, including El Paso and León, Mexico. The private jet, personal driver, three thousand dollar suits, and unlimited credit card all pointed to wealth beyond what could be made in the rodeo stock business. From what Gage could tell, cattle sales outside the rodeo business didn't make up the difference. Each passing week seemed to bring more questions with few answers, which worried him no small amount.

"I am. Please join me." Ivan nodded at the bottle of scotch he held. "It's already been a long day, my friend."

"I'll take a short one. I don't usually drink before leaving the office, but you're right. Today has provided more than the usual number of challenges." Gage sat down, exchanging the papers he'd been holding for the glass of scotch. Tilting it toward Ivan, he took a slow sip, deciding he still needed to keep his suspicions to himself. Whatever he did suspect had to involve Ivan, and that troubled him. He'd spoken to his good friend, Thad Montgomery, twice. Both times, he'd been told there wasn't enough to trigger an investigation. Today's discovery of lost time on the cattle delivery might change Thad's mind.

******

Cold Creek, Colorado

"Are you sure Lainey can't use my help packing?" Cassie sat down across from Cam as he finished loading his books and files into a box.

"She told me it's all covered. We're hiring people to do most of the packing. It's a good thing she already hired a manager for the preschool or I'd have myself one stressed out wife."

Cassie laughed, understanding Cam's joke. Lainey had to be one of the calmest women she'd ever met. Even when she'd been the target of a stalker before she and Cam got together, she'd been tough and calm. It must come from working with preschoolers for a living.

"Have her call me if she changes her mind. And don't even try to get out of here without saying goodbye."

"You sure are getting bossy now that I'm leaving," Cam shot back as she disappeared into the hall.

Checking the time, Cassie made a quick stop in the employee lounge to grab a bag of chips and a soda. She'd skipped breakfast and lunch, but she couldn't ignore the growling of her stomach any longer.

She'd only had a few minutes with Janie before they left for work that morning, but it was long enough to learn the fire had consumed two buildings. One had been the home to several of the town's homeless. Two young men had died. From what Kurt had learned, both had been in the foster care program until a few months before. With no money and unable to obtain work, they'd done what they could to survive. The knowledge had hit Cassie hard.

She and Eric's wife, Amber, had worked with Annie at the MacLaren Foundation, a non-profit organization established to make certain kids exiting the foster care system had the needed skills and resources to make it once their state funding ran out. Prior to the foundation's help, many of the children turning eighteen prior to the end of the school year lost funding before they'd obtained their high school diploma, reducing their chances of finding work. She wondered if this was what had happened to the young men who'd lost their lives last night.

The fires had officially escalated from vandalism to murder, compelling the fire chief and the police chief to establish a joint task force. Its sole purpose would be to find, arrest, and prosecute those responsible.

Vowing to call Annie to see if something could be done for foster children in Cold Creek, Cassie closed her office door, letting her thoughts drift back to Matt.

He and Kade had left for Crooked Tree early that morning, leaving her with an ache that grew with each passing hour. Dinner had been tense, neither of them contributing much to the conversation. Even though they'd said nothing, she felt certain Cam, Kade, and Lainey picked up on the strained vibes between Matt and her. Afterwards, he'd driven to her place, escorting her upstairs. Staring at each other, neither seemed willing to be the first one to speak.

"I'll call you, Cassie. There's still more to say."

"You made it clear what happened earlier tonight was a mistake. If you don't think we have a chance, just tell me. Don't leave town with me wondering."

Stepping forward, he placed a hand against the door, forcing her back. "I don't think either of us believes it's the end." He lifted her chin with his finger. "At least I don't." He studied her face, knowing he'd hurt her. "I was a jerk earlier and I'm sorry. I was angry with myself, not you. Being near you and not having you is harder than I expected. The last thing we need is to jump into a physical relationship before we work through the past. We need time to figure this out, make certain we're ready to try again. Can we at least agree to that?"

Could she do this? Give it her best only to have him walk away again? "All right. What do you suggest?"

"I'll be in Montana with Kade for a few days. I need to schedule the trip to the northwest with you and Skye. We'll carve out some time together while we're away. In the meantime, I'll call you...probably more than you want."

The last caused her mouth to curve into a smile. "I doubt that." She could talk to him all day, every day, and never get tired of it. "The rest sounds good. Really good."

Nodding, he lowered his head, brushing his lips against hers, then stepped back. "I'd better leave before we give the neighbors a show. I'll talk to you tomorrow."

Stepping inside, she listened to the sound of his footfalls on the stairs, then peeked out the window, waiting until he drove away before heading for bed. The pain in her chest had eased with his words. Talking didn't guarantee they had a future, but it was a start.

Pulling herself from thoughts of the night before, she placed a hand on her heart—the heart Matt already owned.

******

Crooked Tree, Montana

Kade kept the phone between his ear and shoulder, listening to his wife's travel plans. Brooke moved from division to division, dealing with team productivity and transitioning new businesses into the corporation. Glancing up as the door opened, he turned away, looking for another moment of privacy.

"Oh, looks like he's still on his call." Skye motioned Gage and Ivan Santiago forward, waving to chairs around the small table a moment before Matt joined them. "Sounds like he's finishing up. May I get you anything to drink?"

"Water would be great," Gage replied, Ivan nodding in agreement.

"I'll be back in Fire Mountain about the time you leave. Let's plan a couple days away when you return... Sounds good... Love you, too." Hanging up, he turned toward the visitors. "Sorry to keep—" He

179

halted, taking a good look at the man sitting next to Gage. "Ivan?"

"Kade Taylor. I had no idea you worked for the MacLarens." Standing, Ivan walked toward him, pulling Kade into an embrace, then stepped back. "It's been a long time. You're looking well."

"As are you," Kade answered.

"My understanding is all divisions are led by someone from the MacLaren family."

"It seems we have some catching up to do. Mother obviously has said nothing to the family, but my father *is* a MacLaren."

Ivan's brows lifted as his eyes grew wide. "You are right. Aunt Reyna has said nothing. Yes, you and I have much to talk about."

Kade's gaze shot to Matt, Skye, and Gage, all signaling their confusion. "Ivan is my cousin. It's been a long time since we've seen each other." Turning back to Ivan, he motioned for him to take a seat. "We'll talk over dinner tonight."

"Excellent. Now, it seems we have business to discuss."

******

Matt, Skye, and Gage sat in the bar, nursing their after dinner cocktails as Kade and Ivan continued to talk in the restaurant. Skye had heard a little of Kade's background from her father, but hearing him discuss it openly with Ivan gave her a different perspective.

"So Kade's mother never told her family about Rafe being his father?" Matt asked, shaking his head.

"Appears not. Kade Santiago Taylor MacLaren...now that's a mouthful." Gage tipped his glass up, sipping his drink, wondering what other surprises would surface. The MacLaren family continued to intrigue him. His hooded gaze shifted to the woman beside him. Each time he met Skye, he left more impressed.

"Yes, it is. Dad has been open with us about his love for Reyna Santiago and his ignorance of fathering Kade. Hearing it from Kade has given me a new understanding of what he went through growing up."

"Cassie and I split up before Rafe mended the riff with Jace and Heath. This is the first I've heard the story." Matt leaned back in his stool, crossing his arms. "They sure don't seem to have any issues now."

Skye chuckled. "They've become tight, although the relationships were strained for several months. Of course, Kade's announcement about his parentage impacted everyone."

"I'd imagine it was hard for you." Gage watched her expression. She seemed to have nothing but affection for her older stepbrother, a man no one knew existed until a couple years before.

"Mitch took it the hardest. Giving up his spot as top dog didn't sit well with him. They've had a few missteps, but I think he and Kade have reached an understanding. And now we learn Ivan and Kade are cousins."

"A wicked we," Matt joked. "It'll be interesting to see how this affects the association with Double Ace."

"It can't hurt and could be a big help going forward. We all have the same goals, and now there's family involved...unless the uncles have an issue with it," Gage said.

"The uncles?" Skye frowned, leaning closer to Gage.

"It's complicated. There are several investors in Double Ace, but the three Santiago brothers own the majority of stock. Ivan's father, Javier, is more of a silent majority owner. He lets his two brothers make the decisions regarding rodeo stock and cattle exports to the United States. Ivan may own a small amount of stock, but it's his father and uncles who have the power. He works for them."

"Could the uncles cause problems?" Matt asked, already aware of the complicated ownership.

Gage shrugged. "Who knows? So far, they've been supportive and have embraced the partnership. They're also increasing their shipments of beef into the U.S. That segment seems to be monopolizing most of their time."

"Do all the shipments still come through the Houston stockyard?" Matt swirled the remaining ice in his glass, deciding against a refill.

"They do. I hired a second crew because of the increase in beef cattle shipments."

"Sounds like a good problem," Skye commented, doing her best not to stare at Gage's profile. Strong and angular with a straight nose and full lips, she hadn't taken the time to appreciate his good looks until now. His thick brown hair, streaked with strands of gold, always seemed to be in need of a trim, resting below his collar and falling into his eyes. And what gorgeous eyes. A piercing deep green with flecks of golden-brown, they seemed to be ever watchful, missing little. Tall and muscular, he projected an air of confidence and power without trying. She bet he'd left a string of broken hearts across America during his rodeo days.

"We'll see. The increased shipments just started. That's why Ivan flew to Houston, so he could observe and report back to his uncles."

"Why would a few additional truckloads of cattle cause so much interest?" Matt's gaze narrowed.

"Good question." Gage didn't elaborate. He had his own questions and was determined to get answers.

"Here they come." Skye set her empty glass down, watching Kade and Ivan approach.

"Everyone ready to head out?" Kade asked, glancing at his watch. "Hope we didn't keep you waiting too long."

"Not at all. It gave us a chance to swap stories and learn more about the two companies." Skye picked up her purse, wishing she'd had more time to learn about the intriguing man next to her. Gage Templeton had many layers, and she found herself fantasizing about peeling back each one.

******

"Hey, it's me." Matt stretched out on the motel bed, an arm behind his head.

"Hey." Cassie's sleepy voice assailed him, making him wish they were in the same room, in the same bed.

"Did I wake you?"

"Not really. I've been reading...about ready to turn off the light." She didn't say she'd stayed awake as long as possible, hoping he'd call. She felt like she did when they'd first started going out—excited, giddy, and scared. "How did the meeting go?"

He tried to think of an appropriate word. "Enlightening."

"That sounds intriguing. What did you get enlightened about?"

"Kade Santiago Taylor MacLaren."

184

She chuckled. Kade never used his full name, and had only started using MacLaren instead of Taylor in the last few months, obstinately sticking to the last name his mother had made up so other children wouldn't tease him about his lack of a father.

"He explained it all to you?"

Matt took a few minutes to explain about Ivan and the relationship between him and Kade.

"It took us all by surprise." Matt shifted on the bed, sitting up to rest against the headboard.

"That's quite a coincidence. You know, none of us have ever met his mother. I believe her name is Reyna. Kade told Brooke she lived in Mexico and never married. A few of us girls wondered if Rafe would get in touch with her after his divorce."

"A few of you girls, huh?" He chuckled, picturing the MacLaren women sitting around, speculating about Rafe and his love life.

"You know how it is when a few of us get together, sharing wine. The topics are endless." She laughed, then grew quiet when Matt didn't respond. "Are you still there?"

"Yeah, I'm here."

She could hear him breathing, and if she didn't know he was a couple states away, she could almost believe he sat next to her.

"Did you ever talk about us?" He breathed out the question, his voice low, seductive.

The question hung between them while Cassie thought back to the evenings she'd spent with Brooke, Amber, Dana, and Lainey, talking of lost loves and future opportunities.

"A little," she whispered.

"Were we a taboo subject?"

"No, not really. It's just that talking about you was difficult for me. To be truthful, I tried to forget you ever existed."

"I can understand that, Cass. I didn't talk about us much, either."

The silence grew once more, neither knowing where to go from there. It would be easier if they were in the same room, able to see each other's reaction and not rely on voices alone. For now, this was all they had.

Cassie cleared her throat. "Did you get a schedule arranged for the northwest trip?"

Matt was glad for the change of subject. "I hope to finalize it tomorrow. Our first stop will be Othello, then Ellensburg. I'll send you the schedule as soon as Kade approves it. I'm looking forward to seeing you."

She hadn't been far from his thoughts since he left Cold Creek. He knew what he wanted, but the odds of making it work after such a tough breakup were slim. The only couple he knew who'd made it work were Eric and Amber. Matt sensed Cassie would be willing to give it a second chance. Knowing her, she'd give it her all, doing whatever she could to make it work. *He* would be the one who'd have a more difficult time with it. As much as he still loved her, he had no intention of putting up with her selfish, inconsiderate actions a second time.

It would be a learning experience for them both, especially if she thought she'd be getting back the same Matt who walked out of her life and didn't look back. He'd also changed. He'd always been strong and knew what he wanted. The problem was the degree he would allow himself to change in order to please Cassie. He'd allowed her desires to take control, suppressing his own for the sake of harmony. That had ended when he left.

"Same here. I miss you, Matt." She tightened her grip on the phone, hoping she hadn't exposed too much.

"You know, this isn't going to be easy. We've both changed, hopefully matured. We may not make it."

If he gave them another chance, she had no intention of screwing it up a second time, but she also knew the odds weren't in their favor. "Eric and Amber made it."

"Yes, they did, and it was a long shot." His voice was controlled, matter-of-fact, as if they were talking about meeting for a burger.

Her stomach twisted as she began to comprehend what he may be saying. "Have you changed your mind about trying again?"

"No. I just don't want to hurt you."

"That goes both ways, Matt. Why don't we meet in Othello and see what happens?"

"Works for me. I'd better let you get some sleep. Goodnight, Cassie."

"Goodnight, Matt." She set the phone next to the bed, placing her open palm on her stomach to loosen the knot. This would not be some fantasy of two lovers coming back together after being forced apart. Matt was right. It would be hard and it may not work, but it was the one shot she had. Nothing in the world could keep her from trying.

Chapter Fifteen

"Hi, Annie. It's Cassie. Do you have a few minutes to talk?"

"Of course. What's going on?" Annie could hear the concern in her stepdaughter's voice.

"Do you remember the fires I mentioned to you the last time we spoke?"

"Of course. Did they catch the person responsible?"

"No, it's gotten worse." Cassie explained about the deaths of the two young men and how the area had nothing similar to the MacLaren Foundation to support those leaving the foster care program. "I checked on both of them. They'd lost their funding and left the system a few months before. They were living in an abandoned warehouse, eating scraps, and still attending high school." Her voice broke. "Oh, Annie, it makes me sick thinking about it."

"Let me talk to Heath and see if there's a way to get something started in Cold Creek. I don't know anything about the legalities or possible funding, but you know we'll do what we can. Are you able to work on it from your end?"

"I'll do whatever I can. With Cam gone, I'm not sure who to talk to about working with the locals."

"I suppose it would be Kade, or possibly Matt. Let me talk to Heath and get back to you. It may be a few days, though." Annie hesitated a moment, then ventured on. "Are you comfortable working with Matt on something like this?"

Although Annie couldn't see it, Cassie smiled at the comment. "Yes. We could work together fine. In fact, well...I think we may be trying to work through the past. It's way too soon to know if it will work between us, but it's a start."

"Oh, Cassie, that's wonderful."

Cassie paused a moment, debating whether to bring up what continued to trouble her. Annie had always been the voice of calm, giving good advice, withholding her opinions unless asked.

"Annie, do you know why Dad did this to me?" The question almost choked her, the sense of betrayal still so raw.

"I don't know what you're talking about. Tell me what's bothering you."

"He knew how much it would hurt me to hire Matt, make him my boss. The only reason I can come up with is he'd like me to quit, find a job somewhere else." Her voice cracked on the last, her grip on the phone almost painful.

"Oh, honey. I'm certain that wasn't his intention." Annie shifted the phone to her other hand, understanding Cassie's confusion. "He thinks you're doing a great job. I can't speak as to the reasons for hiring Matt or making him your boss, but I'm certain they're sound. At least from his viewpoint. You aren't thinking of quitting, are you?"

Her shoulders slumping, Cassie let out a sigh. "Yes, I am."

"Please don't do anything before talking to Heath. If you aren't ready to do that, at least give it time. He and your uncles never make a move without considering all the ramifications. More importantly, if he wanted you to quit, he'd tell you to your face. He isn't one to dance around an issue, not even for family. You know that, don't you?"

She swallowed the lump lodged in her throat. "I suppose so." Her voice trembled with confusion. "Thanks, Annie. I'll think about what you've said."

"You know I'm here for you, no matter what you decide."

Hanging up, Cassie let Annie's words sink in. This didn't call for a quick reaction, but a slow consideration of all the options. She had nothing to lose by taking it slow.

She picked up the schedule Matt had emailed her, trying to refocus. They'd start in Othello, then travel to Ellensburg. Afterwards, they'd drive to Yakima before their last stop in Puyallup.

Making her way into the kitchen, she rummaged in the refrigerator, hoping for leftovers or salad fixings. Settling for what looked like some kind of vegetable casserole Janie had made the weekend before, she heated up a bowl, then curled up in a corner of the sofa. She'd finished the last bite when Annie called back.

"Heath is all for checking out the local resources and putting together a proposal for the board. He suggested working with Matt, but also felt you could work with me if he's too busy."

"That's wonderful news. I'll make some calls and get it rolling." Cassie just wished she'd thought of this before the tragedy of the fire. At least something good might come from it, and working on a local program would give her the time needed to make a sound decision about her job. "How about I give you a progress report at the end of the week?"

"I'll send you some of the material I use when we move into other towns. Use what you feel is worthwhile, adding any suggestions," Annie said. "I'm available anytime, Cassie, for whatever is going on."

Her excitement building, she checked the time. Eight o'clock. Calling local agencies would have to wait until tomorrow. Not one to wait around, she picked up her laptop, creating a folder for MacLaren Foundation, Cold Creek. Checking her email, Cassie downloaded several files from Annie, using one to guide her through the initial process of determining the local need. Reining in her enthusiasm would be hard, but charging in, assuming a program hadn't already been established, could do a great deal of harm. Maybe Cold Creek already had a program and the two young men had fallen through the cracks.

She changed directions, listing two columns. One for any existing programs and one for a new one.

An hour later, she had a good framework for moving forward, not once thinking about Matt or her doubts about work. Now, however, she needed to speak with him. Other than the emailed schedule, she hadn't heard from him all day, which didn't bother her, except she was anxious to tell him about her project and get his ideas. While in college, they'd gone to several foundation fundraisers, and he'd volunteered with her on more than one occasion, even enlisting the help of some of his college rodeo team members when the foundation had bussed a group of kids to the campus for a tour.

When he still hadn't called by ten o'clock, she decided to send him a text. Sending her message, she waited, snatching up her phone when the familiar beep sounded. Reading it, her shoulders slumped with disappointment.

Not tonight. We'll have to talk tomorrow.

Cassie slid her phone back into her purse without responding. She'd get her work done tomorrow, then make a series of calls before lunch. By the time she and Matt spoke again, there'd be considerably more to discuss than what she had on her checklist.

Falling into bed, she found herself wondering what kept Matt from giving her a few minutes of his time tonight. Drifting off to sleep, she told herself it wasn't her business. They weren't a couple, so his time was still his own. The thought didn't give her any comfort.

******

Crooked Tree, Montana

"One more, Matt." The girl who'd plunked herself on his lap leaned against him, pressing her ample curves into his body. Groaning, he wondered how he'd gotten into this situation.

"Sorry, darlin'. I'm done for the night." Extricating himself from the unwanted female took a little maneuvering. "I'm out of here, Sean. Thanks for dinner and drinks."

"You sure you can't hang around a little longer? It's my last night in town before leaving for the dude ranch."

Giving him a sympathetic smile, Matt clasped his shoulder. "You'll have to persevere without me. I'm certain you can deal with it." He looked at the four women sitting around Sean, any one of them willing to help him forget his troubles for the night. "Do you need any help in the morning?"

"I have it covered. Come visit when you have a chance," Sean pleaded, still not certain why he'd been picked to run a ranch targeted at city dwellers who wanted an escape. No matter how much he begged, his father hadn't budged from the decision. He felt doomed.

"Good luck, Sean. Be sure to send postcards," Matt laughed, saluting as he headed for the exit.

"Hey, cowboy. Hold up." A slender arm wrapped around his waist, the owner turning him around, flashing him a brilliant smile. "You *are* a cowboy, right?"

Shaking his head, trying to loosen her grip, he gave her his best cowboy smile. "Yes, ma'am. I've been known to sit a horse." He'd had his share of rodeo bunnies, knowing how to make them smile without getting attached to any. Matt just didn't expect to find them in Crooked Tree.

"Did you hear that, girls? He can sit a horse." She turned back to him. "Can you sit anything else, cowboy?"

Okay, so she might be drunker than he'd first thought. "Not tonight, darlin'." He touched the brim of his hat, making his escape as a new group of women entered. Walking into the parking lot, he took a deep breath, clearing his head. He thought of Cassie's text, feeling a small amount of guilt at not taking the time to call her, but tonight was about Sean and what he wanted to do before leaving. Skye had left with Gage an hour before, offering to drop him off at his hotel. Gage did have a way of attracting the beautiful women, and Skye sure did qualify, even if she'd shown no interest in him. Even if she did,

Gage would blow her off, like he did all his admirers. After a few nights, the woman would be history. His friend's long-term plan didn't include anything beyond a few dates that ended in someone's bed, preferably the woman's. Yep, Skye would do well to stay far away from Gage.

Climbing into his truck, he debated whether to call Cassie. Discarding the idea as being too late, he drove to his hotel. Slipping out of his shirt and pants, he picked up the remote, surfing through the channels until the image of a burning building, the words "Cold Creek" below it, stopped him. Turning up the sound, he caught the last of the news report.

"The names of the two victims have still not been released, but we do know both exited the state's foster care system a few months ago. Their deaths, besides outraging the citizens of this normally peaceful mountain town, have sparked the formation of a joint task force."

Mumbling a curse, Matt turned off the television and tossed the remote aside. She would've heard the report, and he knew her well enough to know how much it would affect her. Maybe that's why she wanted to talk with him. Ignoring the time, he grabbed his phone.

"Cassie, it's Matt."

"Hey," she mumbled, trying to sit up. "What time is it?" She rubbed her eyes, looking toward the clock.

"Almost midnight. Should I call back tomorrow?"

"No. Now's fine."

"I just saw the news about those two foster kids dying in the fire and thought I'd better see how you're doing. I know how much those kids mean to you and your family."

Her stomach plummeted at the reminder. "It's such a tragedy. Neither had even graduated from high school, nor had a place to live, other than the abandoned warehouse." She sighed, feeling the familiar tightness in her chest when she thought of kids getting tossed out of the system with so little preparation. "It's too much to go into tonight, but that's why I called you. Can we schedule a time to talk tomorrow?"

"Sure, sweetheart. I'd better let you get back to sleep. Goodnight, Cass."

"Goodnight, Matt." Hanging up, Cassie couldn't help but smile. He'd called her *sweetheart*. He hadn't called her that since college and it felt great. Slipping under the covers, she closed her eyes, drifting asleep within seconds.

******

Cold Creek, Colorado

"That's all we have. A series of what appear to be arson fires set for fun, not to harm. At least until the last one killed those two kids. We need to find out who's setting these and get him or her off the street." The fire chief stepped aside, letting the police chief take the podium.

"What do you think, Jerrod?" Kurt sat next to his friend, scratching notes as his boss and police chief spoke.

"All I know is they were set by the same person, using similar materials. My first thought was teenagers, but now I'm not so sure. I will say I'm getting worried. Not a single witness has stepped forward with a description, and the last two fires were in the middle of commercial properties. It's as if the arsonist wants the attention. The perp may not have intended to kill anyone, but the game has now changed with the national press, television coverage, and the creation of this task force."

"I'd like to ask our arson investigator, Jerrod James, to step up and give us the latest on his findings," the fire chief announced, looking at Jerrod.

"Looks like you're up." Kurt stood to let him pass, then moved to the side, leaning his shoulder against the wall. He felt the same as Jerrod. Each fire gave the arsonist more confidence, encouraging him to be bolder, seeking buildings in less rural areas. The time between incidences had also shortened. Before, they were set at least a week apart. Now the calls came in every four or five days. The heightened activity also put increasing pressure on the town's available water supply. If this kept up, they'd be in serious trouble.

"All right, ladies and gentleman. You heard investigator James and know the background, as well as the challenge before us," the police chief said. "No one in this room gets any unscheduled time off until we apprehend the person responsible."

The police chief moved toward the mayor, talking in whispers as everyone filed out. Few noticed the lone person standing in the back corner wearing a Cold Creek police uniform, hat tugged firmly in place. Other than a couple polite nods, everyone filed past, lost in their own thoughts about their orders. Waiting until the room emptied, the figure took another look around, then walked out, down the steps, and into a nearby patrol car. Who'd have thought learning what they planned would be so easy?

******

"Hi, Matt. Is this a good time?" Cassie asked, pressing the speaker button on her phone.

"Perfect. Let me close the door so no one barges in. Tell me what's going on."

Cassie explained how she'd spoken with Annie and gotten Heath's approval to check out the local services.

"I've learned a great deal about the foster care program in Cold Creek. They have nothing similar to the MacLaren Foundation, welcoming any help or suggestions to supplement state programs. I could be a huge help to them, Matt."

He understood her excitement and already knew where this would lead. He'd seen it, experienced it. Once she set her mind on a path, little could compete for her attention, including him.

"I'm assuming you need my help." His voice sounded grim, which wasn't what Cassie expected.

"Not if you don't have time. Of course, I won't drop the ball on any of my normal work. I'd do this on weekends and after hours. But I thought you'd want to know since you're my boss and..."

"And what, Cassie? What else am I?"

"I guess I'm not certain. We haven't had time to figure it out yet."

He took a breath, not wanting to curb her enthusiasm, yet sensing they might already be headed off course. "Look, Cass. I'm glad you're doing this and I'll support you any way I can. Extra time off, whatever funding Kade can carve out. You just need to ask."

"Thanks, Matt. I appreciate it." She waited for him to respond. When he didn't, she decided to press on. "This doesn't change anything. I'm still planning to go with you and Skye." Again, she got no response. "We *are* going to spend time together, right?"

"That's the plan. We have a lot to talk through."

Relief coursed through her. For a moment, she thought he'd changed his mind. "Okay then. I'll see you in Othello on Monday."

"I'm also sending you a ticket to Seattle for the following Friday. You'll be taking a different flight than me so Skye doesn't ask questions."

"About what?"

"The fact we're spending a weekend together in Seattle. I don't want her jumping to conclusions or mentioning our private business to anyone until we've had a chance to figure out what's going on with us."

She wanted to scream. Instead, she clamped a hand over her mouth, tempering her excitement. "Sounds wonderful. I'll be all yours for the weekend."

"I'd like that, Cass."

******

Tossing blouses and slacks on the bed, she searched for the perfect outfit to catch Matt's attention. She had no idea where their relationship might go, but she intended to make the most of this opportunity to win him back.

"You know, it's after midnight." Janie walked into Cassie's room, her gaze focused on the pile of clothes on the bed. "What are you doing?"

"Matt sent me tickets to meet him in Seattle after the rodeo meetings in Washington. I want to look great and make him notice me."

"Cass, I may be wrong, but the man already notices you. *A lot.*" Picking up a deep teal silk blouse cut low in the front, she held it out. "This one looks fabulous on you. Whenever you wear it, the men can't take their eyes off you."

"Really?" She took the hanger, holding the blouse in front of her and glancing in the mirror.

"Are you kidding? This, plus those tight white pants are outrageous on you. Add those strappy heels—girlfriend, Matt will never let you out of his sight."

"The weather's predicted to be cold."

"Fine," Janie grinned. "Take your tight black silk pants and boots with the three-inch heels. He still won't be able to resist you." She pulled out a couple other items, hanging them on the doorknob. "Okay, here's what we have." Janie pointed to each outfit, explaining why Cassie needed to take them. "I don't care what you wear for the business meetings, but these are *de rigueur* for your time alone with Matt."

Cassie tilted back her head and laughed. "*Di rigueur*, huh? Where did you learn that?"

"My dear mother used to say it when they traveled to Paris, or London, or maybe it was Rome? Hell, I don't remember, but she loved the phrase."

"Someday, I'm going to get you drunk and you're going to spill all those deep, dark secrets about your way too wealthy family."

"To warn you, you'd have to get me pretty drunk to talk about my family. But hey, if you think you can do it, I'm game. Well, I'm off to bed. Will you be in the office tomorrow?" Janie stifled a yawn, her eyes going glassy.

"It's Friday, and Kade set up a conference call with his group. I don't fly out to meet Matt and Skye in Othello until Saturday. How about you? What are your plans this weekend?"

"If Kurt doesn't get called out, we plan to drive to Aspen and spend the weekend. Keep your fingers crossed that the arsonist gets caught before then. Whoever's doing this is pure evil."

"I agree, the person is a real monster." She glanced up at Janie. "Send me photos from Aspen."

"You do the same. A selfie of you and Matt on your romantic getaway would be great," she suggested, wiggling her brows and closing the door behind her.

A selfie of Matt and I kissing would be even better, Cassie thought, closing her suitcase and setting it beside the door.

Chapter Sixteen

León, Mexico

Ivan sat in stoic silence, watching his father's face shift from surprise to exasperation at the news. He'd thought his father might have known about Aunt Reyna's past. As the oldest brother, he and his sister had always been close, much closer than with either of his younger brothers or their sister. Guilt surrounded Ivan when he realized he'd been the one to reveal a secret she'd hidden for over thirty years.

"You are certain of this? Reyna's son, Kade, is a MacLaren?"

"Yes, Father. Quite certain."

"Have you asked your Aunt Reyna about this?" Javier opened a drawer, pulling out what appeared to be a diary, or perhaps a ledger. Either way, Ivan had never seen the leather-bound journal until now.

"I have said nothing to her. She never told you?"

Flipping open the journal, Javier let his finger move down one page, then another before stopping.

"She said the father was Thomas Taylor, a rodeo cowboy passing through Montana. By the time she knew of her...situation..." He looked up from the ledger, "...the man had left the state. Reyna had no way to reach him. She told me when he did not return for the rodeo the next year, she asked about him and was told he'd died in an accident." Javier slammed the journal closed. "Apparently, all lies."

Ivan could read between the lines. They were a conservative, Catholic family. A pregnancy out of wedlock thirty years ago would not have been welcome news. Reyna had been sent to the United States to live with a distant relative while she finished high school and started college. Giving her family one excuse after another to postpone a return to León, the family hadn't discovered the addition to the Santiago family until well after Kade's birth.

Shoving back his chair, Javier paced around the desk toward the door. "I will learn the truth."

"Father, wait. What is the purpose of this now? Aunt Reyna is happy here. Kade is doing well and is part of a successful family. What is to be gained by confronting her?"

"The truth, my son. A family cannot exist on a bed of lies."

Ivan let the last settle in his mind, knowing he had one other matter of importance to discuss. For now, it could wait.

"Ah, my handsome nephew has returned." Aunt Reyna entered the study, a broad smile on her face as she opened her arms to Ivan. "You have come back sooner than expected."

Stepping away, Ivan studied her face, his own tense, knowing the conversation awaiting them. "You look well, Aunt Reyna."

Her gaze wandered over him, assessing. "You, my nephew, appear tired. Are my brothers pushing you too hard?" She glanced at Javier, her brow raising.

"They do keep me busy."

"Ivan came home to tell us of some news, Reyna. Please, sit down so he may tell you what he has learned."

Looking between the two, Reyna shrugged, her curiosity peaked. "So tell me, Ivan. What is this news you have for me?"

Ivan loved his aunt, having no desire to cause her pain. He sat near her, leaning forward, attempting to close the distance between them, his voice softening. "My meetings took me to Crooked Tree, Montana. Did you not live there for a time?"

Tilting her head, she willed herself to relax at the mention of Kade's birthplace, the town where she'd met and fallen in love with his father. "Yes. I am certain you remember your cousin, Kade, and I lived there for many years."

"I remember." Hesitating, Ivan shot a look at his father, accepting the nod as reassurance to continue. "We have a new partnership. One which we believe will produce many years of profits."

"That is good, Ivan. What does this have to do with me?"

"The company is MacLaren Rodeo. The man in charge is Kade MacLaren."

Reyna's heart jumped into her throat at the mention of her son, even as her face showed no hint of the turbulence building inside. They knew. She could see it in their eyes. The secret she'd kept locked away for so many years had found its way out, as she knew it eventually would.

Instead of feeling fear or condemnation, as she had when her father had learned of Kade, a sense of relief claimed her, giving her life a renewed strength.

"So you saw your cousin after all these years. How is he?" Her question, simple and direct, caught both Ivan and Javier by surprise.

"Is that all you have to say, Reyna? Ivan learns Kade's father is a MacLaren, not Thomas Taylor as you insisted, and you sit before us as if the news does not affect you?"

"Why should it? I've always known the true identity of my son's father."

Ivan pursed his lips so as not to laugh at his aunt's audacity. She'd never been a woman to trifle with, and she continued to prove it

"Why the charade, Reyna? I do not understand the deception you felt necessary?" Javier stood, walking around his desk, resting a hip against the edge. "Was there ever a Thomas Taylor?"

Tucking her shawl around her, she raised her chin. "I am certain there is a Thomas Taylor somewhere. He is just not my son's father."

Looking toward the ceiling, Javier pinched the bridge of his nose, letting out a groan. "I do not understand why you did not tell Father the truth?"

She sighed. The one brother who'd always supported her, even when their father had shunned his unmarried, pregnant daughter, Javier had been there for her. When their father cut off her funds, Javier had set aside part of his own, sending it to her every month until Kade graduated from high school. When even their mother refused to acknowledge them, Javier had. He'd visited several times, bringing presents for his nephew, accepting him.

"Even then, the MacLarens were well-known and quite wealthy. Rafael, Kade's father, had left the family, moving to Montana to find his own way. He worked hard and did well. Rafe did not need to be forced into marrying a woman he didn't love, accepting a child he didn't want." Her unwavering gaze held his. "Our father would have used his family's status against us. I could not let that happen."

"Aunt Reyna, are you so certain Rafe did not love you? That is not the picture Kade gave me of his father." Ivan moved toward her, resting a hand on her shoulder.

Shaking her head, she glanced down at her hands clenched tight in her lap. "I do not wish to speak of him. He is in my past. It is as it should be."

"There is one other piece of news you need to hear." Ivan had not even told his father of his agreement. He could no longer hold it back. "I made a promise to Kade to escort you to Fire Mountain for a visit."

"But—"

"He insisted and I gave my word. You will meet his wife. Would you not like to meet your daughter-in-law?" Ivan's eyes crinkled at the corners, although he held his smile in check. "If you do not agree to go willingly, I will bundle you into our private plane."

"I will also go. I want to meet this Rafael MacLaren, see the man who took so many years from my sister's life." Javier crossed his arms, the decision made.

Standing abruptly, Reyna's face signaled the horror she felt at Javier coming face-to-face with Kade's father. "It is not necessary for you to go. I will travel with Ivan."

"Oh, but it *is* necessary. Pack what you need. We will leave once Ivan concludes his business in León."

******

Cold Creek, Colorado

"At least your weekend in Aspen went well." Cassie sat on the edge of the bed, cradling the phone between her ear and shoulder, catching up with

Janie. Tomorrow morning, she'd have breakfast with Skye and Matt, then they'd part ways. She and Matt would fly to Seattle, while Skye flew home to Crooked Tree.

"We had a wonderful time. We weren't back five minutes before Kurt's boss called, telling him about the change. I haven't seen him since."

"Isn't it the promotion he wanted? He's now Jerrod's assistant arson investigator, right?"

"For now. It may not stick once they find the person responsible for the fires. The fire chief told him it might become permanent, but made no promises. What they need is another person to help Jerrod, and Kurt's the only one with the training. He's excited about the opportunity to put his training to use. You know, there was another fire while we were in Aspen."

"They didn't call Kurt to drive back?"

"Nope. I guess the chief figured they'd have it taken care of before we could drive back to Cold Creek. We heard about it on the news. Thank goodness no one was hurt this time. I hope they find the person responsible and put him away for a very long time," Janie ground out, knowing most people in town felt the same.

"You sound certain it's a guy." Cassie knew the statistics on arsonists. Most were male teens or men. Although women were known to set fires, they weren't the typical arsonist.

"I don't have a clue. According to Kurt, Jerrod believes it's a man, probably in his twenties, and local. Someone who loves to watch the flames, maybe someone with emotional problems. Although I'd think that would be a given," Janie snorted. "Kurt is anxious to solve the puzzle and find the person responsible."

"At least he won't be in the middle of fighting the fires for a while. The one near our apartment opened my eyes to how brutal and dangerous it can be."

"Kurt doesn't talk about it, but I don't believe he even considers the danger. He has several scars from his job, the most visible on his neck. They don't deter him, though. It's his job and he'll do it, no matter what." His dedication was one of the characteristics she loved most about him, even if it put him in danger. "Enough on Kurt and the fires. Tell me about you and Matt."

"Nothing to tell. We've been working all week, doing the best we can to keep our personal plans separate. You are the only person who knows we're going to Seattle, and Matt isn't happy about it. I assured him you wouldn't say anything to anybody. You haven't, have you, Janie?"

"Well...maybe to one person."

"What?" Cassie held the phone closer to her ear. "Who?"

"Kurt. I may have mentioned Matt had a romantic weekend planned in Seattle."

Cassie groaned, falling back on the bed.

"I'm sorry, Cass, but he won't tell anyone. He's happy for you and Matt."

"I guess there's nothing we can do about it now. Please make sure he doesn't let it slip to anyone."

"Are you afraid it won't work out?" Janie's voice grew soft with concern.

"Of course I'm afraid. He still expects me to be the same self-absorbed college girl from his past. I don't know if I'm up for going through this again. What if it *doesn't* work out?"

"You're up for it. If it doesn't work out, at least you tried, and that's the best anyone can do. Besides, you're *not* the same person. Once you graduated, moved back to Fire Mountain, and started working with the foster kids, your priorities shifted."

"I never took much interest until Annie and Amber took me to one of the foster kid events. It had always seemed like any other cause that needed my family's support. Meeting the kids in person made it real for me. That's when I understood how I'd taken my family for granted, expected so much when these kids had so little..." Her voice trailed off, remembering the kids and how grateful they were for any amount of help.

"The fact you're trying to set up a similar program in Cold Creek is proof of how committed you are to the foster kids. Go to Seattle, have a great time, and don't worry about the 'what ifs'.

Remember, Matt is probably as scared as you. He doesn't want to fail again, either."

"Thanks, Janie."

"For what? I'm telling you how I see it. You're a great gal. Matt would be lucky to win you back, and you'd better believe he knows it."

******

Houston, Texas

"I went over each truck twice and didn't find anything unusual, Gage. Maybe you're looking for trouble where there isn't any." Thad Montgomery sat in Gage's living room, a cold beer in his hand. "If the truck will be here a few more days, I can get in touch with my friend who owns the retired field dog used by the DEA. Maybe we'll catch something."

Thad had left the DEA to establish his own corporate investigation company with a couple former agents. They'd done well, growing rapidly, foiling more than one drug smuggling operation the DEA had been unable to crack. Sometimes you had to work outside the system to make a bust happen.

Gage scrubbed a hand down his face. "It's not necessary. Maybe you're right and I'm spooked for no reason."

"Could be, but your gut instincts have always served you well. Just because I didn't find any evidence doesn't mean something isn't going on. I've seen every type of contraband hidden in places you'd never believe possible. Drugs, cash, people…you name it and it's been smuggled." Thad drained the last of his beer, crushing the can. "If what you suspect is true, they'll show their hand. No one can keep an operation like that quiet forever."

"The odd part is I believe Ivan has suspicions of his own. I did every kind of check possible on the company before I started. Each report showed a sterling business record for the Santiago family."

"What about the partners?" From his conversations with Gage, Thad knew a little of the structure.

"From what I know, they have nothing to do with the operational decisions. Believe me, nothing happens at Double Ace without the Santiago uncles knowing about it. If they've moved into another business, I'd be surprised if the other partners know anything about it."

"They'll get their cut, smile, and not ask questions." Thad's chuckle held a cynical edge. He'd seen it before. Silent partners raking in tens of thousands of dollars, acting shocked when they learned the money came from illegal activities, then becoming outraged when criminal charges were filed against them. Deniability didn't account for much when the whole operation tanked. "Let me know if you need anything else. The offer stands if you decide you want me to bring in the dog." Standing, he headed toward the door.

"Thanks, Thad. I trust what you've done and appreciate the time you've put into this." Closing the door behind his friend, Gage decided he needed to put his suspicions behind him. Three shipments and three inspections by Thad. Not one had shown signs of the illegal activities he expected. Time to concentrate on other matters, such as the woman he couldn't seem to get out of his head.

Skye MacLaren had called that morning, asking if he'd be available to meet with Cassie, Kade, and her the following week in Cold Creek. Until the new man started, Gage needed to be the front man for Double Ace. He had no problem with it, except it involved being around the one female who fascinated him more and more with each meeting. The last thing he wanted was to become interested in another woman. The one other time he'd let his guard down, he'd ended up with a broken marriage, an empty bank account, and debts he'd known nothing about. It had taken a few years, and he still had a few loose ends, but he'd emerged a better and stronger, if more cynical, man.

There'd be no issue if Skye were the type for a casual fling with no strings and no future. He didn't have to ask to know the answer. Nothing about her said one-night stand, and he had no interest in anything else. Being a MacLaren didn't help, either.

He needed to stay clear of her and any entanglements jeopardizing the work he'd put into making the partnership a success. Losing a potentially lucrative deal over a woman wouldn't happen. Not even for one as beautiful, witty, and intriguing as Skye MacLaren.

Chapter Seventeen

Seattle, Washington

Gripping her purse in one hand, her computer case in the other, Cassie walked through the incoming passenger terminal, her gaze fixed on the visitor waiting area. Searching the crowd, her chest constricted, as it had throughout her flight. She followed the signs to the baggage area, seeing no sign of Matt.

Picking up her one piece of luggage from the moving carousel, she stepped outside, taking a seat on a nearby bench. A cool, refreshing breeze fanned her face, the smell of saltwater ramping up her excitement and anxiety. Sliding out her phone, she checked for messages. Nothing.

She replayed their last conversation in her head, not remembering if he'd mentioned his arrival time. Five minutes later, Cassie stood at the rental car counter—the agency Matt had mentioned, almost as an afterthought, when they'd parted after breakfast that morning.

"Yes, Mrs. Garner. Your husband has a car reservation for eleven this morning." The woman looked over the top of her glasses at Cassie. "He didn't mention you as a driver. Should I add your information now?"

"No, that's not necessary. Matt usually drives." Cassie cringed at the lie she'd told to learn what she needed. Based on his reservation time, his flight wouldn't be landing for a while. "Thank you so much. I'll just wait for his plane to arrive."

Cassie could feel the woman's gaze burning into her back on the way to the waiting area. Lying had never come easy to her and she guessed the woman knew the truth. At least it got her what she wanted.

Most Saturdays, she went into the office for two or three hours, using the quiet time to catch up on correspondence. At least she could put the wait to good use. Glancing at her phone, she read the messages, sent off a few replies, then slid it back into her purse, her thoughts drifting to Matt. As expected, the butterflies she'd finally tamed roared to life. Excitement mingled with apprehension. This could be a new beginning or a final crash and burn. She wouldn't let herself think of the latter.

******

"You'll need to put that away now, sir." The flight attendant passed by his seat, nodding toward Matt's laptop. "We'll be landing in a few minutes."

Closing it, he tightened the seat belt, resting his head against the seat. He'd spent the last few days doing his best to dampen his anticipation of time alone with Cassie. It would be unwise to expect too much from this weekend. Old hurts were hard to overcome, an old love harder to rekindle.

Desire had never been an issue between them. Making love to her would always be a pleasure, never a hardship. Making it work over time, keeping the desire going, and not falling back into old patterns would take a lot of work. Their efforts could go south in an instant, leaving them wishing they'd left their relationship where it had been—in the past.

Grabbing his bag, Matt walked straight through the terminal, looking through the large window and spotting Cassie sitting on a bench. Making his way outside, he stopped in front of her, careful to keep his hands at his sides.

"Hi." Cassie breathed out, forcing herself to stay rooted in place. She wanted to wrap her arms around him and plant a kiss on his lips. It would have to wait.

"Hi, Cassie. I hope you had a good flight." Short and to the point. No emotion involved at all, which was what he wanted until he saw her smile fade.

She nodded, gripping the handle of her purse.

"I guess we should get the car." Reaching out, Matt grabbed her bag, pulling it along as she walked beside him. The confused look on her face made him wonder if she already thought spending a full weekend together had been a mistake. By the way he'd acted, he wouldn't blame her.

"Stop." Letting go of the bag, he slipped Cassie's bags from her shoulder, setting them on a nearby chair, her dismayed look almost comical. "I forgot something." Wrapping an arm around her waist, he tugged her close. "I've wanted to do this all week." Lowering his head, he kissed her, ignoring the promises he'd made to keep his distance. Groaning as she melted into him, he deepened the kiss, wishing they were alone instead of standing on a public walkway. Breaking the contact, he rested his forehead against hers. "Better?"

"Much,'" she whispered, taking a reluctant step back.

He chuckled, glad to see the light return to her smile.

"All right. Let's get that car."

******

"Just sign here, Mr. Garner. Would you like your wife to sign as an additional driver?" The same woman stood behind the counter, a knowing smirk on her face.

"My what?" Matt looked up from signing his name, his eyes wide.

Gripping his arm, Cassie stepped beside him, leaning in close. "I don't need to drive, sweetheart. When I stopped by earlier to check on the car, this nice woman offered to add me. You so seldom let me drive, I declined." She kissed his check, letting her lips linger a moment longer than necessary.

"Uh...good idea." He could feel the heat rise as his eyes narrowed, although they held a hint of humor. "I'll be the only driver, ma'am."

"Well, if you're certain, here is the key. The car is parked in the second row back. Thank you for renting with us, Mr. Garner."

Slipping an arm through his, Cassie leaned against his side as they walked away from the counter. "Thanks...honey."

"You told her we're married?"

"A small lie. You weren't here and I thought the best way to find out about your flight was to check for a rental. She didn't give me details, but at least I knew you were still joining me." The catch in her voice signaled her concern that he might not show up.

Finding their car, he set down the bags and unlocked the doors, turning her toward him. "Cass, I told you I'd be here."

"You did. The flight and arrival time would've been good information."

"Duly noted for the future." Placing a soft kiss on her lips, Matt tossed the bags inside, more than ready to get on with their weekend. "Hungry?"

"Starving."

"I know the perfect place. We're staying a few miles north. It's a beautiful hotel on Puget Sound with a great restaurant." As soon as the words were out, he winced, realizing he may have said too much.

"You've stayed there before?"

"Once."

"For a rodeo?" She couldn't recall any rodeo where a hotel north of the airport would be convenient. Most cowboys camped in their trailers or stayed in a cheap motel close to the grounds. Just one reason he'd travel to such a romantic spot came to mind. "Forget it. I don't want to know." She focused her attention on the scenery whizzing by, wishing he'd never told her about it.

Reaching across the seat, he pried one hand from where she gripped them in her lap. "You know, Cass, if this is going to work, we have to accept that each of us have had other people in our lives. I won't deny there have been other women, and I'm certain you've had other men."

She snorted. Her social life since Matt had been packed with family dinners, cocktails with girlfriends, ballgames with co-workers, and a couple weekends at the family cabin. She'd dated little, and none had resulted in a real relationship. No one had been able to clear her heart of Matt.

"Cassie?"

Swinging her head toward him, she kept her face neutral. Letting him know how little experience she'd had since him didn't appeal to her. "What?"

"You dated Kurt, and I'm sure there were others. I can live with that. Can you do the same with me?"

"Sure, Matt. Not a problem." Pulling her hand from his, she stared straight ahead, trying to get the visual of Matt with another woman out of her mind. Berating herself for being so ridiculous, she glanced at him, seeing the hard line of his jaw, the twitch of a vein in his neck. "The truth is I've dated, but not that much. School, then work and family took most of my time." Shrugging, she plastered on a smile, keeping her eyes bright and voice light. "Never met anyone worth the effort. I'm certain my experiences are quite the opposite of yours."

The confession surprised him. Gorgeous and talented with a great sense of humor, Matt figured she'd had quite the time after he left.

"You avoided relationships?" His voice held no inflection.

"Didn't you?" she asked.

He hesitated a moment, thinking of the last few years. "I suppose. Moving from town to town didn't allow for more than casual hookups, and besides, I didn't have the interest. I've had two relationships since you, lasting no more than a month or two, and both were in Houston. Neither felt right. I broke off the last one not long ago." He didn't explain, deciding she could figure out the timing and reason behind it herself.

She fell silent after his confession. He didn't know if it was a good or bad sign. He wanted to take her to bed, make love until they were both senseless, and let her know how much he still desired and loved her. It might be too soon, yet perhaps taking her to bed would be the best move he could make— reminding Cassie how good they were together instead of allowing her to wonder about the women from his past.

Shifting in his seat, he focused on the traffic, trying not to read too much into her silence. The reality of how tough a second chance with Cassie would be slammed into him. They'd been each other's first love, learning about passion and pleasure together. He held no doubts about what he wanted from her, and it wasn't a short-term fling. This would either be their one chance to correct the mistakes from their past or bury whatever love they still held for each other and move on. There'd be no half-way for them. They were either both in or it would be all over.

******

"It's as beautiful as you said, Matt." Cassie stood on the outside balcony of her room, letting her gaze take in the churning water and distant islands. Her logical mind knew his decision to have separate rooms made sense. Her rebellious heart felt differently.

Coming up behind her, he rested his hands on her waist, stopping short of wrapping his arms around her to draw her close. No matter his desire to take her to bed, he didn't want to rush it before they'd had a chance to air out the hurt from the past.

"Would it be all right to take a walk?" Turning, she stepped around him, feeling as if she were in a cage. Lunch had been excellent, the conversation pleasant, yet she couldn't escape the feeling that if she made one misstep, disappointed him in some way, their time together would be over. "I need to get out of here for a bit."

"Sure. There's a path along the shoreline. As I recall, it ends near a marina and picnic area." Opening the door, he followed her into the hall, punching the elevator button. "Is everything all right?"

"Fine." She leaned her back against the elevator wall. "We've been cooped up in the car or in meetings so much, I just want to take advantage of the gorgeous weather. I've heard it can change in an instant." Flashing him a smile, she reached over to take his hand. "Will we have time to take a ferry to one of the islands?"

Threading his fingers with hers, he felt the warmth sweep through his body, bathing him in a sense of peace he hadn't known in a long time. "We can do whatever we want. The next three days are about us and nothing else."

The afternoon flew by as they visited one site after another, ending at a cozy restaurant with a great view in the Pike Place Market. Drinking mojitos and snacking on a variety of appetizers, they began to share their lives since they'd been apart.

"Tell me more about what happened?" Cassie picked up a piece of calamari, popping it into her mouth.

"What happened with what?" His brows drew together as he used a finger to brush a crumb from the corner of her mouth.

"Why did you quit the rodeo?"

"It's more like it quit me." Gazing at the water, he remembered his last ride, wincing as if the injury had occurred that day. "It was a saddle bronc event. I'd almost finished the ride on a strong horse who bucked like a sonofabitch. I felt good...too good. One second, I was solid in the saddle, and the next, I was on the ground, pain ripping through my neck and shoulder. Thoughts of healing and getting back into the arena were dashed by one doctor after another. I must have met with six, each one telling me the same thing."

Leaning forward, she fingered the straw, drawing up a small amount of the mojito. "What did they say?"

"Another injury involving my neck would mean some level of paralysis, maybe total. Still, I wanted to try again. It took Pops hauling me home to kick some sense into me." He shrugged, as if the career-ending injury hadn't affected him.

"I didn't know you'd gone home." Her family had insisted on mentioning Matt whenever he went home. She'd learned of his injury months after he'd left the circuit, but not that he'd gone to Fire Mountain to heal.

He reached over, grasping her hand. "You weren't supposed to know. I asked Pops to keep it quiet, let me heal, and decide my next move before I had to face friends."

"Dad would've offered you a job."

Dropping her hand, he leaned back in his chair, his gaze narrowing. "Do you honestly believe that after what happened between us? He would've been more likely to punch me out than offer help."

Cassie studied him, getting a glimpse into how much he'd lost by leaving for the rodeo. He hadn't turned his back on just her. He'd turned away from a family he'd known his entire life.

"He saw you as a son. No matter what happened between you and me, Dad would've been there for you."

"Maybe...maybe not. Regardless, I didn't want or need his charity. I wanted to heal and get out of there with as few people knowing as possible."

Cassie didn't know what to think of the pain she saw on his face. He'd picked the rodeo over her, gone his own way, and made it without anyone's help. Still, he seemed unsettled, as if his achievements meant nothing.

"You're right. Knowing my family, I'm certain they would have rubbed the failure in your face, encouraging you to hunker down and hide from the world. Seems like a reasonable response to me."

His gaze swung to her, his eyes blazing until he saw her mouth tilt up and her eyes sparkle with mischief. She started to laugh, punching him in the arm. "It's good to know you finally snapped out of it and took the job Dad offered. Trust me. He doesn't make those offers without thinking them all the way through. Whatever you did at Double Ace, you must have impressed the brothers."

His eyes widened. "Really? You're happy I'm your boss?"

Finishing her drink, she stood, crossing her arms. "Garner, you will *never* be the boss of me."

Chapter Eighteen

"To a wonderful weekend," Matt said, lifting his glass, touching the edge of Cassie's before bringing it to his lips.

"And great sex," Cassie murmured under her breath, causing Matt to choke. Patting him on the back, she sent him a knowing smile. "Thought I'd throw that out."

Coughing, he stared at her. "If that's a challenge, I'm definitely your man."

Sometime over the last ten hours, they'd settled into a comfort zone they knew well. Joking, mocking, and teasing each other without malice, daring themselves with unsubtle barbs.

They'd finished dinner and settled into a booth in the restaurant's bar, Cassie drinking port wine and finishing the last bite of double chocolate mousse cake while Matt nursed an Irish coffee. The time they'd been apart slipped away. He found himself wondering how he'd ever left her and lived these last few years without any contact. Paying the check, he held out his hand, his eyes darkening.

"Let's get out of here."

Neither spoke as they entered the elevator. When the door slid closed, Matt tightened his hold around her waist, drawing her to him, ravaging her mouth as he pinned her against the wall. His hunger wasn't subtle and neither was hers, each taking as much as possible within the space of a few floors. Hearing the ding signaling a stop, they broke apart, both trying to control their ragged breathing.

"It's our floor," Matt ground out. Gripping her hand, he fumbled with his key card, pushing the door of his room open and kicking it closed. Cradling her face in his hands, he stared into eyes that left no doubt about what she wanted. "My room tonight. Yours tomorrow."

The words were barely out before Cassie drew him down, covering his mouth with hers, letting him know how much she wanted him.

Their frantic hands were everywhere, unbuttoning clothes and tossing them aside. Backing her against the wall, Matt lifted her arms, wrapping a hand around her wrists and pinning them above her head, never losing contact of his mouth on hers.

Cassie moaned as his lips burned a trail along her jawline to the hollow at the base of her neck, sucking lightly before moving lower. Drawing in a breath, she arched into him, wanting and needing more.

"Matt..." she breathed out as his mouth and hands worked their magic.

Lifting her into his arms, he settled her on the bed, stretching alongside, allowing his hands to rediscover the body he'd craved for far too long. Rising up, his hands continued to roam as he stared down, seeing her reaction to his touch. His breath caught, his hunger for her growing with each caress.

Unable to hold back any longer, he wrapped his arms around her, taking her mouth with his, and on a deep groan, made the sweetest love of his life.

******

"You're going to kill me," Matt rasped out, his eyes still closed, as Cassie stroked her hand down his chest to his stomach, being rewarded with an understandable reaction, even as the rest of his body refused to budge.

Leaning forward, she kissed her way from his chin to his chest, exploring with her hands, tracing the path of an unremembered scar.

"How did you get this one?" Her touch felt light as she fingered the angry red mark along his side.

"Bareback event. I got thrown into the fence. It looks worse than it was, but it kept me out of competition for a couple weeks."

"And this one?" She leaned down to kiss a short, jagged scar on his other side.

"Stupid action on my part. I intervened when a guy pulled a knife on one of my buddies. They'd been joking before the guy got angry. I didn't know there were a couple cops in the bar or I would've stayed out of it."

"And your buddy?"

"Not a scratch." Reaching down, he wrapped a hand around her wrist, tugging her up and into his arms. "I'm starving."

"Me, too." Her eyes sparkled as her brows arched.

"For food..." He planted a slow, hot kiss on her mouth, then rolled off the bed. Moving toward the bathroom, he held out his hand. "Join me?"

******

"Breakfast never tasted this good." Matt shoveled another bite of eggs and hash browns into his mouth. He'd gone for the biggest combination plate the restaurant offered, but he didn't think it would be enough.

Shaking her head when the waitress offered a refill, Cassie sat back, enjoying the sight. The shower had taken much longer than normal, but she wouldn't have asked for anything different. Their night together had been wonderful, and he gave her more of the same this morning, all of it beyond her expectations. He'd learned a great deal since they'd last shared a bed. Knowing she had to push such thoughts aside, she gazed out the window, wondering how she measured up to his other lovers. Would she be enough after all this time?

Pushing her empty plate away, Cassie grabbed her purse, reaching inside for a credit card. Matt's hand shot out, halting her motions.

"Don't even think about it. This weekend was my idea." Bringing her hand to his lips, placing a kiss on her palm, he stopped her half-hearted protest. "I'll let you pay some other time."

Some other time. She liked that, hoping it meant he'd become as invested in working this out as her. Even if she hadn't grown in experience, Cassie knew better than to believe sharing a bed, no matter how sweet and satisfying, meant the end to the hurt they'd caused each other. It had taken several long talks, but she'd begun to understand his decision to leave hurt him as much as her.

"Where to next?"

"Let's take the ferry to Bainbridge Island. There are a few shops, a great bakery, a waterfront trail, an art museum..." His voice trailed off when he saw the sparkle in her eyes begin to dim. Taking a breath, he reached for her hand. "It was nothing, Cassie. One of my rodeo buddies moved back to the island after an injury. I was already in Washington for the Othello rodeo, so I took a couple extra days to visit. Although he wasn't up for taking me around, his neighbor was."

"A female?"

"Yeah."

"Pretty?"

"Well, yes. For eighty, she was quite attractive, and a lot of fun. She—"

Slapping his arm, they both laughed, then Cassie's face sobered. "I need to get used to you having a past that didn't include me. It just seems strange. The worst part is it emphasizes how much I didn't do in the time you were gone. You've experienced so much. All I've done is work."

"And volunteer at the foster care foundation. We both took a different path, which is good, Cass. We can share our experiences with each other, build from where we are. Come on. Let's start by exploring the island and see what I can remember."

******

Holding hands, they slowly walked through the airport to Cassie's gate, the air between them filled with tension and unanswered questions. Matt hated to see her leave with so many unknowns between them, yet he had no choice. She'd be going back to Cold Creek, her current home. He'd see her off, then fly out an hour later to Fire Mountain. Neither had talked of the biggest issue hanging between them—their future.

"Well, here we are." Cassie tightened her hold on Matt's hand, looking up to search his face for some kind of validation he'd enjoyed their weekend together. He gave nothing away. He'd been all she

235

could want—charming, fun, a gracious host, and a wonderful lover. The look in his eyes warned her he had something on his mind.

Matt glanced at his watch. "We have a few minutes before you board. We need to talk."

Cassie could feel a knot of unease take hold in her stomach, building into a cold lump as he walked toward seating several yards away. Dismissing his gesture for her to sit, she released his hand.

"What is it you want to say?"

He could see her expression change from hope to curiosity to apprehension. Raising a hand to her face, he stopped when she took a step back and waited.

"I had a good time this weekend. It was all I'd hoped." Stopping, he let out a breath, needing this to come out right.

"But?" she whispered, irritated at the way her voice broke.

Again, Matt reached out toward her, and once more, she stepped aside.

"We had the idyllic time. No stress, no work, no family pressures. Away from everything we'd normally face. These last few days aren't how life is, Cassie. It will take a lot of work to get back what we had. It isn't something we can turn on and off like a switch."

She swallowed, trying to regain the composure which had escaped her the moment he'd asked to talk. Her face began to throb with embarrassment, a pulsing sensation that assaulted her when she expected bad news. In a heartbeat, she realized what she'd prayed for wasn't going to happen.

"Just say it, Matt. If you don't think I'm up to handling our relationship in the *real world*, or if you don't want what we had this weekend to continue, tell me."

Blowing out a breath, he threaded fingers through his hair. He'd already made a mess of this conversation, seeing no way to untangle it in the few minutes left to them.

"I guess I don't want either of us to have unreasonable expectations about the future."

Biting her lower lip, Cassie crossed her arms. "So you're saying this weekend was more of a test. Some wicked experiment to see if you still felt anything for me?"

"That's not it," he ground out, his voice hard.

"Then explain it to me because I have no idea what you're trying to say."

When he reached out this time, she didn't back away, letting his hand rest on her shoulder.

"I care about you, Cassie. I—"

"You *care* about me?" She shook off his hand, not wanting to hear the rest. "After our past and what we had this weekend, that's how you feel? Fine. I *care* about you, too, Matt. But unlike you, I'm not afraid to say I love you." She swallowed the bile in her throat, refusing to let the tears welling in her eyes fall. "I loved you in high school, in college, and after you left me. And as God is my witness, I love you now. If you can't say the same, there's nothing more to discuss." Bending down, she grabbed her purse and computer, squaring her shoulders. "I'm glad you had fun. I'd hate to think I hadn't delivered." Turning, she put a few steps between them before Matt's hand closed on her arm.

"Stop, Cassie. Don't leave like this."

Spinning toward him, eyes blazing, she stared at his hand. "Let go of me, Matt."

"Not until I finish."

Blinking, she swiped at an escaping tear, irritated at her own lack of control. "Fine. You have one minute."

Dropping his hand, he stepped closer. "I just don't want either of us to expect too much. We don't know where this is going."

"Do you love me?"

Narrowing his gaze, his brief hesitation gave her the answer before he could speak.

"Forget it. I can already see it's a tough question for you." She closed her eyes, feeling like a fool for thinking they had a chance. "Don't worry. I won't tell anyone of this weekend. You're free to go on with your life as if this never happened."

Her chest tightened as she tried to control the pain ripping through her. There'd be no way she could ever face him at work or family gatherings. She'd made a huge mistake believing he'd come back to her after experiencing life on his own. He didn't need her, love her, or want to work through their issues. All he'd wanted was a quick weekend fling with no strings and no future. Lowering her voice, she moved a step closer. "You can take this as my two weeks' notice. I'll let you deal with it any way you see fit."

"Cass…"

This time, she didn't turn around. It took all her effort to keep her face neutral as she handed the boarding pass to the flight attendant, walked onto the plane, placing her bag in the overhead, and took her seat, thankful she'd reserved one on the aisle. Taking several deep breaths, she snapped the seat belt closed and rested her head against the seat, praying whoever sat next to her wasn't the chatty type. In the span of five minutes, she'd quit her job and lost the man she thought would be her future. Humiliation burned her cheeks. He cared about her, but nothing more. How could she have ever been so blind? Closing her eyes, searching for a way to forget this weekend ever happened, she let her hand rest on her chest. Perhaps if she pressed hard enough, the intense ache would disappear in time.

******

Every swear word Matt had ever learned streamed through his mind as he stalked toward his own gate. How had he let their conversation deteriorate so much, she not only walked away, but quit her job? A resignation he had no intention of honoring.

Tossing his bag in the overhead, he plopped into the window seat, staring at the tarmac. Thinking back, Matt winced over what he'd said. He'd screwed up the conversation from the beginning, and wondered if she'd ever talk to him again. The first thing out of his mouth should have been *I love you and I want to make this work.* Instead, he'd voiced his concerns, leaving her to think, well...exactly what she did think. When he started the conversation, he had no intention of calling it off between them. All he'd wanted was to express his concerns, discover if she had any doubts, and figure out how to move forward. Then he'd hesitated when she asked if he loved her. All he had to say was yes and the rest would've taken care of itself. Instead, he'd wavered.

Pinching the bridge of his nose, he accepted he'd made a mess of it. Now he had to figure a way to make it right, get her to talk to him, and believe it when he told her how much he still wanted her. And yes, loved her.

Feeling a hand on his arm, he looked over to see an elderly woman watching him, her eyes full of concern.

"Are you all right, young man?"

Hell no, I'm not all right, he thought. "Yes, ma'am. I'm fine. Thanks for asking."

"You just looked so lost, I had to ask." She folded her hands in her lap, leaving him to his own thoughts.

Lost. A lady he'd never met before had described him in one word. The accurateness of it felt like a hot poker to his chest. He *had* been lost. Ever since leaving Cassie to compete, he'd been slogging through each day, thinking he'd been doing all right, but never making much progress, wishing he still had her in his life. He'd been lost and didn't realize it until right now.

Glancing at the woman, he let his mouth tilt into a grim smile. She'd figured him out in an instant and now he had to find a way to get out of the mess he created...and it had to start as soon as the plane touched down.

Chapter Nineteen

Cold Creek, Colorado

Janie glanced at the phone on the kitchen counter, seeing Cassie's gaze shift to the screen from where she stood in front of the stove. Matt. Shaking her head, she continued stirring the marinara sauce, feeling the sting of his rejection.

"Aren't you going to answer it? He's called, what? About twenty times in the last few days. No matter what happened, he's still your boss."

"I'll talk to him when I'm ready."

Crossing her arms, Janie leaned against the counter, frowning. "Does this seem like déjà vu to you?"

Stopping, Cassie cocked her head, turning toward Janie. "What do you mean?"

"Isn't this what happened when he tried to reach you over and over the last time? He finally gave up and left town."

"This is nothing like the last time," she snapped. "He called it off at the airport. Now he just wants to ease his conscience or try to talk me into staying at my job. Neither is going to happen."

"That isn't exactly how you described it when I picked you up at the airport." Janie leaned over Cassie's shoulder, checking the sauce's progress. "Smells great."

"Don't change the subject. What do you mean it isn't what I said Sunday?"

"You said he didn't answer when you asked if he loved you."

"Well, he didn't."

"And how many seconds did you give him? One, two...maybe three?" She watched Cassie's mouth tilt into a frown. "You also told me he kept trying to get you to wait and talk to him, but you were so upset, you left him hanging. Sorry, hon, but it doesn't sound to me like Matt called it off. It sounds more like you did."

Cassie's face sobered as her shoulders slumped. Playing back the conversation over the last few days, she'd already conceded Janie was right. She'd been scared, then on edge when he said they needed to talk. He never did say he wanted to end it.

"Somewhere inside, you must know Matt loves you and wants to try again. He never would've suggested a weekend away if he wasn't pretty sure you're what he wants. Somehow, I think you got your wires crossed."

Letting out a sigh, Cassie lowered the heat under the sauce and set the spoon down. Burying her face in her hands, she slumped against the counter. "It's my stupid pride, isn't it?" she groaned. Of all her faults, it was the one characteristic that continued to trip her up.

"Well, since you asked..."

Cassie held up a hand. "Never mind. I know I messed up. Again."

"After three days, he's still reaching out to you. Don't you think Matt deserves a break? If you intended to make him squirm a little, fine, but it may be time to give him a chance."

Picking up her phone, Cassie turned toward the bedroom. "Go ahead and eat. I'll be out in a bit."

"Take your time." Janie grabbed a plate, hoping she'd done the right thing by encouraging Cassie to speak with Matt.

******

Cassie listened to the last message. He'd said pretty much the same in all of them—he wanted to talk, explain his side, and there was no way he would accept her resignation. The fact he hadn't mentioned he loved her or wanted to continue seeing her had been why she hesitated calling him back. She didn't want to feel worse than she already did. Blowing him off as she'd done before didn't set well with her. He did deserve his say.

Punching in his number, she paced to the window, watching the traffic whiz by. One ring, two, then three before she heard his voice.

"Cassie, hold on. I'm here. Give me a sec." He sounded out of breath, as if he'd been running. "Okay, I'm back. I had to close the door."

"We can talk later if I'm interrupting something."

"No. UPS delivered a large package for Pops. I helped bring it in from the truck." Matt hesitated, the silence growing as each waited for the other to speak.

"Are you sure this is a good time?" Cassie shifted the phone from one ear to the other, her hands shaking.

"Now is good."

"I got your messages. It just took me a little time to calm down from Sunday and call you back." She mentally kicked herself for not taking more time to decide what to say before she made the call.

"That's all right. We both needed time to clear our heads. I know I did."

"Me, too. Matt, I may have overreacted..."

"No, Cass, you didn't. I screwed it up from the start, made you think I didn't want to keep seeing you, and I'm sorry for that."

"You still want to see me?" The shock in her voice didn't surprise Matt. He already knew how much he'd botched the whole conversation.

"Yes, I do. I've never wanted anything more." Matt's stomach began to curl in on itself when she didn't respond. Maybe he had misunderstood the way she felt. "Cassie, are you still there?"

She swiped at the tears running down her face, the relief she felt so immense, talking became hard. "Uh-huh."

"Okay, that's good." He let out a breath, steadying the thumping in his chest. "What I should've said was how much I want this to work out. Instead, I told you my fears, making you believe I'd changed my mind."

"You haven't?" She smiled, her voice catching.

"Hell no. There's no way I want to stop seeing you. Last weekend made me realize how good we are together. We need to see this through...if you're willing to give me another chance."

"I'd like that, Matt. Very much."

He'd never felt such a strong sense of relief. "What are you doing this weekend?"

"Spending it with you?"

He chuckled. "Absolutely. I'll fly in Saturday morning and get a room—"

"Only if the room is for both of us," she laughed. "Unless you'd rather stay at my place." Cassie didn't know what Janie and Kurt had planned, but she could always kick them out for the weekend.

"You're okay with that?"

"More than okay." Swallowing her pride, she drew in a breath. "Thanks, Matt."

"For what?"

She could hear the confusion in his voice. "Hanging in there with me. Not giving up."

His voice sobered. "I could say the same to you. We'll thank each other on Saturday."

"Sounds great. Goodnight, Matt."

"Goodnight, Cassie."

Hanging up, he slouched onto the sofa. He'd been granted a reprieve, a chance to prove how much she meant to him. No woman would ever make him feel as whole and at peace the way Cassie did and he meant to tell her.

"You okay, Matt?"

He sat up, looking over his shoulder. "Yeah, Pops. I'm fine."

"You work things out with Cassie yet?"

Standing, Matt turned to face his grandfather. "Excuse me?"

"Don't try to bullshit me, boy. You're still in love with her, and if you let this chance pass you by, you'll be the biggest fool in the family. And let me tell you, we've had some world-class fools, me included. Now, help me bring that package back to my office."

A grin splitting his face, Matt shook his head. Seth Garner was nobody's fool, no matter what the old man said. If any Garner was a fool, it was him, and he was darn well going to fix that this weekend.

******

"What are you telling me, Jerrod?" Kurt crossed his arms and leaned a shoulder against a wall in the staff room.

"We have a serial arsonist. At first, I thought we were dealing with a couple prank fires, then perhaps a copycat. Comparing lab results presents a different story. I'd bet my career the same person set all the fires."

"Any idea as to the motivation?" Kurt pushed away from the wall, taking a seat across the table. He welcomed the news. Tracking down two or three separate arsonists would've required more manpower and more time. Identifying one arsonist as skilled as this one would be difficult, but more within the scope of their limited resources.

"The list is endless. Let's start with what I *don't* believe is the motivation. First, it's not some teenager looking for a thrill or trying to get noticed, as I'd first thought. The accelerants are too sophisticated. They weren't set for monetary gain, and I seriously doubt vandalism played any part." Jerrod stood and filled his cup with coffee, resting a hip against the counter's edge. "The arsonist is unstable with severe emotional issues. He's trying to get the attention of someone or a group of people, possibly in retaliation for a perceived wrong."

"You're saying this person is after revenge?" Kurt leaned forward, resting his arms on the table.

"In my opinion, yes."

"A cry for help?"

"I'm not sure about that. I've studied the videos of each fire, scanned the crowd, and matched faces. In most cases, a person seeking help can't stay away from a fire they set. Our team has been thorough at capturing images of spectators. I couldn't find a single match."

Kurt scrubbed a hand down his face, picturing the locations of the earliest fires. "Several were in remote locations with few onlookers, but had excellent tree or brush cover. What about that?"

"Could be our arsonist hid in the trees, but I doubt it. From everything I've studied, we're dealing with someone with a need for revenge. He'll keep setting fires until the person or persons he's after have suffered."

"Or died," Kurt muttered.

"Yes, that's always a possibility, but the main motive is to make the person suffer because of a perceived wrong or slight. Killing them doesn't accomplish that goal."

"Do you still believe it's a man?"

"It's probable we're looking for a male in his twenties or thirties, but I can't rule out a female. Most females seeking revenge target something more personal than an empty building. They hit cars, homes, possibly a storage unit with personal affects. These fires don't fit that profile." Taking a sip of coffee, Jerrod joined Kurt at the table. "We've had six fires. The latest ones, although set in abandoned or vacant buildings, have brought a higher degree of risk to surrounding structures. One caused the death of two young men. I believe the arsonist didn't know they were in the building, hunkered down in the storage closet. It doesn't excuse the murders. I'm saying the killings were not part of the arsonist's motivation."

"Where do we go from here?"

"The police chief has requested additional assistance for patrolling potential targets, we're scouring the databases for matches with any known arsonist, and we're working with a profiler to see if we can come up with a possible identity."

Kurt had worked with Jerrod ever since returning from Aspen. The fires, lack of sleep, and stress had taken a toll on his friend. Bloodshot eyes were rimmed with dark circles, his normally clean-shaven face sported at least a three-day beard, and the worry lines around his face had deepened.

"What aren't you telling me?" Kurt asked, studying his friend.

Jerrod glanced up from studying his shaking hands, another consequence of the increased fires. Normally calm and in total control, he seemed increasingly edgy.

Jerrod shook his head, unsure of his conclusion, unable to say what haunted him. *I think I may know the identity of the arsonist.*

******

"Thanks, Gage. I appreciate you flying up." Kade stood, shaking Gage's hand after a successful day of meetings with Skye, Cassie, and him. "When do you fly out?"

"Not until Friday morning. I have some other business to take care of tomorrow." Gage glanced at Skye. He'd hoped to spend some time with her, preferably alone, but the schedule hadn't allowed for it. Instead, they'd taken their meals as a group. Which, as he thought on it, might have been for the best.

He didn't need any entanglements. Instinct warned him nothing about Skye would be temporary or easy, and he certainly didn't want anything more. After tomorrow, he'd finally escape the last claws his ex-wife had in him. They'd meet, sign documents dealing with their final joint piece of property, and he'd never have to deal with her again.

"Let's meet for dinner." Hearing his phone, Kade checked the caller I.D. "Excuse me while I take this." He laughed at whatever the caller said as he disappeared into the hall.

"Mind if we join you?" Beyond his fine physical attributes, quick mind, and easy smile, Skye didn't know what drew her to Gage. Distancing herself would be the smart move, but then she'd never learn why her body coiled in knots at his mere presence. For a woman not at all interested in encumbering herself with a man, the feelings he triggered were unsettling and unwanted.

"That'd be great." Gage glanced at Cassie. "Any suggestions?"

They settled on a restaurant a few miles from the motel where Gage and Skye had rooms, agreeing to meet in two hours as Kade finished his call and walked back into the room.

"Are we set?"

"We are. Cassie and I will meet you and Gage for dinner. He'll give you the details. If you'll excuse me, I have some calls to make." Skye walked out with Cassie, seeing her try to contain a smile. "What?"

"Why don't you ask him to meet you for drinks before dinner? You know that's what you want." Cassie's eyes crinkled at the corners. From the first time they met in Houston months before, she'd watched the two of them dance around each other. Nothing had changed. If anything, the sparks between them became easier to detect with each encounter.

"He's a hunk, no question. Too bad I have no interest in him or anyone else."

"Have you ever been told you're a bad liar, Skye?"

She choked out a laugh, knowing there'd be no getting away from Cassie's all too keen observation.

"Guess I need to work harder at it," she grinned, knowing a relationship wasn't in her future. At least not a future she could see.

******

"Great choice, Cassie." Kade tossed his napkin, along with his credit card, on the table. "Do you need a ride to your motel, Skye?"

"I'll take care of it. We're staying at the same place." Gage stood, pulling out Skye's chair, a gesture hammered into him since he was a small boy. Pulling out chairs and opening car doors were as ingrained in him as taking off his hat in a restaurant. Anything less felt out of character. If a woman balked at graciously accepting either gesture, he figured she'd have to learn to deal with it.

"Are you sure? Cassie has to drive right by there." His offer surprised Skye. In fact, she hadn't even realized they were staying in the same place. The knowledge put a strange, not unpleasant twist on the end of their evening.

"No sense having her stop."

Skye glanced at Cassie, who stood to the side, working to control a knowing smile. "Do you mind, Cassie?"

"It's fine with me. We can talk tomorrow about meeting Janie for dinner." Grabbing her keys, Cassie stepped into the cool night air. The change allowed her that much more time on the phone with Matt. A call she'd looked forward to all day.

"Good luck with your meeting tomorrow, Gage." Kade held his gaze for a second before turning toward his car. The two hadn't discussed the reason for Gage staying an extra day. Somehow, Kade didn't believe he looked forward to it.

Peering around the lot, Skye shot a questioning look at Gage. "Which one is yours?"

"The black car on the end."

Her eyes widened at the sight of a brand new Corvette. "That's some ride." Her hand traced the contour of the beautiful sports car from the trunk to the passenger door. "Yours?"

He laughed. "Hardly. It's a rental. My normal ride is a pickup." Opening the door, he stood as she slid in, unable to stop himself from appreciating the sight of her slim, shapely figure. It hadn't been the first time he'd let himself enjoy the gorgeous woman who needed to stay at arm's length. Anything more would be foolish, hazardous to the partnership they'd worked so hard to forge.

"You've never said how you came to work for Double Ace." Skye tried not to stare at his profile as Gage pulled into traffic. Mesmerized by the strong, angular lines of his face with an aquiline nose and full lips, she startled when his gaze turned toward her, his unusually deep green eyes flashing.

"That's because you never asked." The smile transformed his face from solemn and contemplative to almost playful.

"Right. Well, I'm asking now." She shifted in her seat, doing her best to control the flash of heat his attention and closeness caused, hoping he didn't notice her discomfort.

"It's no secret. I decided my time competing in rodeos was over and put out word I'd be looking for another job. It didn't take long before a few companies showed an interest. Most were small, without the resources to grow much beyond being a family operation. Nothing wrong with that, except I wanted more—a chance to show what could be done, maybe a chance at ownership in the future. Double Ace seemed the right choice. It didn't hurt that I felt a solid connection with Ivan."

"Kindred spirits?"

He chuckled at the thought. "Perhaps. The oldest son of the oldest brother in the Santiago family, he felt compelled to prove himself, the same as me. We're about the same age, neither of us married, all our focus on growing the business." He shrugged, as if his description covered it all.

"You've never married?" Skye cringed at the question, even though she wanted the answer.

He glanced at her, his smile dissolving. "I didn't say that."

His tight expression, the hardening of his face,
signaled her question hit a nerve. When he offered
nothing more, Skye clamped her mouth shut,
counting the blocks until their motel came into view.

Chapter Twenty

Gage killed the engine, walking around the car to open her door. Holding out his hand to help her out, he felt a tinge of regret at his abrupt answer to her question. Divorce wasn't a crime or cause for embarrassment. The fact his marriage had been a fiasco dogged him more than any other reaction to the failed union.

They walked in an uneasy silence through the doors and toward the elevator. He could feel the tension radiating from her, wanting to find a way to return the easy banter during their ride from the office.

"What floor?" he asked as the elevator door closed.

"Three...please."

He leaned against the wall, glad the older machine moved at a slow pace. "It's been a couple years since my divorce and I'm still dealing with the last complications."

"I'm sorry you had to go through it. My parents' divorce dragged on a while. He had a hard time with it, even though the marriage ended years before they both gave up. She, uh...had a long-time boyfriend."

"Geez," he breathed out.

"Yeah. He knew about the guy long before the rest of us found out." She looked up at him, a wistful look on her face. "He's much happier now. Reuniting with his brothers helped a lot, as well as all the new responsibilities. Maybe it will be the same for you."

The elevator slowed, the doors opening.

"My floor," she said, stepping into the hall.

"Mine, too. Which room?"

"The very end." They walked side by side, brushing arms on the way to her room, her stomach churning at his nearness. She needed to get inside her room, close the door, and end the uneasy feelings of desire undulating through her. "Here we are."

Neither spoke as he studied her, not wanting to leave just yet, even though he had no reason to prolong their time together. "I have some things to do tomorrow, but if you don't have plans, I'd like to take you to dinner when I get back."

Her eyes widened at the invitation. She had hoped he'd say something to show his interest. Sighing, she fiddled with the strap of her purse. "I'd love to, but I'm meeting Cassie and Janie for dinner."

"No problem. Another time." The husky reply held a touch of regret. "I guess I'd better head to my room."

"Guess so," she replied, although neither moved.

Lifting a hand, he let his fingers skim down the curve of her cheek, tucking a loose strand of hair behind her ears. When she didn't pull away, he inched closer, his hand moving to the back of her neck, drawing her toward him. Lowering his head, he waited, expecting her to pull back. Instead, her lips parted as her gaze met his.

Touching his lips to hers, he kept the contact light, then settled his mouth on hers. What started as a brief kiss escalated as her hands moved to his shoulders, then circled his neck, drawing him down. Adjusting his stance, Gage wrapped his arms around her back, pulling her tight, aligning their bodies.

She didn't know how much time passed as the feel of him, the heat raging through her body, swamped her senses. His touch, scent, feel of his silky hair slipping through her fingers escalated her passion to a precarious level, one she held no defenses over. If he'd taken the key to her room, opened the door, and pulled her inside, she'd let him. The realization forced her to pull back.

"This is probably a mistake," she whispered against his mouth.

"Probably," he groaned, not easing his hold.

"We should stop before we get carried away." Although the intensity of her desire and her actions spoke otherwise, Skye knew they had to end this craziness before it went too far.

On a ragged breath, Gage let his arms slip from around her, taking a reluctant step away.

"Wow," he breathed out, his husky voice signifying the affect she had on him.

"Yeah…"

"It would probably be a mistake to take this any farther." Gage searched her face, not believing his own words, wanting to ignore the pulsing desire Skye's touch created.

"Yes, I'm sure you're right." Skye hated to agree, wanting to continue more than anything, knowing it wouldn't be wise.

"Am I?"

A throaty laugh answered his question, her mouth quirking into a smile.

"I don't think we should jump into anything. After all, you live in Texas, and I'm in Montana. To be truthful, I'm not interested in a quick one-night stand. It's better to let it go before we make a mistake."

"Who said this would be a quick one-nighter?" Gage leaned a shoulder against the doorframe, crossing his arms, his body adjusting to the loss of contact.

"Are you saying you're looking for something more?"

Sighing, he thought of his past experience, the ex-wife who wouldn't let go, the deep regrets he couldn't ignore. "No, Skye, I'm not."

Even though she was prepared for the answer he gave, she'd hoped for a different one.

"Then I guess this is best." Feeling the loss of someone she never had a chance of having, she pulled the key card from her pocket. "Thanks for the ride back."

"My pleasure." He waited as she stepped inside, glancing at him once more before closing the door. "Damn," he ground out, shoving his hands in his pockets as he walked away.

He didn't know how he'd be able to keep his hands off her after tonight. The sweet, intense reaction he had to their contact had him shaking like a teenager. All the warning signs had been there. He'd ignored them all. Now he knew, without a doubt, Skye MacLaren was dangerous to his peace of mind and determination to steer clear of any kind of relationship. Love and commitment, no matter the woman, had no place in his life. Stopping it here was best for them both, he reasoned, closing the door behind him, tossing his hat on the bed. Yep, no doubt about it. Definitely best for them both.

******

Finishing another chapter of a romantic suspense story, Cassie reread the last line. *Guard your heart.*

The book's cautionary warning had her wondering if she might be jumping into a relationship with little chance of success. During their brief phone conversation, Matt's words were clear, yet the tone of his voice, how he'd hesitated a few times, couldn't be ignored. If it hadn't come a few days after their disastrous conversation at the airport, the one that still haunted her, it might not have bothered her so much. She didn't need or want him to continue seeing her because he felt bad about the way they'd parted. She needed him to be all in, not worried about her leaving her job or breaking her heart.

Setting her book aside, she glanced at the clock next to her bed. Almost eleven and still no word from Matt. His email had indicated he'd call after having dinner with his grandfather and brother, Troy, who'd driven home from college to spend the weekend. Figuring he'd lost track of time, she turned off the light and slid under the covers. Closing her eyes, she thought once more of the book and the last few words. *Guard your heart.* She felt her own heart surge a moment before sleep claimed her.

******

Fire Mountain

"I'm glad you ignored Seth's grumbling and brought him here. We'll keep him overnight, do a few more tests to see if we can figure out what's causing his dizziness and pain. It doesn't appear to be his heart, but I'd rather be safe and have it checked." The doctor made a few more notes, looking over his shoulder to where Seth sat with a disgusted look on his face. Chuckling to himself, he glanced at Matt. "You don't need to stay. We'll give him medication to help him sleep. I've scheduled an angiogram for seven in the morning."

Matt rubbed a hand at the back of his neck. It had been a long day with nonstop phone calls, meetings, and proposal reviews before driving home to find Troy had driven up from school to surprise them. As Matt barbequed steaks and Troy fixed a salad, Seth had decided to have his first beer in weeks. It had been a perfect evening...until Seth stood to take his empty plate to the kitchen and fell back in the chair, gripping his side. His breaths came in short gasps, punctuated by his face wincing in pain.

Twenty minutes later, the boys had him at the emergency room entrance, the older man fighting them every step of the way. He'd been wise enough to keep his comments to himself while the doctor examined him and ordered some tests, asking Matt and Troy to wait in the lobby. Two hours later, they'd finally met with the doctor.

"We'll say goodbye to Pops, then be back in the morning." Matt stepped past the doctor, Troy following as they entered his room to see their grandfather sitting on the side of the bed. "What do you think you're doing?"

"Going home. I'll come back in the morning for the test." The message came out as more of a snarl than a statement.

"The hell you will, Pops. You're staying here and no arguments." Matt grabbed Seth's pants, tossing them to Troy.

"You think I care about leaving here in a gown. Well, I don't. Might give the nurses a little thrill." He started to stand, then gasped at the pain near his rib cage. "Damn, that hurts."

"And that's why you're staying here tonight. Maybe longer if you don't behave yourself." Matt grabbed a chair, pulling it toward the bed. "The doc says he's not convinced it's your heart, but wants you to have the angiogram."

"I know. He told me," Seth groused. "Can't stand hospitals. They wake you up to give you a sleeping pill so you can rest. Then wake you up an hour later to take your blood pressure to make sure you're still alive. Then wake you once more to make sure you can pee. I tell you, it isn't humane or dignified."

Troy clamped his mouth shut, then coughed to cover a laugh.

"What you laughing at, boy?" Seth glared at his youngest grandson. They were too young to remember their grandmother's time in the hospital. The way her body withered away as the cancer ravaged her body. Seth visited twice a day for weeks to hold her hand, read, and do his best to keep her spirits up, even as they both knew her time was limited. She'd refused to go into hospice, begging him to let her die at home. He'd slept with her until the morning he awoke to find her gone, passed away in the middle of the night. A few years later, his son and daughter-in-law died in an accident and he'd been forced to pull himself out of a deep emotional hole to take care of his two grandsons. He'd never regretted a moment of it.

"You know, Pops, your grumbling isn't going to get you out of here. It may be best if you turned on the television and got lost in one of those fishing shows you're so fond of." Troy picked up another chair and set it opposite Matt. "We can stay and hold your hand if you want."

Matt laughed as Seth shot Troy a wicked look. "For a smart kid, you've got a mean mouth."

"All right, you two. Visiting hours are long over." A tall, lean nurse stood in the doorway, hands on hips, shifting her gaze from Matt to Troy, then Seth. "And you...I don't want to hear a peep about how much you don't want to be here."

"Now, Geri, you know I can't promise that."

"Just as ornery as you were in high school. I thought you would've grown out of it by now." She grabbed his pants from a table near the door. "You may want to take these with you." She handed them to Troy. "I don't want him trying to sneak out."

"Yes, ma'am. We completely agree."

"Get some sleep, Pops. We'll be back first thing tomorrow." Matt squeezed his arm before walking out.

"Love you, Pops. Don't be giving Geri a hard time." Troy nodded at the nurse before following Matt to the entrance, then to the parking lot. "At least he's being watched by someone who won't take his bull."

"Helluva way for you to spend your long weekend."

"Don't worry about it, Matt. The tests will probably come back clean and we'll bring him home tomorrow. So, what's new with you?"

Troy's question had him halting, then muttering a curse, remembering his promise to call Cassie.

"What's wrong?"

"I was supposed to call Cassie tonight. All this with Pops..."

Troy stared at Matt, his eyes narrowing. "Are you two back together?"

Shaking his head, he regretted saying anything. He and Cassie had agreed to keep it low-key until they felt firm. His reservations were few, but they still clung to him, like dampness on a cold, foggy evening. They just needed time without any interference from family, no matter how good the intentions.

"We're talking about it. Please don't say anything to Pops or her family."

"No worries, bro. It's got to be tough with her in Colorado and you here." He clamped a hand on Matt's shoulder. "If you're interested, I hope you make it this time."

"Thanks, Troy. So do I."

Climbing into the truck, he checked the time, deciding two in the morning was too late to call her. He'd wait until after the angiogram, hoping there'd be good news to report. He had no doubt she'd understand and would probably want to fly out to check on Seth herself.

He wouldn't let her. Seth would need his rest, and Matt wanted to spend time with Troy. They saw each other on holidays and a couple other times a year, but it wasn't enough. Matt glanced over at Troy, who scrolled through the screen on his phone, laughing at one of the posts.

"You did say no one knows about you and Cassie, right?" Troy stared at an image posted by a high school friend to one of the social media sites.

"We both agreed to keep it between us. Why?" Matt pulled into the drive, turning off the engine.

"Take a look."

He grabbed Troy's phone, his eyes widening at the image of Cassie and him, their arms around each other at the airport before flying to Seattle. Cursing, he glanced at the name of the *friend* who posted the picture, then handed the phone back. "I'm going to strangle that guy," he groaned, sliding out of the truck and slamming the door.

Chapter Twenty-One

Cold Creek, Colorado

"You haven't heard from Matt at all?" Janie checked out the new restaurant while they waited for Skye to join them. "Have you tried calling him?"

"Not yet. He's supposed to fly in tomorrow morning, so I'll wait. I'm sure he's buried with work." Cassie scrolled through her emails, noticing a post she'd missed from a friend. Opening it, her jaw dropped. "Oh no..."

"What is it?" Janie leaned forward, taking the phone from Cassie's hand. "It appears your secret is out. I assume you know this guy."

"I knew him in high school. He's a year or two younger, a friend of Matt's brother, Troy. For some reason, we've kept in touch."

"You didn't see him in Washington?" She handed the phone back, spotting Skye walking toward them.

"No. Maybe Matt did." She cringed, guessing he might have already seen this. "Do you think this is why he hasn't called me?"

"Hi, girls. Sorry I'm late, but I got a call from one of the rodeo committees. What are you drinking?" Skye sank into a chair between the two.

"Um…I have a margarita." Cassie slid the phone into her purse, wondering how many people had seen it and if Matt was one of them.

"Are you okay, Cassie? You look a little pale."

"I'm fine. A little tired after the last couple weeks."

"And last weekend." Skye winked at her, a smile curving the corners of her mouth.

"Last weekend?" Cassie tried to keep her face neutral. Janie's laugh didn't help.

"Oh, come on. I know you and Matt flew to Seattle for the weekend. Is it a secret?"

Cassie sank back into her chair, wishing she were a better liar. "Not so much a secret as we're still trying to figure it out ourselves. We decided to keep it quiet until we're certain of how we feel."

"The way you two look at each other, I think it's pretty obvious." Skye leaned over and squeezed Cassie's arm. "So I shouldn't be talking about it to Mitch or Sean or—"

"Especially not family. They'd get these expectations and feel compelled to ask us about it."

"I assume Janie knows. Anyone else?" Skye glanced at Janie, tilting her drink toward her.

"Just you. At least that's what I hope." Hearing her phone, Cassie grabbed it, seeing Matt's image appear. "I need to take this." She moved away, trying to find a quiet spot in the noisy restaurant. "Hi,

Matt. I hope you can hear me. I'm at dinner with Janie and Skye."

"Should I call back?"

"No, now is good. Are you still coming tomorrow?" She held her breath, hoping he hadn't changed his mind.

"That's why I called. Pops is in the hospital. Troy is here, but I don't think I should leave. Sorry about this."

"There's nothing to be sorry about. What happened?" Cassie could hear the despair in Matt's voice and wished she could be there with him.

"Troy and I brought him in last night. By the time we left, it was about two in the morning. That's why I didn't call. They ran a bunch of tests on him today, but haven't found anything specific. When they decided to keep him another night, I had to make a decision."

"I understand. Do you want me to fly out?"

"No. It's best if Troy and I deal with whatever is going on. Hopefully, we'll be able to bring Pops home tomorrow. The doctor said the angiogram showed nothing...the same as the other tests. Keeping him another night is a precaution." He let out a breath. "I was looking forward to seeing you."

"Same here, but Seth needs you. Are you certain you don't want me there?"

He didn't answer right away, and she wondered if she'd pushed too hard.

"Let's plan on next weekend. I'll try to fly out Friday and stay until Monday morning."

"Sure, Matt. Whatever works best for you." She thought of the image on her phone. "Did you happen to see a photo of us online?"

"You mean the one at the airport? Yeah, I saw it and I'm going to call him about removing it. He came up to me after you flew out, but never mentioned taking a picture of us. I still can't believe he posted it."

"It's not a huge deal. He probably thought we were back together and decided it would be fun to post the photo." She waited a moment, not getting a response from Matt. "Are you still there?"

"I'm still here. Are we back together, Cass, or are we still figuring it out?" He felt tired, way too tired to have this conversation.

"I know what I want. I'm just not sure about you. I'd hoped we could talk about it this weekend." She turned away from the noise, moving into a hallway.

"Let me be clear. I want this to work. This isn't a game to me, it's serious...real serious. Unless you tell me otherwise, we're together, Cassie."

The pounding of her heart added to the noise from the crowd, but she heard every word.

"We're together, Matt. No doubt in my mind." She smiled, wishing she could jump into his arms. Instead, she leaned against a wall, relief washing away the stress of the last few days.

"It's good to get that settled. I'd better get going. I want to see Pops once more before they kick us out."

"Call me tomorrow and let me know how he's doing."

"You know I will."

******

"Kurt, there's a call for the arson investigator. Jerrod isn't here. Do you want to take it?"

"Sure." He took the phone from his fellow firefighter's hand. "This is Kurt Dobson."

"Where's Jerrod James?"

Kurt focused on the voice, unable to tell if it belonged to a male or female. "He's not here right now, but I work with him. What can I do for you?"

"This message is for Jerrod only. Can you pass it along?"

"Sure. What is it?"

"Ten-fifty Lake Drive. That's all he needs to know."

"Did you say—" He stopped when the line went dead. Cursing, he took off out the door toward the parking lot, punching Jerrod's number into his phone. "Jerrod, it's Kurt. Call me as soon as you get this message. We need to talk."

Jumping into his car, he wasted no time. Located in a rundown neighborhood of dilapidated buildings a few miles from the station, Lake Drive had been the site of a fire a few months before the arsonist started his activities. They'd lost the building.

Parking, Kurt grabbed a flashlight and notepad, then scanned the area, looking for movement, sniffing the air for signs of a fire before walking toward the building. Broken glass littered the sidewalk in front and parking area on the side. As expected, the front door was locked, as were the windows. Walking to the side, he tried two other doors, then moved to the back, surprised at the size of the building. Glancing around at the sound of crunching gravel, he turned in a circle, scanning the area, seeing no one.

The structure seemed to go on forever. From the front wall to the back had to be at least three hundred feet, about the length of a football field, making it one of the biggest industrial buildings in Cold Creek.

Resuming his search, he tried the back door. Unlocked. Pushing the door open, he pointed the flashlight inside, revealing a dark interior strewn with trash and torn sleeping bags. Cringing, remembering the deaths of the two young men weeks before, he stepped further inside.

Kurt searched three empty offices before returning to the room where he'd entered, a few feet inside the back door. Spotting another door in the room, he set his notebook against the wall, then turned the knob, exposing what appeared to be a large storeroom with a few windows up high and no exterior door. Boxes lined the walls, which seemed odd given the building had been abandoned for years. Setting the flashlight on the floor, Kurt picked up a box and placed it on the floor in front of him. Using a knife, he slipped it across the tape, searching the contents. Nothing except wadded up newspaper. Trying two more, he found the same crumpled paper in each.

Settling fisted hands on his hips, he took one more look around, then picked up the flashlight, deciding to take one more look through the warehouse before leaving. Approaching the door, Kurt heard a loud crash a moment before the door to the storeroom slammed shut.

******

"All right, Skye. I've fessed up about Matt and me. It's your turn to tell us about Gage." Cassie looked over the rim of her glass, eyes sparkling.

Skye tilted her head, a frown drawing down the corners of her mouth. "What about Gage?"

"It's obvious something is going on between you two. He insisted you ride back to the motel with him. Spill."

Janie's eyes widened a little, although she kept her thoughts to herself. She'd seen Gage and Skye together a couple times, returning from lunch or when she delivered sales data Kade requested for their meeting. Even she noticed the connection.

"It's not at all what you think. He didn't *insist* I ride with him. He offered to take me since we're staying at the same motel." Skye squared her shoulders, deciding the best defense was to deny everything. "Gage is a business partner. I'd be a fool to start anything with him."

"But you'd like to," Cassie added.

"Who wouldn't? He's handsome, intelligent, and from what I understand, available. Even so, nothing is going to happen between us."

At the sound of her phone, Janie reached behind her for the purse slung over the back of her chair. "Hello?"

"Janie, it's Jerrod. Kurt left me a message to call, but I can't reach him. Is he with you?"

"No. As far as I know, he's at the station. Have you tried there?"

"They said he took off about the same time he left the message for me. Well, guess I'll wait until he tries back. Hold on a moment." Janie could hear Jerrod talking to others before he came back on the line. "I've got to go. Another fire has been reported. Sorry to bother you." Jerrod hung up, leaving Janie with a knot building in her stomach.

"What is it?" Cassie asked.

"Jerrod is trying to find Kurt. He thought maybe he was with me." She swallowed. Something wasn't right. Holding her phone, she texted Kurt, then Jerrod, asking him to let her know as soon as Kurt got a hold of him. She glanced up, seeing her friends staring at her. "Then he got a call about another fire and hung up. I'm sure it's nothing."

"Do you want to drive to the station or swing by his place?" Skye asked, signaling the waitress for their check.

"No. He's probably at one of the sports bars with a buddy. It's his way of unwinding."

Walking outside, Janie heard her phone again. "Hello?"

"It's Jerrod. We found Kurt's car at the scene of the fire. We can't find him, Janie."

"Where are you?"

"It's not wise for you to come here. Let us do our job and I'll call you."

"Where...are...you?" she demanded. If he didn't tell her, she'd drive around town until she found it.

"Ten-fifty Lake Drive. But Janie—"

She turned toward Cassie and Skye, her stomach churning. "They found Kurt's car. It's at the scene of the fire, but they can't find him."

"I'll drive while you give me directions," Cassie said, sprinting toward her truck.

******

Not deterred by the road block, Cassie turned around, driving down the next street. Parking, Janie grabbed bottles of water as they jumped from the truck, handing one to each of her friends as they dashed between buildings and toward the fire. Coming to a stop at a fence about eight feet high, Cassie ran from one end to the other.

"Down here," she shouted, already pulling back loose fencing. "If we can open this wide enough, we might be able to squeeze through."

It took several tugs before they could shimmy through the opening, coming to a halt at the back of the building. What they saw stopped them. The building was so large the firefighters hadn't even reached the back yet. Smoke billowed from broken windows as firefighters worked to knock down the flames at the front of the building.

Seeing a door ajar, Janie took a couple steps toward it, stopping when Cassie gripped her arm, tugging her back.

"You can't go closer, Janie. Let them do their job."

"Let go of me." She wrenched her arm free, dashing toward the open door, oblivious to the danger. "I have to find him before the flames reach the back."

"Janie, stop! The smoke will get you before you get ten feet inside," Skye called, running after her, followed by Cassie.

"Dammit, Janie. Stop!" Cassie yelled as Janie disappeared inside, pouring the bottle of water over her head. "Skye, let the firefighters know about Janie. I'm going to try and stop her."

"Are you crazy? Don't you dare go in there." Skye glanced around, seeing no one at the back. Everyone seemed to be clustered at the front, trying to stop the fire from spreading. "I'll find someone and be right back. Promise you won't go in there."

Cassie nodded, waiting until Skye disappeared, then removed her blouse, soaking it with the bottled water. Placing it over her face, she dashed inside, staying low.

"Janie!"

"Here," Janie choked out. "Help me get this door open."

Cassie took a breath through the soaked cloth, then handed it to Janie. "Get out of here. We need to wait for help."

"He's in here. I'm certain of it." She pointed to a notebook leaning against the wall. On her hands and knees, she bent lower, trying to get a breath of fresh air. "I can't leave him."

Before Cassie could reply, a roaring sound came from above them a moment before the ceiling gave way, crashing down around them.

Chapter Twenty-Two

"You're certain Janie went inside?" Jerrod asked, running toward the back of the building with Skye, the fire chief, and several firefighters.

"Positive. We tried to stop her, but…" Rounding the corner, her chest constricted when she didn't spot Cassie.

Grabbing Skye's arm, Jerrod pulled her away from the back entrance. "You've got to get back to the front or behind that fence. You can't stay here."

"Part of the ceiling caved in. Let's get to work," the chief shouted, pointing toward the door.

"Cassie!" Skye's gaze darted from one side of the building to another, looking for any sign of her cousin. "She must have followed Janie inside. Cassie!" she shouted again, trying to hear over the sounds of the fire, sirens, and onlookers.

"Did you hear something?" Jerrod turned toward the other men. "Inside. I'm certain I heard someone."

"Clear the opening." The chief turned toward Skye. "You have to leave. Now. If they're inside, we'll get them out." When Skye hesitated, he grabbed her by the shoulders. "Do I need to escort you?"

Her frightened gaze latched onto the chief's, fear pounding through her body. "No. I'll get back." She didn't head toward the front. Instead, she took a position at the fence, arms crossed as she paced, praying they'd find them in time.

"There, Chief," one of the men pointed. "They're no more than five feet inside, against a doorway."

Working quickly, they had the debris cleared before Skye had a chance to dash back to the building.

"I told you to stay back." Jerrod glowered, pointing toward the fence, stopping Skye midway. Shaking her head, she backed up, not shifting her gaze away from the building.

In less than a minute, one of the men carried Janie outside, another carrying Cassie, both coughing...both alive. Skye sagged with relief, ignoring orders to stay away as she ran to Cassie, hearing the chief bark orders into his phone. Seconds passed before shouts drew her attention to the paramedics racing toward them.

Jerrod crouched next to Janie, brushing hair from her face, his hand supporting her back as her coughing eased. Gripping his arm, Janie tried to stand up.

"Hold on, Janie. The paramedics are just about here."

"Kurt...he's inside that last room. You've got to get him." The panic in her face, her wild-looking eyes, had Jerrod dashing to the doorway.

"Kurt's in that room. We've got to get him out," Jerrod shouted to the chief as he ran past.

Nodding, the chief directed the men, shouting orders, watching as they worked the lock and additional metal barrier which held Kurt captive. Skye stood back as the paramedics worked on their reluctant patients, Janie's and Cassie's attention fixed on the back of the building. Cassie reached over, touching Janie's cut and bruised arm.

"They'll get him out." Cassie's voice, rough and raw, barely reached a whisper.

Her eyes burning with tears, a nod was all Janie could offer in response. Swiping at her dirt-streaked face, she squirmed, trying to move out of the grasp of the paramedic.

"You need to stay here, ma'am. They'll get him out." The woman's soothing voice and gentle touch as she checked Janie's injuries had her settling back, even as the lump in her stomach turned into an icy knot.

"Got him!"

Janie heard the man's shout a moment before he emerged from the building, a limp form in his arms, clothing black and charred. Without a word, the two paramedics began working on an unconscious Kurt, not taking the time to acknowledge the emergency vehicle pulling to a stop next to them.

"What have we got?" the driver shouted, opening the back doors.

"Kurt Dobson. Unconscious..."

The woman's voice drifted into the distance, every motion seeming to slow as Janie focused on Kurt, repeating a silent prayer over and over. Jolting at a hand on her shoulder, she glanced up, eyes heavy with despair.

"I'll drive you and Cassie to the hospital, unless you want to wait for another ambulance." Skye crouched next to Janie.

"I'll go with Kurt."

"Ma'am, it would be best to follow us." The paramedic's eyes narrowed in sympathy. "There isn't much room. We'll take good care of him. You have my word."

******

Fire Mountain

"You boys go on home. No use sticking 'round here, listening to me gripe." Seth's mood had deteriorated through the afternoon as one test after another came back normal. He saw no reason to stay another night, not hesitating to tell the doctor his opinion. If he hadn't been through recent prostate surgery, the doctor might have been more inclined to go along with Seth's wishes.

"Tired of us already, Pops?" Troy smiled, setting aside the magazine he'd been rifling through.

"Hell no. I'm tired of this room, the food, and not getting any rest. Now, get out of here and let me have some peace."

"Guess we don't have a choice." Matt leaned over and brushed a kiss on Seth's forehead. "We'll be back by seven tomorrow morning."

"And bring me some clothes. I'm not leaving in this flimsy thing." Seth scowled as he lifted the thin cotton gown.

"Will do. Try to sleep, Pops." Matt glanced over his shoulder once more before walking down the almost empty corridor with Troy. "Other than telling us what it isn't, the tests haven't given us any clues as to what happened the other night."

"The doctor said it could be indigestion or pleurisy. All we can do is keep an eye on him." Troy slipped his hands in his pockets. "I talked to my advisor and he'll let me finish my last two classes online. All I'll need to do is drive back down to take the final and collect my stuff."

"Are you sure that's what you want to do?"

"I'm more than ready to get out of school and move back home. Other than Pops insisting, I had no reason to get my masters. I'm just checking a box for him." He also knew how much his presence would mean to Matt. His new job had him traveling considerably more than he'd anticipated. And now with Cassie back in his life, he'd be going to Cold Creek more often.

"Hold on a sec." Matt pulled the phone from his pocket, noticing Skye's number. "Hey, Skye. What's up?"

"There's been a fire, Matt…"

Coming to a halt, he turned to face Troy, his eyes already signaling his fear.

"Tell me."

"Kurt got caught in a building. When Janie ran inside to find him, Cassie followed, and—"

"I'm on my way."

"Matt, wait. Let me finish." Skye stared at the phone, which signaled an ended call. She punched in his number again, getting his voicemail. "Matt, she's in the hospital, but will be okay. They'll probably let her go home tonight. Anyway, call me back."

Ignoring the incoming call from Skye, Matt ran to his truck, explaining to Troy as he dialed Heath's number.

"I already heard," Heath answered before Matt could say anything. "Get yourself to the airport. The plane leaves in half an hour."

Heading toward the airport, Matt's mind went on autopilot. "Heath has the pilot going through preflight. You'll have to explain to Pops. Don't tell him about the fire until I know what happened. Tell him it's for work." Matt gripped the wheel, trying to stay five miles per hour over the speed limit. A ticket wouldn't help anything.

"No problem. You take care of Cassie. I'll handle Pops." Troy studied his brother, seeing his hands trembling, his knuckles turning white on the steering wheel. "Maybe you should try calling the hospital before the plane takes off. Get more details."

"Here." Matt handed Troy his phone. "Skye left a message. Tell me what she said."

Troy listened, relaying the message to Matt. "Sounds like Cassie will be fine," he commented, sliding a little in his seat as Matt made a hard left turn into the airport.

Matt's death grip on the wheel loosened at the news. It didn't change the fact he'd be going to Cold Creek with Heath. Pulling to a stop, he jumped out.

"I'll be back as soon as I can."

"Don't worry about Pops. I've got it handled. Call me when you know more."

******

Heath filled Matt in on what he'd learned from Skye. He'd called Rafe, then Kade, who would notify everyone else, telling them not to worry. Cassie didn't need a houseful of MacLarens and Sinclairs showing up at her door.

Matt stared out the window, refusing refreshments and ignoring Heath's questioning glances. He didn't need to go into details about Cassie and him now. Instead, he thought of what a fool he'd been to not come right out and tell her he loved her, wanted her as his wife. Matt closed his eyes, resting his head against the seat, wondering why it had taken a scare like this to bring him to his senses, force him to see what mattered most.

Feeling a slight jolt as the plane touched down, Matt drew in a deep breath. Once he made certain Cassie was okay, he'd lay it all out, explain how he felt, and close this gap between them once and for all. No more missteps. No more taking it slow. No more being a fool as Pops had accused. He loved her and would make it his life's mission to be sure Cassie knew it.

******

"We're still here, Heath. Do you know where the hospital is?" Skye gave him directions. Neither Cassie nor Janie had been released. Most of the emergency room resources were focused on Kurt and the victims of a highway accident involving a big rig. She paced, knowing both Cassie and Janie would be fine, but needing to see them to confirm it for herself.

When the entry doors slid open, she dashed into her uncle's open arms.

"Any word?" Heath asked as he dropped his arms and stepped back.

"Nothing. I know they have their hands full with Kurt and a highway accident, but I can't see why no one can give me any information. I told the nurse both of them were my cousins." Her tired eyes and grim smile told of her frustration and worry.

"Let me check with them."

Skye stood close to Matt as Heath spoke with a lady behind the desk. "She is going to be fine, Matt. I was with both of them from the time they brought them out of the building. They rode with me here, not in an ambulance. It should be a routine check, making sure there's no smoke damage, then they'll be able to leave."

Matt nodded, seeing Heath pull something from his wallet and handing it to the lady. A few minutes later, he turned around, signaling for them to follow.

"I swear, Uncle Heath can accomplish darn near anything," Skye said, lines of worry etched on her face.

Following Heath through a door, Matt passed several glass enclosed rooms before coming to a stop in front of one of the last ones. Inside, Cassie and Janie sat on the exam table talking to a young man.

Staring at Cassie through the open door, her face and arms dotted with cuts, her hair a tangled mess, Matt scolded himself again for not making his love clear when they were in Seattle. She never should've boarded the plane with the doubts he created. As always, Cassie had expressed her feelings without a hint of hesitancy, while he'd kept his under tight control. She deserved better, but she loved him, and he'd be a fool to deny his love any longer.

Looking up, Cassie smiled when she spotted her father. Then her gaze moved to the man standing beside him. "Matt," she whispered. Sliding to the floor, she covered the distance in a few steps, throwing herself into his arms. "Oh, Matt. It was awful. Janie ran inside to find Kurt, and I followed, and..." Her composure faltered as his strength engulfed her. Matt stroked her hair as she melted into quiet sobs.

"I know, baby," he whispered against her ear. "You're going to be fine. I'm here." Holding her until the sobs turned to quiet sniffles, he lifted her chin. "I love you, Cassie, and I'm here for you."

Instead of the radiant smile he expected, she dissolved into sobs, gripping him as if she never intended to let him go. Matt glanced toward Heath, whose shrug told him he was on his own.

So focused on each other, they didn't notice another man slip past them and into the room, closing the door.

Skye watched through the glass as he spoke to Janie, her face crumbling, tears streaming down her cheeks. "Please, God. Don't let it be Kurt," she prayed, getting Cassie's attention.

"I have to go to Janie." She broke from Matt's embrace, using the gown to wipe the dampness from her face, then turned. Walking into the room, she slipped an arm around Janie, kissing her forehead. "Is this about Kurt Dobson?"

The doctor glanced at her. "Are you a relative of Mr. Dobson's?"

"She's my closest friend, and a friend of Kurt's," Janie stuttered. "You can talk in front of her."

"As I told Mr. Dobson's fiancée, his injuries are serious. He has significant smoke damage to his lungs and throat, and burns over both legs and part of his back. It will be a long, slow, and quite painful recovery." The doctor glanced at the chart before finishing. "He has requested no visitors, specifically mentioning Miss Bonds. I'm sorry."

Cassie tightened her arm around Janie, anger sweeping through her. "I know he's in pain and probably not thinking straight, but does he know Janie saved his life? Does he know that without her, he'd still be inside that burning building?" Her voice rose, the pain in Janie's face more than she could bear. "Does he know she risked her life and almost *died* trying to save him?"

Sympathy showed in the doctor's eyes and voice. "I'm sorry, but those are his wishes."

"That's hogwash," Cassie said, looking up to see Matt step up beside her.

"Cassie, please," Janie breathed out through her sobs. "It's not the doctor's fault. Kurt just needs time. Right, Doctor?"

"I wish I knew, Miss Bonds. In his case, I certainly hope time heals him. And I do hope he changes his mind about seeing you. Sometimes those we love are the perfect medicine." He reached into a pocket, pulling out a card, making a notation on the back. "Call this woman. She's a miracle worker when it comes to situations like this one."

Janie watched him go, staring at the name on the card. "What am I going to do, Cassie?" The stricken look on her face broke Cassie's heart.

"I don't know, but it's going to work out. I promise you."

******

"You're under arrest for the attempted murder of Mr. Kurt Dobson."

"But he's not who I wanted!" the woman screamed, her face contorted in anger, craziness in her eyes. "He's not—"

"Ma'am, anything you say..." The officer pulled her arms behind her, continuing to inform her of her rights, ignoring her rants about getting the wrong man.

A dozen feet away, Jerrod watched the scene, listening to his ex-wife rant about how she wanted *him* dead, not Kurt. The woman he'd fallen in love with in high school and married a few years later had sunk into mental illness in her late twenties. He'd done everything the doctors suggested, using all the insurance available, spending every dime, borrowing on their home, then losing everything to bankruptcy. He'd still be with her if she hadn't, in one of her more lucid moments, filed for divorce. They'd fought over it until he had no more fight left.

It had been three years since the divorce became final. Three years of nothing from her...until the fires. It took until the sixth one for him to start piecing it all together, yet he still couldn't bring himself to accept it. The first clue had been her following him around town. He hadn't even known she'd returned to Cold Creek from Denver, where she'd somehow gotten a job in one of the marijuana dispensaries.

When he saw her watching his apartment from across the street, he planned to confront her, but the fire investigations took up almost twenty hours a day of his time. Thinking of the last two fires, before the one tonight, sent chills through him. He'd found a ring and a metal box of pictures at the scene of the second-to-last fire. His heart sank as he studied them. Although charred, images of his ex-wife and him couldn't be ignored. Tagging them as evidence, he mentioned his findings to Kurt earlier in the week, taking what he had to his fire chief. If the police chief hadn't been called away, they would've met with him today, a few hours before the fire that almost killed Kurt. A fire meant for him.

"Who do you think you're looking at?" she yelled.

Jerrod looked up, realizing she'd directed her tirade at him. She didn't even recognize him. He already knew the outcome. She'd plead insanity, be institutionalized, and two young men and his good friend would be the consequences of her incapacitated state. In time, she'd be forgotten and so would the crimes...by everyone except him and Kurt.

******

"Do you feel like taking a walk?" Matt sat beside Cassie, holding her hand and watching television as Janie puttered around in the kitchen. It had been five days since the fire, and Kurt still refused to let Janie near him.

Matt had stayed, working out of the Cold Creek office a few hours each day, then returning to the girls' apartment. Cassie would be going back to work tomorrow, Janie the following Monday, although Heath had told them to take two weeks off. Both needed to get their minds back on something productive, and Janie needed to focus on anything other than Kurt.

"Can we drive to the river and walk toward the campground?" Cassie's eyes brightened at the idea.

Standing, he drew her up. "Perfect."

"We're going for a walk. Do you want anything from the store?" Cassie grabbed her purse, hating the blank look on Janie's face. She wished she could do something to fix the break with Kurt. Janie had only told Cassie about Kurt's proposal, asking her to keep it quiet. They'd planned to announce it to their friends during a dinner at his place. A dinner that now may never happen. Still, Janie refused to take off the ring, saying if Kurt wanted it back, he could damn well ask for it.

"No, I'm good." Janie continued reorganizing shelves she'd worked on the day before. At least she kept herself busy.

The drive took ten minutes. The path meandered along the river, going inland for several yards, then back again, ending at an open meadow surrounded by campsites. Few were being used, which gave them a sense of privacy.

Settling an arm around her shoulders, Matt guided her toward a beautiful place on the river. "Someday, I'd like to camp at this exact spot. Maybe bring fishing poles and teach our kids to fish. Teach them how to—"

"Wait. Teach our kids to what?" Her eyes grew wide. It was the first time he'd spoken of their future.

"Fish. You know, toss a line in the water, pull out a fish." He smiled. "Of course, to do that, we need to have some kids first. And to do that..." He reached into his pocket and dropped to one knee, "...we should probably get married."

Cassie's gasp, hand flying to her mouth, was all he needed.

"I love you, Cass. I have since we were in high school and I've never stopped. You're all I want. Always. There's no way I'll ever get over you if you say no. So please, say yes. Marry me."

As her head bobbed up and down, he took her left hand, sliding the ring on her finger. When he stood, she jumped into his arms, tears streaming down her face.

"I'll take that as a yes," he laughed, twirling her in a circle, then setting her down. "You know, I've never seen you cry as much as you have the last week. I hope today's tears mean something good."

Pulling back, she looked into his face. "These are the best tears ever. I love you, Matt. I always will."

Epilogue

MacLaren Ranch, Fire Mountain

"I warned you. You should've done what Dana and I did." Mitch MacLaren looked across the sprawling front lawn, where the men played football most Sundays, and winced at the number of people who'd come to witness and celebrate Cassie and Matt's marriage. "Saying your vows in front of a couple hundred people...whew."

Matt shrugged. "This is what Cassie wanted. Who am I to say no?" He looked toward a group of women, his wife included. Most were part of his new family and he couldn't be happier. Seeing Janie standing apart, doing her best to hide the pain of Kurt's rejection, he felt a strange urge to knock some sense into the man. Too bad he still occupied a bed in the acute care section of the hospital.

"Guess I'd better ask Dana to dance." Mitch finished his drink, setting the empty glass on a table. "I'll never hear the end of it if she doesn't get at least a couple in before we leave."

Matt started to walk toward Cassie, then stopped when Gage joined him.

"I just got a text from Ivan." Gage looked at his phone, trying to read the message in the waning sunlight. "His plane was delayed, but he's on his way and bringing a couple guests. He'll be here in time for most of the party."

Matt watched Gage drop his arm, his gaze wandering back to the circle of women. One woman in particular.

"Why don't you go ask her to dance?" Matt asked.

"Who?"

"Skye." Matt tilted his glass in her direction. "Either get her out of your system or go after her. Put yourself out of your misery."

Gage stared at Matt. "Spoken by the man who only months ago got a broken nose from the woman he never planned to get near again," he chuckled. "And now you're married to her."

"Life can surprise you." Matt's smile focused on the one woman who owned his heart and always would. He'd never be able to explain it to Gage, a man who'd experienced nothing but pain and betrayal during his own marriage. "You know, Skye isn't anything like your first wife. When she commits to a man, I guarantee you, the marriage will stick."

Gage slugged down the rest of his drink. "You ever think that's what keeps me away from the woman?"

Matt's brows drew together in a frown. "I don't understand."

"Hell, neither do I." Gage shook his head, then turned, stalking toward Skye like a moth drawn to a flame. He knew it would never work, yet there was no reason he couldn't have a few dances with her, feel her in his arms, hear her laughter. Allowing himself that would be worth heading back to Houston alone.

Hearing an outburst of laughter coming from the front entry, Matt turned, shielding his eyes from the afternoon sun. Heath, Rafe, and Jace walked toward the food table, lost in their own conversation.

"They're having a fine time today."

Matt turned at the sound of Cassie's voice. Wrapping an arm around her, he tugged her tight against him, capturing her mouth with his. Giving the guests a brief show, he pulled back. "When can we leave?"

Cassie tossed her head back, laughing. They'd spent more time in bed the last few weeks than at work. "We should probably stay at least until we cut the cake." At the sound of a car engine, she turned to see a sleek silver limousine park at the back of a long line of cars. "Who do you think that is?"

Matt watched as a tall, slim man with ink black hair emerged, offering his hand to someone inside, as a second man exited the car from the other side.

"That's Ivan Santiago. You remember. He runs Double Ace for his father and uncles. He's Gage's boss. Come on. Let's greet him."

"Oh my," Cassie gasped. "Isn't he Kade's cousin?"

"That's what I understand." He tugged her along, confused by her hesitation. "Ivan, we're so glad you could make it." Matt held out his hand. "Let me introduce you to my wife, Cassie MacLaren Garner. Cassie, this is Ivan Santiago."

"You are as lovely as Matt said." He turned to the woman next to him. "This is my aunt, Reyna Santiago, and my father, Javier Santiago. Aunt Reyna, Father, these are the newlyweds, Matt and Cassie Garner."

Cassie caught her breath as the woman stepped forward. Of average size, she had an almost regal bearing and a classical beauty most women would envy. Cassie also knew she stared at her cousin Kade's mother, her aunt Reyna.

"It's so lovely of you to invite us to celebrate your marriage." Reyna held out her hands, taking Cassie's in a warm embrace, her gaze penetrating in its intensity. "I do believe we have someone in common."

Cassie cleared her throat, already liking the woman. "Two, if I'm not mistaken."

Matt stood beside Cassie, his brows drawing together at the unusual exchange. He started to ask about it when he noticed Javier Santiago take a protective stance next to Reyna a moment before Kade, Heath, Rafe, and Jace came to a halt next to him. The air became thick as tension radiated through the group.

Before Matt had a chance to introduce them, Rafe stepped forward, his deep voice slicing through the silence.

"Reyna?"

She smiled up at him, her face glowing. "Rafe. It's been a long time."

Thank you for taking the time to read No Getting Over You. If you enjoyed it, please consider telling your friends or posting a short review. Word of mouth is an author's best friend and much appreciated.

Please join my reader's group to be notified of my New Releases at:
http://www.shirleendavies.com/contact-me.html

I care about quality, so if you find something in error, please contact me via email at
shirleen@shirleendavies.com

About the Author

Shirleen Davies writes romance—historical, contemporary, and romantic suspense. She grew up in Southern California, attended Oregon State University, and has degrees from San Diego State University and the University of Maryland. During the day she provides consulting services to small and mid-sized businesses. But her real passion is writing emotionally charged stories of flawed people who find redemption through love and acceptance. She now lives with her husband in a beautiful town in northern Arizona.

Shirleen loves to hear from her readers.

Write to her at: shirleen@shirleendavies.com

Visit her website: http://www.shirleendavies.com

Sign up to be notified of New Releases:
http://www.shirleendavies.com/contact-me.html

Books by Shirleen:
http://www.shirleendavies.com/books.html

Comment on her blog:
http://www.shirleendavies.com/blog.html

Facebook Fan Page:
https://www.facebook.com/ShirleenDaviesAuthor

Twitter: http://twitter.com/shirleendavies

Google+:   http://www.gplusid.com/shirleendavies

LinkedIn:
http://www.linkedin.com/in/shirleendaviesauthor

Pinterest: http://www.pinterest.com/shirleendavies

Tsu: http://www.tsu.co/shirleendavies

Other Books by Shirleen Davies

http://www.shirleendavies.com/books.html

Tougher than the Rest – Book One
MacLarens of Fire Mountain Historical
Western Romance Series
"A passionate, fast-paced story set in the
untamed western frontier by an exciting new
voice in historical romance."
Niall MacLaren is the oldest of four brothers, and the undisputed leader of the family. A widower, and single father, his focus is on building the MacLaren ranch into the largest and most successful in northern Arizona. He is serious about two things—his responsibility to the family and his future marriage to the wealthy, well-connected widow who will secure his place in the territory's destiny.

Katherine is determined to live the life she's dreamed about. With a job waiting for her in the growing town of Los Angeles, California, the young teacher from Philadelphia begins a journey across the United States with only a couple of trunks and her spinster companion. Life is perfect for this adventurous, beautiful young woman, until an accident throws her into the arms of the one man who can destroy it all.

Fighting his growing attraction and strong desire for the beautiful stranger, Niall is more determined than ever to push emotions aside to focus on his goals of wealth and political gain. But looking into the clear, blue eyes of the woman who could ruin everything, Niall discovers he will have to harden his heart and be tougher than he's ever been in his life...Tougher than the Rest.

Faster than the Rest – Book Two MacLarens of Fire Mountain Historical Western Romance Series
"Headstrong, brash, confident, and complex, the MacLarens of Fire Mountain will captivate you with strong characters set in the wild and rugged western frontier."
Handsome, ruthless, young U.S. Marshal Jamie MacLaren had lost everything—his parents, his family connections, and his childhood sweetheart—but now he's back in Fire Mountain and ready for another chance. Just as he successfully reconnects with his family and starts to rebuild his life, he gets the unexpected and unwanted assignment of rescuing the woman who broke his heart.

Beautiful, wealthy Victoria Wicklin chose money and power over love, but is now fighting for her life—or is she? Who has she become in the seven years since she left Fire Mountain to take up her life in San Francisco? Is she really as innocent as she says?

Marshal MacLaren struggles to learn the truth and do his job, but the past and present lead him in different directions as his heart and brain wage battle. Is Victoria a victim or a villain? Is life offering him another chance, or just another heartbreak?

As Jamie and Victoria struggle to uncover past secrets and come to grips with their shared passion, another danger arises. A life-altering danger that is out of their control and threatens to destroy any chance for a shared future.

Harder than the Rest – Book Three MacLarens of Fire Mountain Historical Western Romance Series
"They are men you want on your side. Hard, confident, and loyal, the MacLarens of Fire Mountain will seize your attention from the first page."
Will MacLaren is a hardened, plain-speaking bounty hunter. His life centers on finding men guilty of horrendous crimes and making sure justice is done. There is no place in his world for the carefree attitude he carried years before when a tragic event destroyed his dreams.

Amanda is the daughter of a successful Colorado rancher. Determined and proud, she works hard to prove she is as capable as any man and worthy to be her father's heir. When a stranger arrives, her independent nature collides with the strong pull toward the handsome ranch hand. But is he what he seems and could his secrets endanger her as well as her family?

The last thing Will needs is to feel passion for another woman. But Amanda elicits feelings he thought were long buried. Can Will's desire for her change him? Or will the vengeance he seeks against the one man he wants to destroy—a dangerous opponent without a conscious—continue to control his life?

Stronger than the Rest – Book Four MacLarens of Fire Mountain Historical Western Romance Series
"Smart, tough, and capable, the MacLarens protect their own no matter the odds. Set against America's rugged frontier, the stories of the men from Fire Mountain are complex, fast-paced, and a must read for anyone who enjoys non-stop action and romance."
Drew MacLaren is focused and strong. He has achieved all of his goals except one—to return to the MacLaren ranch and build the best horse breeding program in the west. His successful career as an attorney is about to give way to his ranching roots when a bullet changes everything.

Tess Taylor is the quiet, serious daughter of a Colorado ranch family with dreams of her own. Her shy nature keeps her from developing friendships outside of her close-knit family until Drew enters her life. Their relationship grows. Then a bullet, meant for another, leaves him paralyzed and determined to distance himself from the one woman he's come to love.

Convinced he is no longer the man Tess needs, Drew focuses on regaining the use of his legs and recapturing a life he thought lost. But danger of another kind threatens those he cares about—including Tess—forcing him to rethink his future.

Can Drew overcome the barriers that stand between him, the safety of his friends and family, and a life with the woman he loves? To do it all, he has to be strong. Stronger than the Rest.

Deadlier than the Rest – Book Five MacLarens of Fire Mountain Historical Western Romance Series
"A passionate, heartwarming story of the iconic MacLarens of Fire Mountain. This captivating historical western romance grabs your attention from the start with an engrossing story encompassing two romances set against the rugged backdrop of the burgeoning western frontier."
Connor MacLaren's search has already stolen eight years of his life. Now he is close to finding what he seeks—Meggie, his missing sister. His quest leads him to the growing city of Salt Lake and an encounter with the most captivating woman he has ever met.

Grace is the third wife of a Mormon farmer, forced into a life far different from what she'd have chosen. Her independent spirit longs for choices governed only by her own heart and mind. To achieve her dreams, she must hide behind secrets and half-truths, even as her heart pulls her towards the ruggedly handsome Connor.

Known as cool and uncompromising, Connor MacLaren lives by a few, firm rules that have served him well and kept him alive. However, danger stalks Connor, even to the front range of the beautiful Wasatch Mountains, threatening those he cares about and impacting his ability to find his sister.

Can Connor protect himself from those who seek his death? Will his eight-year search lead him to his sister while unlocking the secrets he knows are held tight within Grace, the woman who has captured his heart?

Read this heartening story of duty, honor, passion, and love in book five of the MacLarens of Fire Mountain series.

Wilder than the Rest – Book Six MacLarens of Fire Mountain Historical Western Romance Series
"A captivating historical western romance set in the burgeoning and treacherous city of San Francisco. Go along for the ride in this gripping story that seizes your attention from the very first page."
"If you're a reader who wants to discover an entire family of characters you can fall in love with, this is the series for you." – Authors to Watch
Pierce is a rough man, but happy in his new life as a Special Agent. Tasked with defending the rights of the federal government, Pierce is a cunning gunslinger always ready to tackle the next job. That

is, until he finds out that his new job involves Mollie Jamison.

Mollie can be a lot to handle. Headstrong and independent, Mollie has chosen a life of danger and intrigue guaranteed to prove her liquor-loving father wrong. She will make something of herself, and no one, not even arrogant Pierce MacLaren, will stand in her way.

A secret mission brings them together, but will their attraction to each other prove deadly in their hunt for justice? The payoff for success is high, much higher than any assignment either has taken before. But will the damage to their hearts and souls be too much to bear? Can Pierce and Mollie find a way to overcome their misgivings and work together as one?

Second Summer – Book One
MacLarens of Fire Mountain Contemporary Romance Series
"In this passionate Contemporary Romance, author Shirleen Davies introduces her readers to the modern day MacLarens starting with Heath MacLaren, the head of the family."
The Chairman of both the MacLaren Cattle Co. and MacLaren Land Development, Heath MacLaren is a success professionally—his personal life is another matter.
Following a divorce after a long, loveless marriage, Heath spends his time with women who are

beautiful and passionate, yet unable to provide what he longs for . . .

Heath has never experienced love even though he witnesses it every day between his younger brother, Jace, and wife, Caroline. He wants what they have, yet spends his time with women too young to understand what drives him and too focused on themselves to be true companions.

It's been two years since Annie's husband died, leaving her to build a new life. He was her soul mate and confidante. She has no desire to find a replacement, yet longs for male friendship.

Annie's closest friend in Fire Mountain, Caroline MacLaren, is determined to see Annie come out of her shell after almost two years of mourning. A chance meeting with Heath turns into an offer to be a part of the MacLaren Foundation Board and an opportunity for a life outside her home sanctuary which has also become her prison. The platonic friendship that builds between Annie and Heath points to a future where each may rely on the other without the bonds a romance would entail. *However, without consciously seeking it, each yearns for more . . .*

The MacLaren Development Company is booming with Heath at the helm. His meetings at a partner company with the young, beautiful marketing director, who makes no secret of her desire for him, are a temptation. But is she the type of woman he truly wants?

Annie's acceptance of the deep, yet passionless, friendship with Heath sustains her, lulling her to believe it is all she needs. At least until Heath drops a bombshell, forcing Annie to realize that what she took for friendship is actually a deep, lasting love. One she doesn't want to lose.

Each must decide to settle—or fight for it all.

Hard Landing – Book Two
MacLarens of Fire Mountain Contemporary Romance Series

Trey MacLaren is a confident, poised Navy pilot. He's focused, loyal, ethical, and a natural leader. He is also on his way to what he hopes will be a lasting relationship and marriage with fellow pilot, Jesse Evans.

Jesse has always been driven. Her graduation from the Naval Academy and acceptance into the pilot training program are all she thought she wanted— until she discovered love with Trey MacLaren

Trey and Jesse's lives are filled with fast flying, friends, and the demands of their military careers. Lives each has settled into with a passion. At least until the day Trey receives a letter that could change his and Jesse's lives forever.

It's been over two years since Trey has seen the woman in Pensacola. Her unexpected letter stuns him and pushes Jesse into a tailspin from which she might not pull back.

Each must make a choice. Will the choice Trey makes cause him to lose Jesse forever? Will she

follow her heart or her head as she fights for a
chance to save the love she's found? Will their
independent decisions collide, forcing them to give
up on a life together?

One More Day – Book Three
MacLarens of Fire Mountain Contemporary
Romance Series

Cameron "Cam" Sinclair is smart, driven, and
dedicated, with an easygoing temperament that
belies his strong will and the personal ambitions he
holds close. Besides his family, his job as head of IT
at the MacLaren Cattle Company and his position as
a Search and Rescue volunteer are all he needs to
make him happy. At least that's what he thinks until
he meets, and is instantly drawn to, fellow SAR
volunteer, Lainey Devlin.

*Lainey is compassionate, independent, and ready to
break away from her manipulative and controlling
fiancé. Just as her decision is made, she's called into
a major search and rescue effort, where once again,
her path crosses with the intriguing, and much too
handsome, Cam Sinclair. But Lainey's plans are set.
An opportunity to buy a flourishing preschool in
northern Arizona is her chance to make a fresh
start, and nothing, not even her fierce attraction to
Cam Sinclair, will impede her plans.*

As Lainey begins to settle into her new life, an
unexpected danger arises —threats from an
unknown assailant—someone who doesn't believe
she belongs in Fire Mountain. The more Lainey

begins to love her new home, the greater the danger becomes. Can she accept the help and protection Cam offers while ignoring her consuming desire for him?

Even if Lainey accepts her attraction to Cam, will he ever be able to come to terms with his own driving ambition and allow himself to consider a different life than the one he's always pictured? A life with the one woman who offers more than he'd ever hoped to find?

All Your Nights – Book Four
MacLarens of Fire Mountain Contemporary Romance Series
"Romance, adventure, cowboys, suspense— everything you want in a contemporary western romance novel."
Kade Taylor likes living on the edge. As an undercover agent for the DEA and a former Special Ops team member, his current assignment seems tame—keep tabs on a bookish Ph.D. candidate the agency believes is connected to a ruthless drug cartel.

Brooke Sinclair is weeks away from obtaining her goal of a doctoral degree. She spends time finalizing her presentation and relaxing with another student who seems to want nothing more than her friendship. That's fine with Brooke. Her last serious relationship ended in a broken engagement.

Her future is set, safe and peaceful, just as she's always planned—until Agent Taylor informs her she's under suspicion for illegal drug activities.

Kade and his DEA team obtain evidence which exonerates Brooke while placing her in danger from those who sought to use her. As Kade races to take down the drug cartel while protecting Brooke, he must also find common ground with the former suspect—a woman he desires with increasing intensity.

At odds with her better judgment, Brooke finds the more time she spends with Kade, the more she's attracted to the complex, multi-faceted agent. But Kade holds secrets he knows Brooke will never understand or accept.

Can Kade keep Brooke safe while coming to terms with his past, or will he stay silent, ruining any future with the woman his heart can't let go?

Always Love You– Book Five
MacLarens of Fire Mountain Contemporary Romance Series
"Romance, adventure, motorcycles, cowboys, suspense—everything you want in a contemporary western romance novel."
Eric Sinclair loves his bachelor status. His work at MacLaren Enterprises leaves him with plenty of time

to ride his horse as well as his Harley...and date beautiful women without a thought to commitment.

Amber Anderson is the new person at MacLaren Enterprises. Her passion for marketing landed her what she believes to be the perfect job—until she steps into her first meeting to find the man she left, but still loves, sitting at the management table—his disdain for her clear.

Eric won't allow the past to taint his professional behavior, nor will he repeat his mistakes with Amber, even though love for her pulses through him as strong as ever.

As they strive to mold a working relationship, unexpected danger confronts those close to them, pitting the MacLarens and Sinclairs against an evil who stalks one member but threatens them all.

Eric can't get the memories of their passionate past out of his mind, while Amber wrestles with feelings she thought long buried. Will they be able to put the past behind them to reclaim the love lost years before?

Hearts Don't Lie– Book Six
MacLarens of Fire Mountain Contemporary Romance Series
Mitch MacLaren has reasons for avoiding relationships, and in his opinion, they're pretty darn

good. As the new president of RTC Bucking Bulls, difficult challenges occur daily. He certainly doesn't need another one in the form of a fiery, blue-eyed, redhead.

Dana Ballard's new job forces her to work with the one MacLaren who can't seem to get over himself and lighten up. Their verbal sparring is second nature and entertaining until the night of Mitch's departure when he surprises her with a dare she doesn't refuse.

With his assignment in Fire Mountain over, Mitch is free to return to Montana and run the business his father helped start. The glitch in his enthusiasm has to do with one irreversible mistake—the dare Dana didn't ignore. Now, for reasons that confound him, he just can't let it go.

Working together is a circumstance neither wants, but both must accept. As their attraction grows, so do the accidents and strange illnesses of the animals RTC depends on to stay in business. Mitch's total focus should be on finding the reasons and people behind the incidents. Instead, he finds himself torn between his unwanted desire for Dana and the business which is his life.

In his mind, a simple proposition can solve one problem. Will Dana make the smart move and walk away? Or take the gamble and expose her heart?

**No Getting Over You— Book Seven
MacLarens of Fire Mountain Contemporary
Romance Series**

Cassie MacLaren has come a long way since being dumped by her long-time boyfriend, a man she believed to be her future. Successful in her job at MacLaren Enterprises, dreaming of one day leading one of the divisions, she's moved on to start a new relationship, having little time to dwell on past mistakes.

Matt Garner loves his job as rodeo representative for Double Ace Bucking Stock. Busy days and constant travel leave no time for anything more than the occasional short-term relationship—which is just the way he likes it. He's come to accept the regret of leaving the woman he loved for the pro rodeo circuit. The future is set for both, until a chance meeting ignites long buried emotions neither is willing to face.

Forced to work together, their attraction grows, even as multiple arson fires threaten Cassie's new home of Cold Creek, Colorado. Although Cassie believes the danger from the fires is remote, she knows the danger Matt poses to her heart is real.

While fighting his renewed feelings for Cassie, Matt focuses on a new and unexpected opportunity offered by MacLaren Enterprises—an opportunity that will put him on a direct collision course with Cassie.

Will pride and self-preservation control their future? Or will one be strong enough to make the first move, risking everything, including their heart?

Redemption's Edge – Book One
Redemption Mountain – Historical Western Romance Series
"A heartwarming, passionate story of loss, forgiveness, and redemption set in the untamed frontier during the tumultuous years following the Civil War. Ms. Davies' engaging and complex characters draw you in from the start, creating an exciting introduction to this new historical western romance series."
"Redemption's Edge is a strong and engaging introduction to her new historical western romance series."
Dax Pelletier is ready for a new life, far away from the one he left behind in Savannah following the South's devastating defeat in the Civil War. The ex-Confederate general wants nothing more to do with commanding men and confronting the tough truths of leadership.

Rachel Davenport possesses skills unlike those of her Boston socialite peers—skills honed as a nurse in field hospitals during the Civil War. Eschewing her northeastern suitors and changed by the carnage she's seen, Rachel decides to accept her uncle's invitation to assist him at his clinic in the dangerous and wild frontier of Montana.

Now a Texas Ranger, a promise to a friend takes Dax and his brother, Luke, to the untamed territory of Montana. He'll fulfill his oath and return to Austin, at least that's what he believes.

The small town of Splendor is what Rachel needs after life in a large city. In a few short months, she's grown to love the people as well as the majestic beauty of the untamed frontier. She's settled into a life unlike any she has ever thought possible.

Thinking his battle days are over, he now faces dangers of a different kind—one by those from his past who seek vengeance, and another from Rachel, the woman who's captured his heart.

Wildfire Creek – Book Two
Redemption Mountain – Historical Western Romance Series
"A passionate story of rebuilding lives, working to find a place in the wild frontier, and building new lives in the years following the American Civil War. A rugged, heartwarming story of choices and love in the continuing saga of Redemption Mountain."
Luke Pelletier is settling into his new life as a rancher and occasional Pinkerton Agent, leaving his past as an ex-Confederate major and Texas Ranger far behind. He wants nothing more than to work the

ranch, charm the ladies, and live a life of carefree bachelorhood.
Ginny Sorensen has accepted her responsibility as the sole provider for herself and her younger sister. The desire to continue their journey to Oregon is crushed when the need for food and shelter keeps them in the growing frontier town of Splendor, Montana, forcing Ginny to accept work as a server in the local saloon.

Luke has never met a woman as lovely and unspoiled as Ginny. He longs to know her, yet fears his wild ways and unsettled nature aren't what she deserves. She's a girl you marry, but that is nowhere in Luke's plans.

Complicating their tenuous friendship, a twist in circumstances forces Ginny closer to the man she most wants to avoid—the man who can destroy her dreams, and who's captured her heart.

Believing his bachelor status firm, Luke moves from danger to adventure, never dreaming each step he takes brings him closer to his true destiny and a life much different from what he imagines.

Sunrise Ridge – Book Three
Redemption Mountain – Historical Western Romance Series
"The author has a talent for bringing the historical west to life, realistically and vividly, and doesn't shy away from some of the harder aspects of frontier life, even

though it's fiction. Recommended to readers who like sweeping western historical romances that are grounded with memorable, likeable characters and a strong sense of place."

Noah Brandt is a successful blacksmith and businessman in Splendor, Montana, with few ties to his past as an ex-Union Army major and sharpshooter. Quiet and hardworking, his biggest challenge is controlling his strong desire for a woman he believes is beyond his reach.

Abigail Tolbert is tired of being under her father's thumb while at the same time, being pushed away by the one man she desires. Determined to build a new life outside the control of her wealthy father, she finds work and sets out to shape a life on her own terms.

Noah has made too many mistakes with Abby to have any hope of getting her back. Even with the changes in her life, including the distance she's built with her father, he can't keep himself from believing he'll never be good enough to claim her.

Unexpected dangers, including a twist of fate for Abby, change both their lives, making the tentative steps they've taken to build a relationship a distant hope. As Noah battles his past as well as the threats to Abby, she fights for a future with the only man she will ever love.

Dixie Moon – Book Four
Redemption Mountain – Historical Western
Romance Series

Gabe Evans is a man of his word with strong convictions and steadfast loyalty. As the sheriff of Splendor, Montana, the ex-Union Colonel and oldest of four boys from an affluent family, Gabe understands the meaning of responsibility. The last thing he wants is another commitment—especially of the female variety.

Until he meets Lena Campanel…

Lena's past is one she intends to keep buried. Overcoming a childhood of setbacks and obstacles, she and her friend, Nick, have succeeded in creating a life of financial success and devout loyalty to one another.

When an unexpected death leaves Gabe the sole heir of a considerable estate, partnering with Nick and Lena is a lucrative decision…forcing Gabe and Lena to work together. As their desire grows, Lena refuses to let down her guard, vowing to keep her past hidden—even from a perfect man like Gabe.

But secrets never stay buried…

When revealed, Gabe realizes Lena's secrets are deeper than he ever imagined. For a man of his character, deception and lies of omission aren't negotiable. Will he be able to forgive the deceit? Or is the damage too great to ever repair?

**Survivor Pass – Book Five
Redemption Mountain – Historical Western
Romance Series**

He thought he'd found a quiet life...
Cash Coulter settled into a life far removed from his days of fighting for the South and crossing the country as a bounty hunter. Now a deputy sheriff, Cash wants nothing more than to buy some land, raise cattle, and build a simple life in the frontier town of Splendor, Montana. But his whole world shifts when his gaze lands on the most captivating woman he's ever seen. And the feeling appears to be mutual.

But nothing is as it seems...
Alison McGrath moved from her home in Kentucky to the rugged mountains of Montana for one reason—to find the man responsible for murdering her brother. Despite using a false identity to avoid any tie to her brother's name, the citizens of Splendor have no intention of sharing their knowledge about the bank robbery which killed her only sibling. Alison knows her circle of lies can't end well, and her growing for Cash threatens to weaken the revenge which drives her.

And the troubles are mounting...
There is danger surrounding them both—men who seek vengeance as a way to silence the past...by any means necessary.

Reclaiming Love – Book One, A Novella
Peregrine Bay – Contemporary Romance
Series

Adam Monroe has seen his share of setbacks. Now he's back in Peregrine Bay, looking for a new life and second chance.

Julia Kerrigan's life rebounded after the sudden betrayal of the one man she ever loved. As president of a success real estate company, she's built a new life and future, pushing the painful past behind her. Adam's reason for accepting the job as the town's new Police Chief can be explained in one word— Julia. He wants her back and will do whatever is necessary to achieve his goal, even knowing his biggest hurdle is the woman he still loves.

As they begin to reconnect, a terrible scandal breaks loose with Julia and Adam at the center.

Will the threat to their lives and reputations destroy their fledgling romance? Can Adam identify and eliminate the danger to Julia before he's had a chance to reclaim her love?

Our Kind of Love – Book Two
Peregrine Bay – Contemporary Romance
Series

Selena Kerrigan is content with a life filled with work and family, never feeling the need to take a chance on a relationship—until she steps into a social world inhabited by a man with dark hair and penetrating blue eyes. Eyes that are fixed on her.

Lincoln Caldwell is a man satisfied with his life. Transitioning from an enviable career as a Navy SEAL to becoming a successful entrepreneur, his days focus on growing his security firm, spending his nights with whomever he chooses. Committing to one woman isn't on the horizon—until a captivating woman with caramel eyes sends his personal life into a tailspin.

Believing her identity remains a secret, Selena returns to work, ready to forget about running away from the bed she never should have gone near. She's prepared to put the colossal error, as well as the man she'll never see again, behind her.

Too bad the object of her lapse in judgment doesn't feel the same.

Linc is good at tracking his targets, and Selena is now at the top of his list. It's amazing how a pair of sandals and only a first name can say so much.

As he pursues the woman he can't rid from his mind, a series of cyber-attacks hit his business, threatening its hard-won success. Worse, and unbeknownst to most, Linc harbors a secret—one with the potential to alter his life, along with those he's close to, in ways he could never imagine.

Our Kind of Love, Book Two in the Peregrine Bay Contemporary Romance series, is a full-length novel with an HEA and no cliffhanger.

**Colin's Quest – Book One
MacLarens of Boundary Mountain –
Historical Western Romance Series**

For An Undying Love...
When Colin MacLaren headed west on a wagon
train, he hoped to find adventure and perhaps a little
danger in untamed California. He never expected to
meet the girl he would love forever. He also never
expected her to be the daughter of his family's age-
old enemy, but Sarah was a MacGregor and the
anger he anticipated soon became a reality. Her
father would not be swayed, vehemently refusing to
allow marriage to a MacLaren.

Time Has No Effect...
Forced apart for five years, Sarah never forgot
Colin—nor did she give up on his promise to come
for her. Carrying the brooch he gave her as proof of
their secret betrothal, she scans the trail from
California, waiting for Colin to claim her.
Unfortunately, her father has other plans.

And Enemies Hold No Power.
Nothing can stop Colin from locating Sarah. Not
outlaws, runaways, or miles of difficult trails.
However, reuniting is only the beginning. Together
they must find the courage to fight the men who
would keep them apart—and conquer the challenge
of uniting two independent hearts.

Find all of my books at:
http://www.shirleendavies.com/books.html

www.ingramcontent.com/pod-product-compliance
Lightning Source LLC
Chambersburg PA
CBHW060245210726
48292CB00002BA/494